A Sweet Lowcountry Proposal

A Sweet Lowcountry Proposal

A Novel

Preslaysa Williams

AVON

An Imprint of HarperCollinsPublishers

A SWEET LOWCOUNTRY PROPOSAL. Copyright © 2022 by Preslaysa Cielita Williams. All rights reserved. Printed in the United States of America. No part of this book may be used or reproduced in any manner whatsoever without written permission except in the case of brief quotations embodied in critical articles and reviews. For information, address HarperCollins Publishers, 195 Broadway, New York, NY 10007.

HarperCollins books may be purchased for educational, business, or sales promotional use. For information, please email the Special Markets Department at SPsales@harpercollins.com.

FIRST EDITION

Designed by Diahann Sturge

Flower petal illustrations © wacomka/Shutterstock

Flower bouquet © Anna Kasyanova/Shutterstock

Library of Congress Cataloging-in-Publication Data has been applied for.

ISBN 978-0-06-323698-1

22 23 24 25 26 LSC 10 9 8 7 6 5 4 3 2 1

For my children, Hannah and Samuel.
You encouraged me to write and edit this
story when I wanted to quit.
This book is for you.

All Her human powers failing,
Sorrow's sword, at last prevailing,
Stabs and breaks Her heart of love.
My dear Lady, full of sorrow,
From Your love, I ask to borrow,
Love enough to share Your pain.
Make my heart to burn with fire.
Make Your love my own desire.

—Paraphrased excerpt from *Stabat Mater*

A Sweet Lowcountry Proposal

Chapter One

*J*aslene Simmons sat on a leather chair and scrolled through her iPad in her chic, yet tiny, office space in downtown Charleston. November's autumnal sunshine cast its glow through her windows, brightening up the space. She'd spruced it up in the hopes that it would help her get focused for once. Added a potted plant near the entryway. Hung teal curtains on the bay windows. Set a vanilla-scented candle on the wooden coffee table in the reception area. It helped her continue working . . . a little.

She glanced to the right at a faded picture of her late sister, Hope, standing in front of the ocean at Myrtle Beach, her curly hair blown by the wind, happy and carefree. Jaslene blinked back the threat of tears. "I'm trying, sis. I'm really trying."

Hope's smile lit up the photograph.

Jaslene checked the time on her iPad. It was 11:50 A.M. Her next client would arrive in about ten minutes. Jaslene would go over the details of the nuptials, sign the contract, and commence with the work of wedding planning.

She clicked on the appointment detail icon to get more information about this client.

Sasha Harrington.

Her shoulders tensed. Jaslene hadn't spoken to Sasha in a long time. Maintaining friendships had grown tougher since Hope died. Now Jaslene would have to face her old friend.

Seconds later, the door to Jaslene's office space opened. Sasha stepped inside and waved. "Hey, girl, hey!"

"Hey," Jaslene said, a low note in her voice.

"It's been so long since we've seen each other."

Sasha glowed, but then again, she was the glowy type. Sasha's long black hair hung to her waist. She could win the Miss Universe pageant with her liquid brown eyes, high cheekbones, and statuesque frame. Whatever "it" was that made folks turn heads, Sasha possessed it. When they were in college together, she always captured the attention of folks on campus. Yet Sasha was never the vain, self-centered type. That was probably why they became fast friends.

"How've you been?"

"Greg and I got engaged last week. He proposed right before he left for a submarine tour." Sasha showed off her huge engagement ring. "I want you to be my wedding planner."

Oh brother. Jaslene could help, but if they worked together, would Sasha get all Sasha-y on her and probe into her life? Probably. Sasha never missed a beat when it came to reading people. "You're sure you want to hire me?"

"Positive. I spoke to most every wedding planner in the state of South Carolina. They don't get it."

"Get what?"

"I tell them that I want the arras, and the eternity cord, and the veil for my wedding. I tell them I want to jump the broom too. They look at me strangely. People around here don't know about all of that. You, on the other hand, understand."

As a Blasian woman, Jaslene definitely understood. The trademark of Fairytale Weddings was incorporating a couple's cultural traditions into their wedding ceremony, and Jaslene was well aware of both Filipino and African American wedding rituals. Jaslene incorporated those same rituals in her own wedding with Marcus . . . well, what would've been her wedding with Marcus. "You're positive you want us to work together? We haven't spoken in a while."

"Correction: *you* haven't spoken to *me* in a while, Ms. Lady."

Jaslene tugged on her silver-and-gold bracelet, not liking the turn of this conversation. Distancing herself from friends had become a great way to avoid those inevitable conversations about her canceled wedding and her sister's death. Jaslene thought about Hope every single day. Talking about her would be hard, though. Keeping to herself was the best option.

"I tried contacting you, but you didn't answer my messages. What happened?" Sasha asked.

"A lot of things happened. You know that."

Sasha's eyes softened. "I know, but I'm here to support you. We all are. You're not alone."

Alone.

Jaslene swallowed the lump in her throat and checked her phone, a much-needed distraction. Alone wasn't so bad. It was better than putting herself out there and trusting people—loving people—only to lose them. "So tell me about your wed—"

"I still consider you a friend, even though we haven't spoken in a while." Sasha's gaze didn't waver. "When Greg and I became engaged, I couldn't help but think about the conversations we used to have about getting married one day. Remember?"

She remembered. They used to scour the internet for venues and dresses and cakes and flowers. It had become a shared obsession among the three of them—Jaslene, Hope, and Sasha—a fun one, something to focus on as they procrastinated on studying for midterms and final exams at South Carolina State. Jaslene hadn't obsessed about it in a while. Not since everything went downhill.

"I'm going to email *Southern Bride* to see if they want to feature my wedding in their magazine. They made a call for submissions on their website for brides of color." Sasha cheesed. "Wouldn't it be great to be in their publication?"

"Oh yes. Great." Jaslene hadn't thought of being in that publication in a while. When they were undergraduates, they'd chatted endlessly about how the brides in the fancy wedding magazines never looked like them. There wasn't a brown face in sight.

Actually, that was the very reason Jaslene and Hope had started this business and made it culturally focused. They had planned to change the wedding narrative. Sasha would've partnered in their venture, but she went to Paris for graduate school, earning a degree in art history. Nonetheless, they vowed to one another that when they got engaged, their photos would be featured in one of those bridal magazines.

Jaslene stared at her bare ring finger. At least Sasha was keeping up her end of the bargain, but getting married didn't matter to Jaslene anymore. Running this business and taking care of her seventeen-year-old niece, Imani, did. "Let's get started, shall we?" She pulled out one of her client contracts. "When is the date of your wedding?"

"January twelfth. My birthday."

"I love that. Two celebrations in one." Jaslene scribbled the date down in a notebook. "That gives us two months to plan. That's not a lot of time to reserve venues and place orders with vendors. I might be able to pull some strings, but I can't guarantee it."

"That's all right. Greg and I don't want to wait. I already spoke to Pastor Clark. He agreed to officiate our wedding ceremony."

A weight pressed on her chest. Pastor Clark was Marcus's grandfather. He was supposed to officiate Jaslene and Marcus's wedding at New Life Church two years ago, but when Hope died that day, Jaslene called it off. Jaslene hadn't spoken to Pastor Clark ever since, and she hadn't stepped foot in that church either. Jaslene wouldn't ever return to New Life. "Will your ceremony be there?"

"Oh no. It won't."

The tension in Jaslene's chest relaxed. "Good. Where were you thinking?"

Sasha's face flickered. "Well . . . before we discuss venues, I wanted you to also design the overall aesthetic for the ceremony and the reception. Can you do that?"

When Hope was alive, she was in charge of the logistical planning for their clients while Jaslene cast a vision for every single wedding. She used to love adding beautiful touches to each event space, something that was unique to each couple and their shared love for each other. Jaslene had created a floral theme for her own wedding. Orchids accented the altar where she would take her vows. They were her favorite flower. Yet shortly after the funeral, her creativity dried up. "Um, no."

"No?" The volume of Sasha's voice increased two notches. "You create the most gorgeous centerpieces, and I love the way you bring your artistic eye to physical spaces. The way you and Hope coupled event planning and design was one of a kind. What happened to that?"

The question poked at her. She shifted in her seat and focused on her cell phone—again. This time she pulled up photos of Imani.

"You're avoiding my question, sis."

"I wasn't . . . I was just . . . you know. Anyway, we have a very short time to plan, and so we better get to it," Jaslene said. "Have you booked your reception at a hotel yet?"

Sasha did that face flicker thing again. "No."

"I see." Jaslene tapped her pen on her chin. "Nailing down a reception hall will be tough. Most places are booked for the upcoming winter. Our options will be limited."

Sasha hesitated and twirled her finger around her hair, apparently uncomfortable. "I have a few ideas for my ceremony and reception. My first choice is a museum."

A museum. That was unique. About 80 percent of weddings were held at churches. Whenever her clients chose a different venue, that location held particular importance to the couple. "Oh, really? What museums were you thinking of?"

"The Lowcountry African American Heritage Museum."

Jaslene froze. "The one where Marcus works?"

"That's the one."

Jaslene set her pen down. "Sasha, you're my friend and all, but there's no way in the world that I'll coordinate a wedding there. Marcus and I haven't spoken in years."

"I knew you were going to say that."

"Of course I was going to say it." She closed her notebook and set it aside. "It'd be too awkward."

"I know it's been hard. I really do. That's another reason why I made an appointment with you," Sasha continued. "Even though we haven't spoken, I've been worried. I thought giving you your space would help, but I want us to talk again."

"I'd like that too." Jaslene kept the emotion out of her voice.

"Wonderful." Sasha tilted her head slightly. "And I know you have your qualms about the museum, but I have noble reasons for wanting my wedding there."

Noble reasons? This was getting interesting. "And what are these noble reasons?"

Sasha set her phone on Jaslene's desk. "I don't know if you heard, but I recently joined a volunteer committee at the museum. We're trying to coordinate cultural events there. I wanted to help continue the work that your sister started."

Her breath caught. Hope was a founding member of that committee. She was very involved in it, often telling Jaslene about all the historical tidbits that she discovered. "That's so thoughtful. I can't believe you did that. Well, actually, I can believe it. You've always been cool."

"It's what a friend should do," Sasha said, her eyes exuding warmth. "I've been to the museum a few times since joining the group. The building is older, but it has so much potential. Having my reception there might inspire Harold, the museum director, to finally give the place a newer look. I thought you could help with that."

"You already spoke to Harold about all of this?"

"I told him about the wedding part, not about sprucing up the museum part. He's supportive of me having my reception there. I scheduled an appointment for Friday to figure out the seating arrangements for my guests . . . and I'd like my wedding planner to come with. Pretty please?" She crossed her fingers.

Oh brother. "I don't know."

An invisible weight settled on her. Working on a wedding at the museum could be a way to try her hand at event design again.

Could be. It could also just blow up in her face.

She glanced at that picture of Hope again. If she were alive, she would probably love the idea of Sasha celebrating her nuptials at the museum.

But Jaslene would most definitely bump into Marcus.

Being around Marcus would be . . . There was no way she could visit. "I'll see what I can do and let you know."

"Thank you so much. That's all I ask." Sasha hugged Jaslene.

Worry filled the vacant spaces within Jaslene's heart. Perhaps she could make up an excuse for not going to the meeting on Friday. Then Jaslene wouldn't have to risk seeing Marcus. Seeing Marcus would dredge up the past, and Jaslene wasn't ready for it.

She never would be.

Marcus Clark had perfected the art of hiding from the world. A museum was the perfect place to do so.

Sitting at his desk, tucked inside the recesses of the museum, Marcus archived old photographs of people long gone. People he would never see in person. That was a good thing. It meant Marcus would never let them down.

He grasped the bottle of glue and dotted the four corners of a photo dated from 1820. It was a picture of a brown-skinned woman with two children at her side. The woman wore a wide-brimmed hat, and she had a piece of straw in her mouth. A worn-down shack was behind them. The older child wore a pair of ratty pants held up by suspenders and a white button-down shirt. His skinny arm was wrapped around the other child, presumably his younger brother.

The older brother held his sibling close, protective like. The kind of brother who would never be so careless as to risk a loved one's safety.

Marcus pressed the photograph onto the backing board, being careful not to smudge it or leave fingerprints. He wanted to trace the history of New Life Church by using photos like this one, showcasing its members from the past. Sasha and the rest of the volunteer committee helped gather pictures too. He planned to display some of these photos for an exhibit, one that he'd temporarily abandoned shortly after Hope died. If he could pull that off, then maybe he would get some forward motion in his life.

He also wanted the exhibit to bring in more visitors; it was hard to get people inside of the building. Marcus would change that—at least that was his goal.

He sifted through the stacks of photos on his wooden desk for the picture of Hope—taken when she was on the event committee. Worry set in. He'd have to contact Jaslene soon and give it to her. He'd been avoiding making the call for two years. Two years too long.

He had tried to console Jaslene after all that happened, but she kept pushing him away. He didn't blame her, given the fact that Jaslene probably blamed him for the car accident that led to Hope's death. Once again, Marcus hadn't been able to mend the broken. Looking back, not getting married was the best choice.

He gathered the pictures in his arms and headed down the hallway for the three o'clock meeting with his boss, Harold Jenkins. Marcus would finalize the plans for the exhibit's design with Harold. They had been working on it for months, and they could taste the completion.

He made a right down the dimly lit hall leading to Harold's workspace. The overhead lights flickered on and off, and he made a mental note to talk to maintenance.

A glow spilled into the hallway from the half-opened door to Harold's office. The closer he got, the louder Harold's voice became.

"You sure of that? I mean, because I have a preponderance of evidence that shows we're doing some real good in the community."

No response. He must've been talking on the phone. Marcus stopped outside, not wanting to interrupt the conversation.

"We've been around for years," Harold continued. "The local schools have reached out to us for their education programs. I've had people from out of state contact us. They want to visit. All of those folks think we're worth keeping. How can the Lee Ray Foundation think otherwise?"

Marcus's chest tightened. What was going on?

"All right, well, I have a meeting in a few minutes. I'll have to think this one through. There's no way for me to have an answer for you today."

The phone slammed into the cradle. That wasn't a good sign. Marcus tapped on the door lightly.

"That you, Marcus?" Harold said, his voice gruff.

"Yes, it is."

"Come on in."

He stepped inside. A trail of smoke from a cigarette floated up to the ceiling. Harold usually took all his smoke breaks outside. The man must've been stressed. Harold quickly snuffed out the cigarette.

This office hadn't been tidied in decades. He sat behind his desk, drumming his fingertips on the phone receiver. Next to him, an old Royal typewriter with a permanently half-typed letter stuck inside rested proudly on top of a stack of books. Harold said it had belonged to his mother, and he wanted it cataloged and displayed in the museum. He'd never gotten around to getting that done. Harold was holding on to it for sentimental reasons, just like Marcus was holding on to things that he had discovered while working on his genealogical records. Those precious items were hard to let go.

Marcus glanced at the pictures in his arms, ready to get approval for the exhibit. "I'm prepared to set things up. I need your go-ahead to—"

"We have a problem," Harold said.

"What problem?"

Harold scratched the side of his nose. "I got off the phone with the chief financial officer for our largest donor. He's sympathetic to us and wanted to give me a heads-up. They're going over the proposed budget for the upcoming year. The museum probably won't receive funding from them for the next fiscal year . . . or ever again."

Marcus's pulse raced. This could have ripple effects on everything else associated with the museum. The Lee Ray Foundation's grant covered everyone's salary and funded all the museum's much-needed research, programs, and exhibits. "Why?"

"A group of Confederate history enthusiasts want a share of that funding for their programs."

"Did they state the reason?"

"You know the reason." Harold picked up a newspaper and pushed it to the edge of the desk. "It made today's headlines. Over the weekend protesters knocked over two statues of Confederate generals in Columbia. The Confederate history folks believe that if they're going to knock down Confederate statues, then in a 'fair and equal' society, our museum shouldn't exist either."

This was not good.

"More board members are supporting the effort too. There's been a preliminary motion to defund our museum."

Marcus's eyes widened. "What?"

Harold didn't miss a beat. "It was a shocker to me too."

A pain shot into the base of Marcus's neck, and numbness began to spread. The exhibit on the history of New Life would never come to be. He glanced at the pictures tucked underneath his arm, sadness coursing through him. Their stories would remain untold. "So that's it? We're going to shut down?"

"No. I'm not giving up that easy. You know me. I've been here for over thirty years. This place means everything to me."

Marcus smiled. Harold had worked at the museum since the mid-eighties. He was the first Black curator in the South, a history maker in his own right. He helped to make it a place where tourists and locals would come to learn all of South Carolina's history, not the watered-down information taught in schools. If anyone had more passion about this place than Marcus did, it was Harold. "What can we do?"

"I don't know." He fumbled for another cigarette but then set it on the desk. "I have to brainstorm. In the meantime, we'll have to figure out ways to bring in funding. Our individual donors have decreased considerably over the years, except for donations from Heather Gates."

The governor's daughter became a huge supporter of the museum after she discovered that her great-grandmother was a Black woman who had passed for White.

"It's ironic Heather Gates wants to help, but her father is staying out of it," Harold added.

Marcus could understand. Memories of his strained relations with his grandfather rose to the surface. Pastor Clark didn't approve of Marcus's career choice, but history was his passion. "Family gets like that sometimes."

"I know." Harold rubbed his temples. "We have to figure something out. I don't want to make any more cuts."

Marcus's breath shortened for a split second. It had

been only two months since Harold let go of Dorothy, the exhibit designer, and some of the fundraising staff because of budget constraints. It would be a matter of time until Marcus lost his job too. Then what would he do?

This was the only place where he found a sense of stability.

"One funding idea just dropped into my lap. Sasha called me this morning. She wants to rent the museum for her wedding ceremony and reception."

Marcus's brows lifted. "Oh, yeah. Last week, Greg asked me to be the best man before he left for a tour. I agreed, of course. He mentioned that they were thinking about having their wedding here."

"Good you already know. She wants to meet on Friday to figure out the seating arrangements. I'm glad she chose this place for her big day, despite its need of an update." Harold glanced at his desk filled with paper and clutter. "If she could've seen the inside of my office, then she would have certainly changed her mind."

Marcus chuckled. "It's not that bad."

"Yes, it is." Harold let out an easy laugh. The strain in Harold's voice was palpable, despite his joking. "I'm going to take off for the rest of the day. I need some time to figure this out. If I can think of a viable solution, then maybe our museum will stand a chance after all. I wish I could've kept Dorothy. She would've boosted the optics of this place. That would help in giving us more foot traffic."

"Do you plan to meet with the board of directors at the foundation?"

"Yes, most definitely. They have a meeting coming up. I'll be there."

"I can go with you."

"You? No. All of those folks who want this museum closed will bother you too. Believe me, you don't want that stress in your life."

Marcus's shoulders tensed. Harold didn't need to take on the majority of that stress. He was getting up there in years, and those Confederate supporters would be at those meetings. They weren't friendly toward people like Harold either. "Is someone going with you to the meeting?"

"Nope. Just me. I'll be fine, Marcus. Don't worry." He clasped his hands. "I do need your help in a different way, however. If we lose funding, then we'll have to raise money to keep this place going. We need to step up our fundraising efforts, and I can't afford to hire new staff. I'll need you to find volunteers to help the fundraising manager. Folks experienced in that arena. We'll need them as soon as possible." Harold shifted uncomfortably. "Also . . . I can't go ahead with the church exhibit right now."

"What?"

"We need to focus our efforts elsewhere."

Marcus felt his resolve fold in on itself. He'd been looking forward to the grand opening. If the exhibit didn't happen . . . Marcus didn't even want to consider it. "I can find the time to work on the project without interfering with fundraising efforts."

"I'm sure you can, but we need this budget issue resolved. That's the priority." Harold tapped his fingers. "I know you've done a lot for the project. But we have to take this new direction. Can you support it?"

Could he? "I could lose the gains I'd been making on the exhibit. A lot of people want to see the exhibit happen."

The frown lines on Harold's forehead deepened. "I know. You have a point. But we can revisit the project after I have enough buffer money raised for the museum's operations. I really need your help with this."

A memory resurfaced, a memory from when his grandfather, Pastor Clark, had asked him to reconsider his plans to become a museum archivist. He'd wanted to retire from the ministry, and he was looking to Marcus to fill his shoes. When Marcus turned down his offer, his grandfather had been deeply disappointed. That look of resignation and apathy on his grandfather's face when they made eye contact . . .

Marcus would never live that down.

"Marcus?" Harold's voice interrupted his musings. "What do you say?"

Harold's expression hit a little too close to home. Marcus couldn't bear to see that disappointment again. Still, the exhibit was also a way for Marcus to show his grandfather the value in his work. He had hoped that it would win his grandfather over, but now even that would be put on hold. "I can help. I'll . . . ask Sasha and the rest of the cultural events committee if any of them would be interested in volunteering to fundraise. I'll have to let them know that plans for the exhibit will be cut, since they've been looking forward to it."

"Thank you, Marcus. And don't worry. Once we get a footing financially, we can redirect our efforts toward the exhibit again. By the way"—Harold flicked a yellow sticky note from his desk and showed it to Marcus—"I'd like you to meet with Sasha this Friday and show her the options for seating arrangements. I won't be here on that day."

He took the sticky note. They were changing their focus from exhibits to weddings and fundraising. What did he know about either? Nothing. Yet they'd need to do this if Marcus hoped to keep his job. "I'll give Sasha a call and see what she needs for Friday's meeting."

"Good. Also, post a message on our social media pages to ask for volunteers," Harold added.

A bittersweetness arose within him. "I can do that."

The frown lines returned to Harold's mouth. "We'll get that exhibit up and running. I promise."

"I hope so." He tried to sound confident, but the possibility of the exhibit never happening planted a seed of worry in him.

And no matter how much he tried, Marcus couldn't uproot it.

Chapter Two

The following day, Jaslene pulled her blue Toyota Corolla into an empty parking space at the Flowertown Center for Performing Arts and turned off the ignition. Imani's violin lesson would end in fifteen minutes. Driving her niece around felt like a part-time job, but Jaslene wouldn't have it any other way.

Although Imani would soon qualify to get her driver's license, Jaslene enjoyed taking her niece to violin lessons, music rehearsals, and performances. Hope used to do this, and Jaslene had vowed to support her niece's endeavors. It also gave Jaslene a rhythm to her busy days—and she wanted to keep Imani close.

Today, Imani's music teacher wanted to meet up with Jaslene to discuss Imani's career options after high school. Jaslene was eager to discuss that. She'd spent a lot of time researching state schools and hoped Imani would become a music major at South Carolina State. Imani would do well there, and she would still be local.

The redbrick building stood proud with its crisp American flag at the entrance. Perfectly manicured bushes encircled the parking lot. A private security guard stood at the entrance, watching.

She exhaled, and unbuckled, shifting in her seat, unable to get the conversation with Sasha out of her mind. Should Jaslene go to the museum on Friday? The fact that Sasha volunteered there as a way to honor Hope moved her. The least Jaslene could do was show up and talk seating arrangements. Yeah, that's what she would do.

The alarm on her phone buzzed—time to pick up Imani. No time to think about Friday's meeting.

Jaslene exited her sedan and headed to the performing arts center. After walking through the door, she hooked a left toward the rehearsal area. A small crowd of musicians spilled out of the room across from Imani's, each one toting a flute or a stringed instrument. They chatted and laughed among themselves.

Jaslene waited outside Imani's room and waved to them as they passed by. Once the last musician left, all was quiet. The sonorous strains of Imani's violin echoed into the hall. Jaslene closed her eyes and inhaled the melody. She pressed her hand against the wall. Each note reverberated on her palm.

Imani's composition traveled slowly and softly. The ebb and flow of the sound sent pinpricks of longing through Jaslene, a longing for something distant and too far gone. Her niece's music often stirred buried feelings within her, feelings Jaslene had forgotten.

The music stopped, and Imani's instructor spoke. Seconds later, the door clicked open and Mrs. Carlisle popped her head out and waved. "Come on in, Ms. Simmons. So glad to see you this afternoon."

Jaslene greeted her. Inside the lesson space, neat rows of music stands were lined up in front of a whiteboard that displayed handwritten half notes and whole notes. A keyboard stood in the far left corner, right next to Mrs. Carlisle's empty violin case. The walls displayed sketches of Beethoven, Bach, and Mozart.

Imani sat on a metal folding chair and carefully placed her violin on her lap. Her brown eyes exuded the satisfaction that could only come from being in creative flow. Jaslene used to have that same look whenever she finished designing a space for a wedding client—at least that's what others had told her.

Mrs. Carlisle smoothed the front of her gray pleated skirt and sat in the chair next to the two of them. "As you know, Imani has been a student of mine for fourteen years now, and she's worked hard to bring her skills to the professional level."

At Hope's encouragement, Imani had started playing the violin at three years old. It was a cute hobby, but as the years passed, the hobby morphed into a calling. When other kids played video games, Imani played concertos. When other kids performed at the school's Nativity play, Imani performed as a guest artist with the Charleston Symphony.

A glint of sunshine streamed through the windows and cast a glow on Mrs. Carlisle's countenance, accentuating the light in her eyes. "Imani could succeed as a chamber musician. She's built a great musical rapport with other performers at the symphony orchestra, and she wants to attend a conservatory after graduation. Isn't that right?"

"Yes, that's what I want to do. I'm excited to apply."

Mrs. Carlisle and Imani nodded in agreement. Imani's mouth curled upward, revealing the dimples on her smooth brown cheeks.

Conservatory? "So you don't want to go to South Carolina State?"

"No." Imani crossed her legs at the ankles and tucked her violin closer to her abdomen.

Jaslene went through her mental files. Were there any in-state conservatories? She had no idea.

"I made a list of potential places for Imani to audition." Mrs. Carlisle reached over to the small wooden desk behind her, lifted an ivory sheet of paper and handed it to Jaslene. "I already discussed these options with Imani."

Jaslene studied the list: Juilliard, Curtis Institute of Music, Manhattan School of Music, Berklee College of Music, New England Conservatory of Music, and more. "I recognize some of these places but not all. Are they all out of state?"

Imani paused. "Yes."

Jaslene's neck muscles tensed, and she took a deep breath against the strain.

Mrs. Carlisle adjusted the bifocals that rested on the bridge of her nose. "Imani has the talent and discipline to succeed at this level. She has a strong chance of getting into at least one of these schools, but it'll be a very competitive process."

Out of state.

"A lot of applicants have already taken extracurricular courses at the conservatories on the list prior to applying, either through summer programs or during the regular school year. Imani hasn't done that. That won't help her case," Mrs. Carlisle added.

"Imani's mother wanted her to enroll in a summer music program, but our business is very busy here. No time to take off."

"Understandable. Nonetheless, Imani has extensive professional experience with the Charleston Symphony. That makes her unique. If she can perform at least once with the South Carolina Philharmonic, that'll make her an even more competitive applicant." The fine lines around Mrs. Carlisle's eyes crinkled. "What are your thoughts, Ms. Simmons?"

Jaslene had so many. When she and Hope were placed in foster care as children, they promised to always stick together. They managed to do that, if only because some divine force honored the silent wishes of two orphaned girls. As time passed, that promise rooted more deeply within Jaslene, despite Hope's death. Jaslene and Imani had to stick together. "All of these schools are so far away. Aren't there great music programs here?"

Imani exchanged a look with Mrs. Carlisle. "There are . . . it's just . . ."

"It's just what?" Jaslene asked.

"It's hard to explain." Imani bowed her head.

Jaslene's resolve softened. The tone in Imani's voice reminded Jaslene of when she had been a senior in high school, when she held big aims of becoming a successful wedding decorator. At the time, not many people in the area knew of wedding decorators, but Jaslene intended to put the profession on the map. As a high school senior, Jaslene had booked a few clients who loved her center-pieces and aesthetic, but then the discouraging words of her high school guidance counselor made Jaslene quit: *It's going to be hard for someone like you to pursue a little-known profession, especially here.*

Someone like you. Jaslene had been stunned at her guidance counselor's words, but her brain couldn't form a retort. That meeting had paralyzed Jaslene for years.

Jaslene didn't want to be a dissenting voice in Imani's life.

Imani lifted her head. "I grew up here. Was born and raised here. I want to see the world."

Big dreams could turn into small ones—and not by one's choice. "That's great, honey. But sometimes . . ." Jaslene focused her attention on Mrs. Carlisle as if she would complete her thought, but Imani's violin teacher couldn't know Jaslene's mind.

"If you apply, I want to make sure we pick out the best audition piece for you," Mrs. Carlisle said. "And you'll have to practice, practice, practice, but you know that already."

"Of course." Imani smiled.

Mrs. Carlisle riffled through a file folder on the desk behind her. "For Juilliard's application, we don't have to record her audition for another month or so. I think the Manhattan School of Music's deadline is a bit earlier. And they may want a sonata. I'll have to double-check."

Jaslene's pulse pitter-pattered. They were moving forward with this. Life would be so quiet if Imani left. Jaslene would no longer chauffeur Imani around for her lessons, rehearsals, and performances. The condominium would be empty. Jaslene loved living with Hope and Imani. They'd been a team of three—and then suddenly a team of two. Without Imani there, Jaslene would end up alone, with nothing, with no one. It wasn't like Jaslene kept up with any of her friends after her sister passed away.

She blinked, blinked, blinked, unable to stop her galloping pulse.

"Here are the application packets for the top conservatories." Mrs. Carlisle handed them to Imani in a ceremonious manner. "Read through everything, and we can discuss more at your next lesson. And start researching audition pieces."

Imani flipped through the pages of a packet, entranced.

"Your niece's level of skill is a rarity in Charleston. Be proud." Mrs. Carlisle clasped her hands together, her tone upbeat. "And let me know if you have any questions."

"I will." Jaslene stood. "Thank you again."

They left and headed to the parking lot in silence. Shortly after the car doors closed, Imani faced her. "You don't want me to go to school out of state, huh?"

"What?" Jaslene clasped her seat belt. "I never said that."

"You don't have to say it. I see it."

How could she tell Imani about her fears and worries? She couldn't. She wouldn't. "I want you to be happy. To pursue your dreams."

Imani tilted her head to the side and gave her a *get real* look. "There's a 'but' in there. I know it."

Jaslene fumbled with the seat belt until it locked into place. "But I will miss you if you leave. It would be another big change for us. And I don't want you to get your hopes up and be disappointed. Those are highly competitive schools."

Frown lines etched into Imani's mouth. Jaslene didn't want to dash her hopes. "Unlike me, you're young. You have the world ahead of you. Don't worry about what I think."

Imani glanced away. The sunlight pierced through the windshield and shone on Imani's cheek, highlighting her glistening eye.

"What's the matter, honey?"

"I was thinking about how proud Mom would've been today." Imani tugged on the hem of her Aaliyah T-shirt, and her lower lip trembled. "I miss her."

"Me too."

"Now that Mom's gone, I have no one," Imani added.

No one. That was a strong statement. It threatened to put Jaslene on the defensive, but she understood Imani's feelings.

"I want to get a head start on filling out the online applications for the New York schools. I can send those now and upload my audition pieces later. But for me to send them, I'll have to pay all of the application fees. And I wasn't prepared for that."

"How much does it cost?"

"About five hundred dollars for each of the New York schools."

"Each school? That's over a grand," Jaslene said.

"I know."

What should I do, Hope? Jaslene gently squeezed Imani's hand. Her niece deserved the world, but the world could be cruel—experience had taught Jaslene that much. Still, she didn't want to dash her niece's aspirations. "You're a young woman. You know what's best for you. I'll try my best to trust your decisions about your future. I'll pay your application fees."

Imani's eyes brightened. "For real?"

"For real."

"Oh, Auntie." She reached over and hugged Jaslene's neck. "Thank you so much."

Jaslene hugged her in return. Perhaps this would turn out for the best. Perhaps Imani would end up with all her dreams fulfilled. Perhaps Jaslene needn't worry.

A tiny ember of expectancy lit within her, but she couldn't count on it burning too bright. She held only a preliminary hope—and a wish. A wish that life would be kinder to her niece than it had been to Jaslene.

On Tuesday evening, Marcus worked late at the museum. He still had to call Sasha to discuss plans for

Friday, but the mere thought of doing so made him anxious.

Anxious about whether he'd ever get back to work on the exhibit.

He pushed aside the feeling, but the conversation with Harold stuck in his mind. Since they were halting the exhibit, he'd have to figure out these fundraising efforts. That, coupled with folks not wanting the museum to exist, challenged him. Navigating it all . . .

Marcus posted a call for fundraising volunteers on the museum's social media page. Hopefully, some folks would respond. He made a note to ask the museum volunteers too.

The faint sound of footsteps grew louder and louder. Moments later, Grandma Clark stepped into his office. "Hey there, grandson."

The singsong tone of her greeting brought a smile to his face. Her presence was like a tray of warm buttered biscuits, comforting and sweet. "Hey. What brings you here?"

"You, of course. I was doing some shopping downtown, and I thought I'd see my grandson. I brought coffee and doughnuts from Bertha's Kitchen." She held up a brown paper bag and a carton of coffee. "You look hungry."

"You showed up at the perfect time. My stomach was rumbling." He inhaled the scent of freshly brewed coffee.

"I'm glad I brought sustenance." She set the food and drink on his desk, grabbed a Ziploc bag of disinfectant wipes from her purse, and proceeded to wipe everything down. The fresh lemon scent filled the space, bringing back memories of sitting at her kitchen table as a child. Grandma Clark always fussed at him about making a mess, and she always had a packet of cleaning wipes on hand for the occasion. He appreciated her preparedness.

"You're looking worried over there." She tossed the dirty wipes in the trash can. "You okay?"

His shoulders stiffened. Marcus wasn't ready to share his concerns. Grandma Clark had a way of telling it like it was, and he didn't want to face her blunt honesty. "I'm great."

"You surely don't look too great to me. Got a furrow in your brow and a frown around your mouth. I know you too well for you to hide your feelings from me. Practically raised you."

That she had. His mother was a busy lawyer, working extended hours on cases. His father often had back-to-back shifts at the hospital. When Marcus was a child, Grandma Clark became his second mother.

She pulled out a chair and sat down, then she motioned to him. "Come on, now. Have a doughnut and talk to me. Tell me what's on your mind."

Grandma Clark took a bite of a chocolate doughnut. Her dark eyes shone with ease. Maybe he should get some fresh perspective. Her perspective was blunt, but she never steered him wrong.

Marcus poured himself a cup of black coffee, and then he emptied a creamer container and one pack of sugar inside of it. "I may be losing my job soon." He then told her all the details, bit by painful bit, including the part about the museum losing funding from its largest benefactor.

"That's a shame that folks don't see the importance of the museum."

He tugged his phone from the back pocket of his khakis and opened some photos of newspaper headlines from the 1800s. He would like to put these on display at the exhibit—if it was still happening.

THE SOUTH STRIKES THE FIRST BLOW.
THE SOUTHERN CONFEDERACY
AUTHORIZES HOSTILITIES.
FORT MOULTRIE OPENS FIRE ON FORT SUMTER,
AT FOUR O'CLOCK FRIDAY MORNING.

He closed the photos. "Old wounds run deep."

"Too deep." The lilt in her voice had dissipated.

"I don't think those wounds will ever be mended."

She pursed her lips and straightened her posture. The folds in her cardigan shifted with the movement of her breath. "Well . . . you might want to ask your grandfather for help. Pretty sure he knows a thing or two about raising money."

His jaw tightened at the mention of his grandfather. "I can't."

"Boy, please. You made your decision. You chose your career path. You need to let it go. Your fool grandfather needs to let it go too."

He warmed his hands on the hot cup of coffee, allowing the steam to rise up to his face, hiding his expression. "You're asking a lot."

"What? That my husband and my grandson should be on better terms? That's not a lot to ask. What's the harm in requesting help?"

Marcus shifted in his chair. Grandma put him on the spot. "Um . . . there's a lot of harm. I ruined his hopes of maintaining the Clark ministerial legacy."

She smiled at him in that *you can't fool me* way. "Your grandfather acts as if the church is going to fall apart if a Clark isn't a pastor there. New Life has suffered far worse, and it will remain, regardless of who shepherds the flock."

Marcus glanced away. She was right. The church had endured a lot since a group of free Black people had held their first services there in the early 1800s. The church had been born out of protest. The congregants had been tired of being relegated to segregated galleries in the house of God, unable to pray and worship alongside the White congregants. They'd endured more than their share of troubled times. "I don't want to talk to Grandpa Clark, though."

"You two are so stubborn," she continued. "I'll ask him myself. If he refuses, I'll insist. The museum is important to us too, you know."

He kept silent. When Grandma Clark was onto something, no one could stop her.

"It's settled then," she said.

He didn't feel settled at all.

After Marcus told his grandfather that he didn't want

to go into the ministry, Marcus still tried to keep the lines of communication open, especially since Grandpa Clark was officiating their wedding ceremony at New Life. Whenever Marcus reached out to him, he never picked up the phone or answered his texts. Marcus never told Jaslene about the disagreement, not wanting to cause her unnecessary stress, but his grandmother knew. She had to convince Grandpa Clark to still officiate the ceremony. Grandpa Clark only showed up for the wedding day, not the rehearsal. His grandfather had sent a clear message, so Marcus kept his distance. Now Grandma Clark was going to shake things up.

Grandma studied Marcus, compassion in her eyes. "Trust me."

Her tone made him uneasy. Nothing had turned out right for him in a while, but Grandma Clark wasn't one for excuses. *Refocus, Marcus.* "I will."

"Good. There's always a silver lining to everything. You have to remember to look up."

She was right in a way, but he'd never acknowledge that. Although everything about Marcus's life had felt empty since he and Jaslene separated, he'd grown comfortable with the void. It was familiar and safe, and Marcus wouldn't upset the cocoon that he'd built.

Chapter Three

$\mathcal{F}$ingers crossed that Jaslene wouldn't run into Marcus today.

Fingers crossed that Jaslene wouldn't see him at all.

The late-afternoon sunlight bounced off the museum's dulled stone walls and dusty windows. The sign on the front said the place was open, but it didn't seem ready for visitors.

Jaslene's breathing shallowed. Inside that building was the man she once loved.

She forced an exhale and put a few coins in the parking meter. Sasha was still sitting in the driver's seat, powdering her nose and putting on lipstick. A cool breeze rustled through Jaslene's hair, tickling her cheek.

"Ready to go inside and see Harold?" Jaslene called to Sasha.

"Harold?" Sasha's voice went high pitch for a moment, and she rolled down her window. "Oh yeah. Harold. Actually, I need a moment."

"Is something wrong?"

"No. I just . . . a phone call. I have to make an important phone call." Sasha snapped her compact shut and offered a lopsided smile.

"Can't it wait until after our meeting?"

"It's very important. You can go ahead of me. I'll catch up in a bit."

Jaslene's pulse somersaulted. No way was she going in there by herself. "I'll wait for you."

"Don't do that. I don't want to keep Harold waiting. Just . . . you know, go in there and check out the space."

"Go in there by myself and possibly run into Marcus? Alone? Not happening."

"You technically won't be alone. I'm sure there are other people inside the museum."

Jaslene rolled her eyes. "Fine. I'll go so we can be on time, but don't take long."

"I won't." Sasha's smile stayed put. How did Sasha manage to talk and smile simultaneously? Who knew?

Jaslene headed to the museum's entrance, her heels clacking against the cobblestone pavement. Everything in Jaslene screamed to turn around, but she didn't. "Be the wedding planning professional." If she repeated this over and over, it would remove her nervousness.

She tried. It didn't.

The OPEN sign at the entrance tapped against the front door, beckoning her to step inside. She stilled. Marcus was most likely inside right now.

A longing bloomed inside of her, a longing for what could have been, but she shook off the sensation. She had ended their relationship. Jaslene refused to give place to longings or regrets or anything of the sort.

She squinted at the entrance. "This meeting will be very brief." Jaslene opened the heavy wooden door and stepped inside the dimly lit space. A small gift shop was on her left, and a narrow hallway stretched before her. She took her mini notepad from her purse and jotted down a bunch of things to discuss about the museum. She would need to measure the perimeter of the space and research various table options. Square. Rectangular. Wide. Narrow. She glanced up. The skylights let in a trickle of brightness. More was needed.

Jaslene walked the hallway and hooked a left toward the Civil War area. A lone man stood in front of the exhibit, his back to her. He wore an unremarkable suit, but she knew that tall, proud bearing anywhere. Marcus.

Her emotions went into overdrive, and she hated that her pulse betrayed her.

"Hey, Sa—" Marcus turned, and his eyes widened. "What are you doing here?"

He saw her. It was too late to run. She gulped. "I'm the planner for Sasha's wedding. We're supposed to meet with Harold. Is he here?"

"Harold? No. Harold wanted me to see Sasha today because he couldn't make it." He rubbed a scuff mark off the tile floor with the toe of his shoe. "I'm sorry. This is awkward and I hate that. When I spoke to her the other day, she never mentioned that you were the wedding planner."

"She didn't?"

"No." His volume increased. "She didn't say a thing."

Jaslene recalled the "phone call" Sasha had to make, and her awareness piqued. Sasha set her up. Not fair. Not fair at all.

"This is awkward," he said again.

"Sure is." Jaslene tapped her notepad against her thigh.

Marcus hadn't changed a bit. His hair was still cropped into a Caesar cut. Thick, dark lashes framed eyes the color of her morning coffee. Marcus's suit didn't do his athletic frame any justice, but she admired it nonetheless. She used to love being in his embrace. *Stop it, Jaslene.*

She cleared her throat. She could do this. Be professional. "Is this the exact space where Sasha wants her wedding reception to be held?" She gestured to the dimly lit atrium where they stood.

"Yes."

His voice was low and deep and way too inviting. A warmth spread through her, but she pushed it aside. Being here wouldn't work. She focused on her notes, but her eyes smarted. The words she'd written on the pages turned into a blur. "The lighting is dim here. Is it usually like this?" She squinted at the skylights again, trying to figure out how to brighten up the place.

"Yes. That's the best we can do for now. I've told Harold about it, but he has more pressing concerns."

"Oh," she said, ensuring that she sounded as matter-of-fact as possible. "Do you think he'd object if we brought in additional lighting for Sasha's reception?"

"I have no idea. You'd have to ask him."

Jaslene wrote a reminder to ask Harold, careful to avoid eye contact with Marcus.

"How've you been?" His voice was softer now.

"Fine," she said, still staring at her notepad.

A hum of electricity buzzed between them. It made her scalp tingle. She tried to squelch the sensation, but she couldn't.

"Wedding planning keeping you busy?"

Was he going to keep trying the small talk? She needed to stay in professional mode. "Very busy." She walked around the space and made more notes. Better to keep her mind occupied while Marcus asked her a million questions.

"Glad to hear. I remember you were worried that you'd have enough business after . . . after everything."

He meant to say *after Hope,* and Jaslene was grateful that Marcus didn't bring her up. She wouldn't know what to do if he did. Two years had passed, but losing her still felt like yesterday. She stopped walking around the space and faced him. "I'm fortunate that people still want to get married in the Lowcountry." The dry humor in her voice loosened the tension between them.

The furrow in Marcus's brow relaxed. Light streamed through the windows and highlighted the angles of his face. "I'd say that people are fortunate to have you as their wedding planner."

The ceiling fan whirred a steady *da-dum, da-dum, da-dum,* but it did little to cool the flushed sensation rising from her neck and spreading to her face. A tingling feeling lingered on her skin too. His focus didn't waver from her. Unnerved, she flipped through the pages of her notepad in search of a talking point. "You were always one for flattery."

"I'm not flattering. I'm stating the facts."

Jaslene resisted the urge to smile at his candor. They hadn't spoken in a long time, and she was feeling her way through this predicament.

"There you are!" Sasha's voice cut into the moment. "Did I miss anything?"

Jaslene flicked a tiny speck of lint from her notepad. Hard. "You missed a whole lot."

"When I called you the other day, you didn't tell me that Jaslene was your wedding planner," Marcus said.

"I didn't?" Sasha feigned innocence. She had definitely planned all of this in advance.

"No, you didn't," Marcus said. "It's fine with me. I wish you would've mentioned it." He glanced at Jaslene with—was that compassion? She didn't need his pity.

"Oh, well . . ." Sasha twisted her engagement ring. "I was planning to tell you."

"When?" Marcus and Jaslene asked in unison.

Sasha stopped twisting. "Soon."

"I doubt that. You had plenty of time to mention that Marcus would be leading this meeting while we were on our way here."

Sasha looked like a child who got caught stealing cookies from the jar. "Before Greg left, he said that I could coordinate the groomsmen stuff until he returned." Sasha did this jazz hands thing, her apparent attempt to lighten their interrogation.

"He mentioned that to me," Marcus said.

"Wait. Marcus is in the wedding?"

Sasha bobbed her head. "Yes."

Marcus nodded slightly.

This was silly. "Why are you doing this?" Jaslene directed her question at Sasha.

"I didn't know how else to get the two of you together." Sasha tucked a stray piece of hair behind her ear. "I was butting in, and I shouldn't have."

"You're right. Especially since you knew my qualms." Jaslene tucked her notepad under her arm.

"What qualms?" Marcus asked. "Had to do with me, didn't it?"

Oh brother. Jaslene was not in the mood to answer that question, but for the sake of this situation, she would. "It was a lot of things."

He shoved his hands in his pockets and nodded. "Understood."

Jaslene's response bothered him. She could tell by the way he took a subtle step backward. He always did that whenever he was on the defensive.

Whew. She still remembered those things about Marcus. That, on top of Marcus making her almost smile earlier, was not a good thing. If she let herself feel anything good toward Marcus, it would betray the promise she had made to herself to not put her heart out there again.

"Now that you two are speaking again, shall we continue with a tour of the space?"

Now that we're speaking again? Is Sasha serious? "I'm not sure if I can plan your wedding reception here."

"Look, I know I messed up. I should've told you that Marcus would be here today." Sasha adjusted her black crossbody bag. "I could've handled this better. It's my fault."

"The fact that you didn't say a word to me is beyond bothersome. If I'm going to work on your wedding, then you can't keep these sorts of details from me."

Marcus gave an imperceptible nod. At least he was in agreement.

The glint of a gold picture frame hanging near the exit sign caught Jaslene's eye. She stepped closer and squinted at it. Her sister's familiar glow was undeniable. Jaslene recognized her instantly. "Hope."

Jaslene traced her finger over the edge of the frame. In this photo, Hope's hair was blow-dried straight. She usually wore it curly. Either way, Hope always wore her hairstyles well. Jaslene was so impressed that she'd tried to blow-dry her hair straight too, but she couldn't do the look justice. Whatever Hope may have said, Jaslene soon reverted to her curly hair.

"I have another picture of your sister in my office." Marcus sounded tired, but—like he missed her too. "I wanted to give it to you. The photo was taken when she volunteered here."

"I brought up the idea of having her photo hung in the

museum," Sasha said. "Marcus asked Harold about the possibility, and he agreed."

Her frustration ebbed. How kind of them. All this time they were apart from each other, but he made that gesture to remember her sister, despite their spats and disagreements.

Jaslene studied the image. Hope stood in front of the museum, satisfaction written all over her face. "Hope used to love coming here to help out."

"She most definitely did, Jazz."

Her scalp tingled. *Jazz?*

Marcus hadn't called her that name in a long time. Jazz was his special nickname for her. He'd made it up after they officially agreed to date, and she liked it. But things were different now.

Should she brush off his words, or should she tell him that she preferred to be called Jaslene?

If she kept quiet, then it would be an invitation to something more, and she wasn't ready for that. If she said something, it would make an already awkward situation worse.

She might as well say something. Nothing lived between them. All feelings had died. "It's Jaslene. You can call me Jaslene now."

His expression flickered. "Of course. My apologies."

Jaslene refocused on the picture of her sister, but the weight of his gaze hadn't left her. This was too much. "I, uh, have to go."

"Did I say something wrong?" Marcus asked.

Yes. "No. But after being here, I don't think I'm the right person to work on Sasha's wedding. This is a lot to take in."

Marcus's expression faltered. "I understand."

"Wait, Jaslene. Let me—"

"Let her go," Marcus said, cutting Sasha off. "She needs to go. This was too much . . ."

Jaslene's eyes smarted again, and, as their conversation continued, she walked to the exit, her footsteps echoing the whole way and drowning it out. Tears threatened to rise to the surface, but she wasn't having it. She'd already cried enough. Jaslene opened the door and stepped onto the sidewalk.

The Lowcountry sky was a clear blue with threads of white clouds on the horizon—calm and free, unlike her. The November breeze cooled her face. She closed her eyes and inhaled the fresh air, hoping her choice was a good one, grasping for a tiny shred of tranquility, at least for this one small moment.

JASLENE WAS GONE. An emptiness settled onto Marcus—an emptiness and a longing.

The sense of disappointment Marcus had felt after seeing Jaslene walk out hadn't left him when he'd gone to sleep last night, and the feeling lingered upon awakening the next morning. He hadn't been aware of the void until now, until Jaslene's presence had filled the room and then abandoned it.

He missed her presence, her voice, her understanding

heart. She still had those same liquid brown eyes that held a world of emotions and dreams—things she'd once shared with him.

Jaslene had looked gorgeous in her split-sleeve silken blouse embroidered with tiny red orchids. Upon seeing her, Marcus's pulse had raced faster than the questions that poured from his lips. At one point, he thought he surmised a smile on her lips, but it could've been the lighting.

Marcus had wanted to touch the stray curl that graced her cheek, but he caught himself. If he had given in to his instincts, then Jaslene would've surely left sooner than she did.

He didn't know whether to be offended by or saddened about Jaslene's reaction when he used her old nickname. Calling her Jazz came as naturally as the easy conversations they used to share. But if she didn't like the name Jazz anymore, then he'd respect that.

Marcus showered, dressed, and drove to the museum. As soon as Marcus arrived, he headed to the half-finished exhibit and surveyed the display. An old hymnal was propped next to a wooden cashbox. The box was once carried by the preacher, since the minister was also responsible for financial accounting back then. A light sheen of dust had settled on both objects. Marcus's fonds, the archive of photographs, records, and artifacts he had personally collected for the church, were quite extensive, but some items needed to be acquired.

Next to the cashbox hung a watercolor, the artist unknown. Marcus had sent the painting to be scientifically dated, and the report estimated that it was created in the early nineteenth century. The painting featured a Low-country sunrise over New Life Church. Speckles of color swirled and blended to evoke the trees and flowers that encircled the church, an idyllic scene and an ironic one, given the church's history.

The picture of Hope hung a few inches from the painting. Her image had rattled Jaslene, and he didn't know why. That bothered him too. Jaslene was still saddened by Hope's death. Seeing her picture in the same place where Marcus worked probably didn't go over too well with Jaslene. Although Jaslene had said she didn't blame him, Marcus blamed himself.

An old, familiar guilt rose to the surface. Marcus longed to be freed of its weight, a weight that he'd been carrying since the day Trey, his younger brother, had drowned at the lake over two decades ago. Marcus swam to his rescue. Despite Marcus's efforts to resuscitate him, it was too late.

And now things were too late for Hope.

"Time to get to work," Marcus said quietly, pushing those thoughts out of his head.

He picked up a drawing of Denmark Vesey, a free Black preacher who was accused and convicted of plotting an alleged rebellion of enslaved people in South Carolina. The rebellion never even happened. The accusations were based on suspicion. Denmark was known for preaching fiery sermons at New Life.

Marcus surveyed the empty white walls surrounding

the exhibit. He could display a lot here: membership rolls, baptismal and marriage records, even old newspaper clippings about the alleged rebellion. That was the most interesting artifact.

The faint sound of footsteps grew louder and louder. Harold was heading his way.

"Morning. Said you wanted to meet with me, but I went to your office and you weren't there."

The casual chiding in Harold's voice made him straighten a bit. "Oh yeah. I forgot. Had a lot on my mind. How'd the meeting with the foundation go?"

Harold studied him for a few seconds, and then he glanced over at the unfinished exhibit. A reservedness came over his expression. "We're going to need all of the help we can get. Confederate history proponents were present as well."

Tension pressed at Marcus's shoulders. "What happened?"

"We're now on a three-month trial period to prove the museum's viability to the community." Harold crossed his arms, obviously upset with the news.

"Viability? What does that mean? How is it measured?"

Harold shook his head. "I asked about that, and it's by visitor count, which hasn't been too high recently, and of course by individual donations."

"By individual donations? After they say they're going to cut off our funding?"

Harold just shook his head. "I know. It's a mess."

Marcus set down the picture of Denmark Vesey, unable

to concentrate on the museum exhibit now. "Do those proponents of Confederate history have to meet the same requirements?"

Harold pinned him with a look. "Now you know they don't."

True. Marcus knew, but he held onto a small hope that things would be fair for them.

"It's great that we're starting independent fundraising. Still, the foundation is our biggest source of income right now. We'll have to try to earn their grant money for this fiscal year."

He nodded, respecting Harold's thoughts on the issue. Still, Marcus held his doubts. If Harold's plans to meet the foundation's requirements proved to be ineffective, then they would lose everything. The exhibit—that seemed like a sure bet to Marcus. It could draw new visitors, and new visitors would help them meet the foundation's visitor requirements.

Then again, why should they work to appease the Lee Ray Foundation? Did the museum exist to only subsist on monies from that organization? No. It served a greater purpose, but somehow, that purpose was lost when acquiring money took precedence over mission.

Marcus stared at the unfinished exhibit. "You know the story of how New Life started. They met in secret. They didn't wait for approval."

"What are you saying, Marcus?"

"We don't have to follow the foundation's requirements during this fiscal year. We can go at this on our own. We can be a completely independent operation. We can raise enough money without them."

Marcus glanced at the image of Denmark and that early congregation at New Life. They must've gone through so much to exist as a unit, to survive. "Whatever Denmark and the first congregation at New Life had to keep them going, I believe we have it too. Our validity, our existence, doesn't rest with the foundation. It shouldn't be that way."

A dimple indented Harold's cheek. "Youthful energy. That's what you have. I ran out of energy a long time ago."

"What do you mean?"

"I like your thinking, Marcus. I really do. But you're gonna have to trust me on this one. We'll need their support. They have a large endowment of funds, and if we were a completely independent operation, without any outside oversight, then people could accuse us of spreading biased information. We don't want that accusation hanging over us either, especially as historians."

The Confederate history enthusiasts are biased, but he didn't say that aloud. Back when New Life Church was started, laws were enacted that prohibited free Black people and the enslaved from gathering without White supervision. Those legislators from the past also wanted to control the spread of "biased information" . . . "I don't see how we can meet the foundation's requirements without having an exhibit to draw new visitors."

Harold paused. "I wouldn't get too dejected. Did you make that social media post?"

"I did. We haven't gotten any responses from folks willing to help with fundraising. I'll ask the current volunteers soon."

"Good. How'd things go with Sasha yesterday?"

"They went fine. I didn't get to ask her about volunteering yesterday because . . ." Marcus paused, thinking about Jaslene.

"Because what?"

"Jaslene is Sasha's wedding planner. She was at the meeting too."

"Oh. How'd that go?"

"It . . . went."

"Sorry to hear that." Recognition colored Harold's features, and he scratched his bald head.

He knew most of what had happened between Marcus and Jaslene. In fact, he and Marcus had a heart-to-heart talk about Jaslene shortly after she broke up with him. Harold tried to get Marcus to see the flip side of the breakup. He advised that it was better for a couple to know they weren't ready for marriage *before* they said I do. Harold had been married and divorced twice, so he spoke from experience. Harold once said that Marcus should consider himself lucky.

Marcus didn't feel too lucky at the time, and years later, he still didn't feel lucky.

The silence between them discomforted him, but Marcus could say nothing. He was still processing the encounter himself.

"Sasha paid a deposit to have her wedding and reception here. I told her she didn't have to do so," Harold continued. "To be honest, the money will help. Although I know this situation with Jaslene is tough for you, I don't want Sasha's wedding fumbled. Can you and Jaslene work together?"

Could they? The answer was a clear no. Marcus didn't want to mention the part where Jaslene already said that she didn't want to plan Sasha's wedding at the museum. Harold was going through enough pressure. Marcus would have to un-fumble his situation with Jaslene somehow. "I'll try my best."

"Do more than try. Succeed." Harold patted his shoulder. "Get past your differences with Jaslene so that this wedding can happen without a hitch."

The look on Jaslene's face when he'd called her Jazz resurfaced in his mind. One word from him upset her. How could he make this work? "You're issuing a tall order."

"You can do it. You're both professionals." Harold checked his wristwatch. "I'm going to answer some emails and reach out to potential donors. You've got this."

Harold left, so sure in his steps. Marcus stayed put, listening to the scuffle of Harold's shoes until the sound faded to a hush. A part of Marcus wanted to run after Harold and say that he and Jaslene couldn't get over their differences.

Another part of him recalled the easy conversation that he shared with Jaslene right before Sasha arrived. That moment sparked something in Marcus. Moments like that could lead to good things.

Outside the museum's window, two mourning doves

fluttered from one tree to another, neither of them apparently aware of the other, both in search of sustenance for their journey. They poked around for a few minutes, finding nothing. After searching for a while, they landed on the same branch. Marcus held his breath, thinking the branch would snap, but it gently bowed underneath the doves' weight. The birds stayed like that for some time, both on a questionable foundation but still together nonetheless. They found something on the nearby leaves and nibbled on the food.

Dappled sunlight danced across the tree branches, and a quiet certainty arose in Marcus. He would stop by Jaslene's office and apologize for calling her Jazz. He would also try to convince her to continue planning the wedding at the museum. Jaslene would hopefully see his resolve, and it would melt any hesitation she held.

Maybe he could also convince Jaslene that, despite their losses, some good existed between them—enough good that she could be persuaded to change her mind about working on Sasha's wedding at the museum. When they met yesterday, he certainly felt it.

If he could earn her trust, he would love another chance with her.

Chapter Four

*J*aslene headed to her office early on Monday. As soon as she stepped inside the space, she plugged in her laptop and proceeded to open a browser to pay Imani's application fees. Though Jaslene had her qualms about Imani moving out of state, she was grateful for the distraction of focusing on Imani's needs. It was much better than the alternative: being at the museum with Marcus.

On top of that, she hadn't done much to support her sister's endeavors at the museum, and she was feeling guilty about that. The more time Hope had spent volunteering there, the more her enthusiasm for history grew.

Then she had gotten into genealogical research, and that had made Jaslene nervous because they'd been part of a closed adoption. The nature of the adoption made the chance of identifying their biological parents virtually nonexistent. All they knew was that one biological parent was Black and the other biological parent was Filipino. No names. No records. No nothing.

Still, Hope had persisted in trying to piece together

their ancestry. A few months before Jaslene was supposed to get married, Hope had asked her to accompany her on a trip to Walterboro to see if they could access their closed adoption records, but Jaslene refused. The conversation bubbled to the surface.

"This place could have the answers that we've been looking for," Hope had said.

Jaslene's neck tensed. "Correction: the answers that you're looking for. I'm fine with not knowing. Our biological parents gave us up in secrecy, and it must've been for a good reason. I'm fine with that."

Hope's countenance changed, as if trying to figure out how to say the next part. "I'm not. We have another family out there. I want to know who they are."

"I don't have to know. I have you. I have Imani. You two are all that I need."

Hope side-eyed her. "And Marcus. You need Marcus. He's gonna be part of our family too. Don't forget that."

Jaslene waved her engagement ring in the air. "True. And that's more reason for leaving things be. We have all the family we need."

Hope didn't seem convinced. "I'll work on our family tree myself. If you ever want to help out, though, you can."

That had been their last conversation on the topic.

She would give anything to go back in time and make another choice, but she couldn't change the past. She could only learn to navigate the effects of it. That was hard though.

Jaslene typed in the web address for the first conservatory on Imani's list, and her cell phone buzzed. It was Sasha.

Great. She got the sigh out of her system before she picked up. Then, "Hey." Jaslene held the cell phone to her ear, trying to sound nonplussed.

"You okay? I couldn't stop thinking about you after you left."

"I'm doing great. Got flustered, that's all." She navigated Juilliard's webpage, in search of where to pay the application fee.

"I'm so sorry for setting you and Marcus up that way. I still feel awful."

She spotted where to pay and clicked the link. "No problem. It happens." *Sort of.*

"I hope we're still friends. I don't ever want us to not be in touch again. I wouldn't be able to bear it if I pushed you away."

Oh brother. Sasha was laying it on thick, but her tone radiated sincerity. "We're still friends. That won't change."

"Oh good. Will you . . . will you still plan my wedding?"

Aha. The question of the hour. She opened her wallet and slid her credit card from its slot. "I don't think I can. That visit made me uncomfortable."

"I know. I promise that I won't ever do something like that again. Whatever happens with you and Marcus will be between you and Marcus."

Only time would tell whether Sasha would keep her word. She had a track record for not keeping her promises.

A knock at the door interrupted her. "Hold on a sec." She set her cell phone and credit card on the desk and opened the office door.

Marcus.

Maybe it was the soft overhead lights or the pale blue of his polo shirt, contrasting nicely with his smooth brown complexion. Something enticed her.

He showed up. After all that happened the other day, Marcus still showed up. Hope used to say that Marcus didn't hide from conflict, and that he wouldn't ever let her down. She sighed. What would her sister say if she were here now?

I told you so, Jaslene.

Yep. Hope would say *I told you so.*

"Is that Marcus?" Sasha's voice blared through the phone.

Heat climbed up Jaslene's neck. "Give me a moment." Jaslene turned her back on Marcus and closed the door behind her.

"Hello? Anybody there?"

"I'm here," Jaslene said, whispering into her cell phone. "Marcus is standing outside the door."

"I knew it. I told you he was moved by seeing you again. Had to show up at your office. I'll leave you two to talk. Chat soon."

Jaslene's phone went dead. She took a breath and re-opened the entrance to her office. "Hi again. Sorry for closing the door in your face."

"Not a problem," Marcus said. "The outside of your door is . . . nice."

The grin on his lips made her smile. They stood there, staring at each other, trying to sort out this moment.

"You busy?" He dipped his chin and looked at the phone in her hand. If she weren't holding it, he would have probably greeted her by kissing the back of her hand, as any southern gentleman would do.

Jaslene was getting ahead of herself. *Stop.*

"Um, I was talking on the phone." She stuck it in the back pocket of her jeans.

"Beautiful." He glanced at her hand.

Jaslene's cheeks tingled. "What's beautiful?"

"That bracelet you're wearing. I like it."

The rustling of trees sounded through the half-open windows of her office. "Oh, this?" She held up her wrist, revealing the silver-and-gold bracelet. "It belonged to Hope."

"May I see it up close?"

The tingling from her cheeks spread to her neck. "Sure."

He held her hand, softly, and she breathed in sandalwood with notes of cinnamon. "Lovely piece of jewelry."

Jaslene let herself be swept up in this moment, even though it wasn't the wisest move. His touch sent an invisible sensation through her skin: gentleness. She'd forgotten how that felt.

After a few moments, she stepped away, reorienting herself. "Why'd you stop by? Did I leave something at the museum?"

"I wanted to talk about this past Friday."

"Everyone wants to talk about Friday. You. Sasha." She

gestured to the phone in her back pocket. "I'm fine. Really and truly fine."

"I don't want you to cut yourself off from planning Sasha's wedding at the museum because of me. If there's anything I can do to make it easier for you to work there, I'll do it."

"Is that so?" Jaslene adjusted the bracelet on her wrist, careful not to let it snag on her pale pink sweater.

"Definitely. If you want, I can be out of the building during the times that you're there."

In the past, she couldn't conceive of the two of them being apart. "That's unnecessary." She glanced outside her window at the Charleston skyline. The white clouds floated across the baby-blue horizon.

"I know. But you seemed so stressed the other day. It's one solution to any misgivings you may have about me."

His tone was gentle, and it reminded her of the times when they would have late-night conversations on life and their future. Who would've known that they would end up in a situation where talking to each other was a rarity? "I never had any misgivings about you."

"I don't believe that for a minute. Despite what you've said, you think I could've prevented her death. I think the same. My one dumb decision changed everything."

The notion had crossed her mind, especially in the days and weeks following the car accident. "I don't blame you, Marcus. I was hurt. Confused. Angry at times. But I never blamed you. Not even secretly in my heart."

Marcus's eyes shifted from right to left, as if trying to take in what she'd said. "Then what was it?"

In that moment, an invisible barrier formed around Jaslene, but she sensed it nonetheless. Jaslene lost one-third of her family when Hope died. She lost one-third of herself. After they had graduated from college, their adoptive parents didn't keep in touch with them. They must've thought that they completed their good deed by raising two orphans, but Marcus wouldn't understand. He had blood relatives: parents, grandparents, extended family. "I don't want to discuss it."

Disappointment colored his features. "Understood."

"So is that all you came here for? To talk about Friday?"

"Yes." Marcus glanced over at her desk and noticed her laptop. "I didn't know you liked classical music."

"Oh, that? It's for Imani. She's applying to Juilliard, along with a few other conservatories. I was on their website to pay her application fee."

"Juilliard. Impressive. She's always been talented. I'm pretty sure she'll get accepted."

"Part of me wants you to be right. And the other part of me wants you to be wrong."

"Why's that?"

"I have growing pains, I guess." Jaslene studied her French manicure, careful to not open her heart to him. "Being an overprotective aunt and all that."

"Understandable. Letting go is hard."

"Agreed," Jaslene said, her tone bittersweet.

Marcus pointed to the photo frame shaped like a seashell. "Isn't that the frame I gave you?"

"Yes." Jaslene nodded, self-conscious.

Marcus picked it up, running his fingertip over its bumpy edges. He had purchased the frame for her when they went on a day trip to Myrtle Beach as undergraduates. That was about fifteen years ago. The frame used to hold a photo of the three of them, Jaslene, Marcus, and Hope, but she switched it to a picture of her and her sister after the breakup.

The sensible side of her should've stopped using the photo frame itself, but Marcus's gift was too unique to give away.

"That was a fun trip," he said.

"Very fun. You refused to wear your baseball hat that day, and it was blazing hot outside," she said, a teasing note in her voice. "You needed protection from the sun."

"I didn't need sun protection. Black don't crack." Marcus set the photo frame on her desk.

"We may stay ageless, but we're not immune to getting skin cancer. You needed a hat and sunscreen."

"Sunscreen makes my face greasy."

"And you needed to cover that big forehead of yours."

"You won't ever let up about my forehead now, will you?" He smiled.

"Not one bit. I could hardly see the ocean with your forehead in the way."

Marcus chuckled, and the air shifted between them. She used to bug him about wearing visors and caps for his forehead. Every year, Jaslene would get him a new hat for his birthday as a running joke the two of them shared.

Jaslene missed joking around with him. She couldn't

stop thinking about whether she should change her mind. Working on Sasha's wedding reception at the museum wouldn't be a bad thing. "I have a question for you."

"What is it?"

"I know you mentioned how I'd feel uncomfortable working on Sasha's wedding at the museum, but what if you didn't stay out of the way? Would you feel uncomfortable with me being there?"

He paused, apparently weighing the question. "As long as you aren't always talking about my forehead, then I think it's fine."

She laughed. "That's gonna be hard to do."

A small light returned to his eyes. "If you can't promise to leave my forehead out of this, then I'll have to figure out how to deal with your jokes."

"You must want me at the museum."

"I do."

Marcus's directness caught her off guard. The corner of his mouth slanted up, and he tipped his head. "It's a win for you," he added, as if covering his tracks. "You'll get to keep working with Sasha as a wedding client. You won't lose her business."

An intensity settled into his dark eyes, and something in her stirred. "This is very true. I'll text Sasha and let her know that I'm fine with her wedding and reception being at the museum. And please don't disappear whenever I'm around. We both have important work to do."

"Good decision." He adjusted the collar of his button-down shirt.

"I'll stop by on Thursday to look at the space again. I didn't get to do a full walk-through the other day."

"I can show you around, if you'd like."

Would she like? She would definitely like. "Sounds like a plan."

JASLENE PULLED UP in front of the museum to check out the space in full this time. Sasha couldn't make today's meeting, but she had said that Jaslene could conduct it without her. She turned off the ignition of her blue Toyota Corolla, grabbed her huge tote from the back seat, and exited the sedan, closing the door behind her.

After years apart, Marcus possessed the ability to make her feel at ease, and she still sensed their connection. They shared a few jokes, but maybe connections and jokes couldn't remove the emptiness that resurfaced in the middle of the night. An emptiness she erased by crying herself to sleep.

This section of Charleston imbued serenity, and she tried to breathe it in. Historic homes lined the street, punctuated by oaks and wrought-iron fences. When they were dating, Jaslene used to daydream about living in this area. She had wanted to plant a white rocking chair on her back patio and spend her days reading as the sun warmed her face. She would have a small garden where she tested out her green thumb. Jaslene envisioned living a quiet and simple life until she grew old and gray, with Marcus at her side.

How many times had Jaslene pondered that version of life? Many.

How would life be today if Jaslene's dream had become reality? She didn't know.

"Morning."

Marcus stood at the entrance of the museum and waved at her in his nerdy-cute way. Jaslene's lips curved up in a smile. His glasses were perched on his nose, and the top two buttons of his shirt were unbuttoned, revealing the beginnings of his collarbone. Her Marcus.

Wait. *Her Marcus?*

The thought startled her, and she shoved it out of her mind. She headed his way and waved in return. "Hey," she said, trying to sound as casual as possible.

His sleeves were rolled up, revealing his toned forearms. Those arms had been wrapped around her so many times in the past, and she had forgotten what it was like to be near him. He would hold her in those tender moments, the tough ones, the soft and quiet ones. The joy of being in each other's presence without any agenda or expectation was something which she almost missed—almost.

Stop it, Jaslene. Who was she to think about this romance-y stuff when her sister wouldn't be around to experience a happiness of her own?

"Looks like you have your entire office in that bag." Marcus's voice pulled her out of her thoughts.

"You're probably right. I keep the files of all of my current clients in here. I'm always driving Imani around to her lessons and rehearsals, and so I try to use my downtime to get work done." Jaslene tried to keep her voice even, but she couldn't stop thinking about how handsome he looked today.

"I can carry that for you."

She hesitated, unwilling to accept his help. "I have it. I'm used to the weight."

"If you say so." He stepped back, and she caught a whiff of his Armani cologne. Hmm. She'd bought that fragrance for his birthday a few years ago. Surprising that he still wore it.

Or was he wearing it because she was there? Ugh. Why overthink everything? This was too much to deal with.

"Follow me."

Marcus held open one of the large wooden doors to the museum. The contrast from outside was stark. The museum was dim and warm compared to the coolness outside. She blinked several times so that her eyes could adjust. The overhead lights flickered.

"Are you going to get that bulb changed?"

He glanced up. "Oh yeah, I plan to do that." Marcus continued walking down the hall, and she followed.

Exhibits from different eras of Black history lined them on each side. They passed by those featuring the early Americas, the Reconstruction period, and the civil rights movement. She made a mental note to stop by each one when she had more time. Marcus had done an amazing job on them, but the lighting posed a problem. How could visitors fully experience this museum when the displays were so dim?

"Lighting would help you bring in more traffic," she

said. "The dimness is a deterrent, in my opinion. First impressions are everything."

"There's a lot more deterring visitors than a simple light bulb change." He walked past the exhibit featuring notable people from the 1970s and 1980s.

"What do you mean?" She kept following.

Marcus tugged on his earlobe. He always did that whenever he was stressed. "It's a long story. Too long for me to explain today. Do you want to set your bag down at my desk so that you're not lugging it around during our walk-through?"

"Sure."

Moments later, they arrived at Marcus's office. His name was proudly displayed on the door: MARCUS CLARK, M.A., HEAD ARCHIVIST.

She smiled at the letters after his name. He'd earned the master's degree that he pursued when they were engaged. Jaslene was done with school, but he loved it. And she also loved seeing the fruits of his labor paying off.

He pushed on the door with his elbow, and it creaked open. When she caught sight of the space, she did a double take. The room was so . . . dank. Was dank a word? Maybe. Maybe not, but the place was dank. Stark gray walls with no pictures. A neatly organized wooden desk stood in one corner of the office. With only one source of light, the green banker's lamp on Marcus's desk, the room was a muted amber—hardly enough to brighten up the space. The white vinyl blinds were in serious need of a dusting—and they were closed.

"You can set your tote on this chair." He pointed to the metal seat that was opposite his.

"Great."

"You want coffee? I brewed some this morning in the break room."

Jaslene tilted her head. "I'm good. Thanks for offering."

"Not a problem." A half-shadow cast across his face.

Jaslene wasn't beautifying spaces anymore, but she couldn't help but think of ways to improve this one. "I suggest opening your blinds. Natural light helps with productivity. An extra lamp wouldn't hurt either."

"You think?"

"I know. It's the little things that make a huge difference."

"I'll see if there's an extra lamp around here," he said.

"Good." Jaslene headed over to the vinyl blinds and grabbed the cord to open them.

"Don't open the blinds."

Jaslene stopped. "Why not?"

"Because . . . um . . . I don't need them opened. Lamps are good enough for me."

His voice held an edge. "How do you work like this?"

"I manage."

"No need to suffer when you can pull on the cord." She jiggled the cord, half joking, half serious.

"I don't want the blinds open." Faint lines that she hadn't seen before formed around his eyes. He shuffled the papers on his desk. Marcus was apparently done with this conversation.

Yet Jaslene wasn't done. When they had been together, his office space was never in near darkness with the blinds closed—shut off from the rest of the world. It was open and filled with natural light. He had mentioned that working in such an environment fueled his creativity. What was he fueling in an office like this?

"Let me show you where the reception will be held."

Marcus wasn't doing good. He might make a good show for others, but she sensed the truth about him. "How long will you be able to keep this up? Closed off and hiding."

"Hiding? I'm not hiding," he said, his tone defensive.

"You're locking yourself in. I can tell by looking at this space . . . and you. We may not have spoken to each other in a while, but I know you, Marcus. I see the change."

"I might agree with you if I were sitting at home all day playing video games. But I'm not shutting myself off. I'm here. I show up to the museum every day. Some people don't want this museum to exist, and that lends even greater importance to the work we're doing here. I'm going to prove them wrong."

"What happened to honoring those who came before?"

His posture straightened. "I do that too."

"But that drive to prove them wrong is slowing you down. It would slow me down." She shook her head. "I want you to be at peace too. Closing yourself in won't bring peace. Trying to prove other people wrong won't bring you peace either. You're chasing the wind if you do that."

"This setup works for me." He shrugged. "I'm working to make unknown stories known. And I like closed blinds."

She smiled at his dry humor. A stack of files caught her eye—was that Hope's? "What's that on your desk? That handwriting . . ."

He glanced at the papers. "Oh, that. Those are for an exhibit that I was working on. When Hope was a volunteer here, she helped me with some cataloging. Those are her notes. I still have to organize them all. There's a lot of good stuff in there."

Jaslene picked up a file and paged through the information. Hope had the prettiest cursive handwriting. She used to get on Jaslene about her sloppy penmanship. "How did she find the time to do all of that and take care of Imani and run Fairytale Weddings?"

"Beats me. But I'm guessing this place inspired her in some way."

Jaslene considered that family tree. What Jaslene wouldn't give to help Hope with it now. She would do anything to spend one more moment with her sister. "What was the exhibit about?"

Marcus told her about the New Life exhibit. "But the project is on an indefinite hold."

"That's too bad." She set the file back in the stack.

"Jaslene?"

"Yes?"

"I know you might be put off by my office setup. And I know you think I'm not the same person as before. But you don't have to concern yourself with me. I'm good."

Her heart pricked. Would it be foolish to believe him? It could be totally foolish, given his physical surroundings. Although they weren't together anymore, Jaslene wanted to see him happy. "How can you be certain?"

"Good question." Marcus scratched his chin. "I can't be. I threw all certainty out the window two years ago."

His voice broke, and the scratching stopped. Worry etched into his expression, and Jaslene wanted to hug him, tell him it would be okay. But saying that would be an untruth. No telling what their tomorrow would bring. "I stopped being certain too. Perhaps we can be certain in our uncertainty."

"Perhaps."

They inhaled the shared space for a long, long moment. Jaslene couldn't fight this pull to Marcus. A pull that grew stronger each time they were together. From the way Marcus fixed his attention on her, he must've felt the same.

"We're going to have to do something about this darkness," she said. "If you're not going to open your blinds, then promise me you'll find a light or something. I'll bring an extra lamp too."

"I promise." The resolve in his eyes spoke clearly, and that filled her with a comfort she hadn't experienced in ages. Jaslene tugged at her bracelet. The alternating gold and silver design sparkled, despite the dimness.

Chapter Five

Talking with Jaslene made Marcus want to get reacquainted with her more, but every time he thought about genuinely pursuing it, doubt returned. What if he brought sorrow to her life again? Yes, Jaslene said that she never blamed him for what happened to Hope, but he still blamed himself. If he knew how to get rid of the feeling, he would.

"This exhibit should be completed," Jaslene said, her voice interrupting his musings. "People should learn more about historic Black churches. And you can do it."

Her tone was confident, and he wanted to live up to her expectations this time. Still, Harold made it clear that he wanted Marcus to focus on fundraising, something that was definitely out of his league. "You think too highly of me."

"No, I don't." She cracked her knuckle and paused. "It may not have worked out between us, but that doesn't mean I don't believe in you."

"I know I've asked you before, but I want to know, Jaslene. Why'd you break up with me?"

"A lot of things were happening after Hope died on our wedding day. Everything overwhelmed me." She tugged at the hem of her black long-sleeved shirt, apparently uncomfortable with his question. "Things seemed off between us after the funeral. We could never agree on the little stuff. If things were like that while we were engaged, then what would've happened if we got married?"

Well, that was a fair question. After Hope died, they argued daily. It was mostly petty disagreements, but those spats built up over time. A wall built between them, and try as he might, he couldn't break it down. "It wasn't a good time for us."

"Not at all."

Things hadn't been all that bad though. His mind flashed memories of dancing with Jaslene, of taking walks with her in downtown Summerville, of talking about their future together . . .

Marcus shouldn't ponder these things. He made himself stop, or at least tried to.

"So are you going to work on the New Life exhibit?"

Jaslene was enthused about this unfinished project, and her interest motivated him. Working on it could repair some of what was broken between them. Maybe make them friends again.

"I might. That would be a feat, however. Harold will likely get upset, and he's been laying off staff lately. I don't want to be the next one to lose a job."

"You won't get fired." Jaslene swept her curly hair in a

loose ponytail and tied it with a black elastic band. "I'm confident that won't happen."

The expectation in her eyes refreshed him. Any time he had doubts about something, she always managed to encourage him. It was nice to see that Jaslene still did that two years later. "Would you like to see the exhibit?"

She blinked, apparently surprised. "Sure. I was secretly hoping you'd show it to me."

"Follow me." Marcus closed the browser on his laptop and grabbed the file folder from his desk. He led the way.

Light flooded the center of the museum where the skylights shone on the hardwood floor. When he became a full-time employee after interning at the museum, he suggested Harold get the skylights to make the exhibits pop. But without an exhibit in this space, it seemed like a wasted investment. He intended for the New Life exhibit to be a highlight for visitors, but the space was currently unkempt and barely any people walked through their doors.

"Here we are," he said, gesturing to the empty display cards and unwritten placards. "As you can see, it needs a lot of work."

A mishmash of boxes stood in the corner of the space, full of an overflow of office supplies. They had to get them out of the closet when a pipe burst last month. Right now, that tower took up most of the space.

Jaslene surveyed the area. "Did you bring Hope's notes with you?"

"I did." He handed the file over to her. "I can make copies of them, if you'd like."

"That'd be great." She flipped through the pages of Hope's writings. Sketches, drawings, and notes filled every corner of every page. "She was quite meticulous with her cataloging. Hope should've considered a second career as a historian."

"I was always in awe of her work ethic," he said.

"I should've paid more attention to all that she did here. I should've listened when she wanted to talk about it." A tinge of regret laced her tone.

"Don't get down on yourself."

Jaslene didn't respond; she kept flipping through pages and pages of notes. He waited and watched as she traced her finger over a sketch of the exhibit's layout. Jaslene must've needed this time, and so he gave it to her. Then, as she looked up, her gaze landed on a letter that was displayed in a glass case. "What's this?"

"A few months ago, I found an electronic copy of this letter. It was written by my ancestor, Janey, and it's dated July 6, 1822. The letter intrigued me, and so I added it to what would've been the exhibit."

Jaslene read it aloud.

"*Dear Solomon, I waited for as long as I could for you, but folks were starting to stare. Where'd you go? I hope you're safe. I can't wait for us to be married. Love, Mrs. Janey Clark.*"

"Janey Clark went to New Life?"

"Yes. And Solomon pilfered the sapphire ring, remember?" He made sure to say *ring* instead of *engagement ring*.

"Sapphire ring?" Her brow crinkled. "The same ring that—"

"Yes, *that* ring," he said.

"Oh." Recognition colored her features.

Prior to Marcus and Grandpa Clark's falling out, Grandpa Clark gave Marcus an heirloom ring and said it should be Jaslene's engagement ring. The ring had been in the Clark family for generations. According to Grandpa Clark, Solomon had stolen the ring from his enslaver.

"Did you ever find out why Solomon took the ring?" Jaslene asked.

"Nope."

"I still think he wanted it to be Janey's engagement ring." Marcus smiled. She said *engagement*. "Maybe."

Jaslene kept looking closely at the letter. "She signed the letter as 'Mrs. Janey Clark.' They couldn't have been married yet if she spoke of wanting to marry him in this letter."

He glanced at Jaslene, and her expression said that they both remembered the same thing.

When they were engaged, Jaslene signed her name as "Mrs. Jaslene Clark," although things weren't official yet. She had said that love couldn't wait.

Jaslene never became Mrs. Clark. The thought stung.

"Do you think Solomon got caught?" Jaslene asked.

"It's a definite possibility."

Jaslene bent to look at the letter more closely. "She could've thought that Solomon didn't love her anymore when he didn't show up."

"I don't think people fall out of love that quickly, especially when they're risking their lives to be together."

A frown line creased the corners of her mouth.

"Did I say something wrong?"

"No. Trying to wrap my mind around all of this, that's all. Back to Hope's notes. My sister had the best cursive handwriting." She flipped the page and held it up for him to see. "She used to bug me about my sloppy handwriting. I tried to tell her that my everyday handwriting was different from my work handwriting."

"Work handwriting? What's that?"

"It's the way I write for my wedding planning clients. I sometimes have to compose place cards and notes. I hand-lettered invitations once when one of our clients lost their invitations in the mail."

"You did? That must've been stressful."

"It was." She looked at Hope's notes and then again at the empty space in the exhibit. She pointed to the alcove. "Was that where this . . . mourners' bench was supposed to be?"

"Yes. Hope figured that was a good spot."

"Interesting," Jaslene said. "I never heard of a mourners' bench before. What is it?"

"It was set up inside of New Life Church back in the nineteenth century, when the church was first formed. It was a place for members to unload their worries. They could be relieved of their burdens—at least temporarily."

"So it was like a spiritual therapy couch?"

"Something like that. That bench was one of the few spots where they could simply be. Of course, laws controlled their gatherings, but that bench was a refuge."

"I couldn't even imagine the half of what they experienced."

"Me neither."

Silence. He tried to imagine the people who had used the mourners' bench. "It was a sacred piece of furniture for them, albeit symbolic."

"I don't think it was symbolic." She gave her right thumb a gentle tug. "It was real."

"It could've been." He smiled at her insight.

"You remember that sword lily Hope gave me?"

Oh yes. Hope's therapy plant. They had both been surprised at her gift. "I do. What's the connection?"

"Hope said I should talk to the plant. It helped." She regarded him for a long moment, her gaze soft. "I felt awkward and stumbly at first, speaking to this plant. But then something changed. The sword lily and its leaves seemed to drink in my words, to savor them. And in return, I received consolation for my troubles. That feeling stayed with me as I went through both the dark times and the daily moments."

"Do you still have it?"

"No. I gave it away after Hope's funeral." She shrugged. "Some things are meant to last for only a season. Know what I mean?"

"Not really." Marcus didn't know what she meant. If he were honest with himself, he still wanted to be with her, in every season. When Hope died, he could admit their relationship turned wintry, cold and bleak. Jaslene obviously didn't like that part of living. He didn't like it either, but as long as they were together, he knew they'd weather it. "I know you said that you couldn't stand our daily arguments, but I wasn't expecting our lives together to be perfect. I was willing to stick it out with you."

Jaslene fiddled with the edge of the paper in her hand until it curled. "Sorry that I couldn't stick it out in return."

Marcus stood closer to her, his unspoken way of accepting her apology. The quiet rise and fall of their breath filled in the quiet between them.

"Where do we go from here?" she asked.

They both needed time. "I don't know. Let's take it day by day." His voice was gentle.

"Day by day. I can do that." Jaslene uncurled the edge of the paper. "Where's the mourners' bench now?"

"Still at New Life. Somewhere in their storage, the last I heard."

"It should be on display here. You should try to acquire it."

Unease formed within him. "I tried."

"What happened?"

"A lot happened." Marcus didn't say anything more. Since Grandpa Clark had been giving him the silent treatment, Marcus had asked his grandmother to see if he would be willing to loan the bench for the exhibit. She had said that Grandpa Clark didn't want to go through the hassle of searching through his shed to retrieve it, and he fiercely guarded his shed. What Grandpa Clark really meant was that he didn't see the value in Marcus's work.

Should he share this with Jaslene? It could give her a better perspective. "My grandmother asked Grandpa Clark if he'd be willing to loan the bench to the museum temporarily. He refused."

"Why?"

"He holds a grudge about my career choice. When we were engaged, he asked me to be the next pastor of New Life, and I turned down his offer."

"I wish I would've known." Jaslene squinted. "Why didn't you tell me before?"

When they were engaged, Marcus rarely talked about the downside of his life. A part of him wanted to ensure that Jaslene only saw his best side and not his pain points. He didn't want Jaslene to think differently of him. Yet Jaslene had discussed the sword lily, and that knowledge expanded his compassion toward her. "I didn't want to weigh you down with my problems. And also—"

"Yes?"

He wanted to say that this slight from Grandpa Clark made him feel as if he would never be good enough for anyone, including Jaslene, but he kept that part to himself. "Nothing . . . I don't know. It's ironic that we're both scared of the same thing."

"What's that?"

"Tough seasons."

Jaslene's eyes softened. "Yeah. We're two scaredy-cats, I guess." A smile formed at her lips.

"At least we found common ground."

She laughed at his sarcasm. "But seriously, you should

ask your grandfather about the bench directly. Break the silence between the two of you. He may change his mind."

"I doubt it."

"You never know. I'd hate to see you give up on your relationship with him. Time isn't guaranteed." She glanced at Hope's writings. "I would give anything to spend one more day with my sister."

"I wish I could give that day to you, and a lifetime after that."

Jaslene's lips parted subtly, apparently surprised. "If it's uncomfortable for you to see your grandfather alone, then I could go along with you for moral support."

"You don't have to do that."

"But I want to go. I haven't seen Pastor Clark since our wedding day. I'd like to catch up with him and your grandmother. I thought about your grandparents after I broke up with you, thought about how kind and welcoming they'd always been to me." She hesitated, looking into Marcus's eyes. "I was going to miss that part."

Her words were a sun ray, casting its glow on falling leaves. He smiled.

"I have a planning meeting with Sasha next week," she continued. "Imani has a slew of rehearsals and lessons that I have to drive her to, but this is important. We should try."

Should Marcus ask Grandpa Clark directly? Should he bring Jaslene along with him? Their efforts could fail, and it would be worse if Jaslene got hurt when Grandpa Clark said no again.

On the other hand, this could have a good outcome. Grandpa Clark could have a change of heart, especially if Jaslene was present. And it might bring Marcus and Jaslene closer together.

Marcus's heart pulled two ways, tugged by their shared past yet prodded by the possibility of bonding with Jaslene. That possibility was still unfinished for him—as unfinished as the empty alcove and half-done displays before them.

Was that how it should be for Jaslene and Marcus? Should things remain undone? The idea bothered him. "We can see if Grandpa Clark will loan me the mourners' bench this time. But nothing's guaranteed."

"I'll keep my fingers crossed that he says yes." Jaslene's smile revealed a beauty that a guy saw only once in his lifetime, if he was lucky.

He was lucky.

"I'll call his church secretary to see if I can get on his calendar," he said. "Grandpa Clark is a busy man. Lots of responsibilities."

"Call the church secretary?" Jaslene scrunched her nose in that too-cute way of hers. "You have to make an appointment to see your grandfather?"

"Yep."

"That's not good." He heard dejection in her voice, as if she knew getting this bench was a futile effort.

"We can still try, though," Marcus continued. "This is one of those uncertainties that we discussed earlier. I want to make this uncertain step with you."

Her mouth curled into a smile. "Me too."

He was *very* lucky.

THE FOLLOWING WEEK, Jaslene readied herself for a planning meeting with Sasha at the museum. She had texted Marcus earlier that day to see if he would be at his office. He said he'd arrive in the late morning, and that it was okay if she met Sasha in his office. This time, she also brought in items for Marcus's office: a lamp, a red area rug, and a vase with one fresh orchid.

The orchid was a bit more personal, given that orchids were a flower of choice for their wedding aesthetic. At first, she wasn't going to get it for Marcus, but the plum-red petals blended well with the area rug.

Yeah, that was the reason . . .

She set everything up, putting the new vase and lamp on the corner of his mahogany desk. While working, Jaslene couldn't help but think of getting the exhibit on New Life completed. She could lay out a project plan on how to complete the exhibit for Marcus, and he, being the history expert, would fill in the details. The mourners' bench would be an asset to the project for sure. If she interpreted Hope's notes correctly, then she probably wanted the bench to be the center of the story that this exhibit would tell.

So many thoughts. But Sasha should arrive at the museum any moment now. Jaslene pulled out her trusty wedding planning template and wrote in key dates for Sasha's upcoming nuptials. Despite her best intentions, her mind hopped on over to Marcus and Grandpa Clark. She stopped writing and tapped her pen on the desk.

Marcus had never discussed his issues with Grandpa Clark when they were together. If she were honest, she never noticed they held tensions with each other. Some things seemed odd, like the time when Jaslene said they should have pre-marital counseling with Pastor Clark. Marcus flat-out refused to be counseled by his grandfather, even though he had a graduate degree in pastoral counseling.

Or the other time when Jaslene read one of Pastor Clark's transcribed sermons, and, moved by his ideas, she shared a printed copy with Marcus. He refused to read the transcription, saying that he had all the advice he needed from Grandpa Clark. Marcus didn't need his grandfather's 'homiletics and hermeneutics,' as he sarcastically phrased it.

Jaslene had written those instances off as minor, but she should've paid attention, just as she should've paid attention to Hope's interest in history.

Marcus had a place in his heart that she could never reach. On top of that, the daily fighting and stress had made things worse. Going with Marcus to his grandparents' house could help her get a better gauge on the tensions between the two.

She doodled on the corner of her pad, thinking about how that would turn out. It might not be wise to butt into Marcus's relationship with his grandfather. That could sour things. Yeah, when she went there, she would be a supportive presence, nothing more.

Jaslene resumed writing more dates into the planning document for Sasha's wedding. She needed to figure out how to configure round tables into the museum space for the reception. Rectangular tables wouldn't do. Jaslene also had to figure out the perfect room for the ceremony. It would be too hard to have the ceremony and reception in the same space. She made a note to ask Marcus or Harold about that too.

Next thing, a knock sounded at the office door. "Hey, girl!"

Sasha's voice brought a smile to her face. Jaslene set her template aside. "Good morning. I'm getting the timeline down for your wedding. Somehow, we'll fit all of your guests in the atrium. Round tables will help. I'll mark the museum's floor to test out my theory, but if it doesn't work, then I have other ideas. I still haven't figured out where to have your ceremony though."

"The W. E. B. Du Bois room is big enough to fit my guests for the ceremony. But I trust whatever you decide because everything you decide is fabulous!"

Jaslene chuckled. In the time that they hadn't been talking, Jaslene forgot how enthusiastic Sasha could be. "Did you contact *Southern Bride*?"

"Oh yes, ma'am. I did. I told them all about you and your centerpieces too."

"What?!"

"Yeah. I told them that you were planning my wedding, and that you're also designing the aesthetic for my ceremony and reception. They're going to cover my wedding." She gave a cheeseburger smile. "They want to see samples of your centerpieces. I told them you'd send them off next week."

"You did not!"

"I surely did."

OMG. This was going to be a disaster. "I can't create centerpieces in a week. I need more time than a week."

"Girl, you're tripping. I've seen you whip things together before at the last minute. You've got this."

A dull ache formed at her temples. How would she pull that off? "I never said that I wanted to have my centerpieces in *Southern Bride*. And we never confirmed that I was going to design your wedding either."

"I know. And I also know that I promised I wouldn't butt in, but I'm not butting into your relationship with Marcus. Which I hope is going well, by the way. I'm butting into your career. Which needs a serious boost. You're more than a wedding planner. You're a wedding visionary."

"Wedding visionary? Stop."

"It's true though. But you have to believe it for yourself."

"How? I don't know if I can be creative again. My brain is fried."

"I'll help you un-fry your brain." Sasha's tone dialed down from super-enthusiastic to empathetic. "I know how hurt you were by everything, but you can't keep letting it get you down."

Jaslene's vision blurred, and she quickly wiped her eyes before the tears started rolling.

Sasha reached across the desk and held her hand. "You'll be okay. I'll walk alongside you every step of the way."

Another tear trickled down her cheek. "How many centerpieces did she want?"

"At least two. But if that's too much, then we can give her one. It's your call."

"I'll do one, but I'll need about two weeks to have it ready. It'll match the aesthetic for your wedding."

Sasha's eyes lit. "Two weeks works. So you're going to design my wedding too?"

Jaslene nodded. "Might as well if I'm making these centerpieces. I'll do something that reflects Black and Filipino heritage. Oh, and I ordered the arras, the eternity cord, the veil, and a straw broom for your wedding. They should arrive in a week or two."

"Great! That's way ahead of my wedding."

"I like to get the smaller details out of the way. Maybe you can ask them for more time so that I can make a second piece."

"I'll certainly do that for you. We'll make this one sample the best sample ever, and she'll be begging for more to feature in the magazine. It'll be great," Sasha said.

"Thank you for being such a great friend."

"Oh, girl. I'm here for you. I hated seeing your enthusiasm for design wither away. Just like I hated to see you and Marcus not talking. But the two of you are talking now." She smiled. "So . . . how is it?"

"How is what?"

"Being at the museum while Marcus is here?" Sasha's voice lowered to a whisper.

"Oh . . . um, it's fine. Just, you know, making sure all things are a go for your wedding day."

"That's good. You seem settled and more at peace."

"I do?"

"Yep. Everything's happening just as predicted."

Amusement filled her. "And what did you predict?"

"That all you needed was to get around Marcus and you'd start to be your old self again. Calm. Focused. Stress-free."

Sasha was a trip. "This was your plan all along?"

"No, of course not." She shook her head, and her long, dark hair whipped around. Sasha was gorgeous even when she didn't try to be. "I just knew this would happen. That's all. I've known the two of you since college. I have you figured out by now."

Jaslene laughed. "Not sure if I should be happy or offended by your take."

"Be happy. Be very happy." Sasha smiled at her. "Have you and Marcus discussed your relationship yet?"

Lordy. Sasha was so nosy. "Not your business. Now can we focus on your wedding, please?"

"All right. I won't say anything more." Sasha pretended to lock her lips and throw away the key.

Good. Jaslene opened the spreadsheet app on her phone so they could discuss.

"Sasha and Jaslene, both in my office. Nice to see the two of you."

Jaslene startled. Had Marcus overheard their conversation about him? She hoped not. He leaned against the doorjamb and tugged on his earlobe.

Oh my gosh. The earlobe tug thing must mean he overheard them.

No. No. No. It didn't have to mean that at all. She was worried over nothing.

"Marcus!" Sasha stood and gave him a side hug. "I didn't know you were coming to the museum today."

"He works here, Sasha." Jaslene's tone turned flat.

"I know that he works here. Duh!" Sasha held both palms up, feigning innocence. "I just figured . . . I don't know. I'm making small talk! Anyway, how are you?"

"Doing good?" He stepped inside and took note of the orchid and lamp on his desk. Then he turned his attention to Jaslene. "Those flowers are nice. You brought them?"

She nodded, nervous.

Marcus sat at his desk and held the vase, studying the petals. Did he draw the connection about the orchids? He must have, because when they were shopping for wedding flowers, they had spent hours looking at different types. At the time, Jaslene was more into choosing the perfect florals than he was, but they had settled on orchids for the pews and tulips for her bouquet.

"The lamp and the rug," he added. "They brighten up my office. Thank you."

"You're welcome."

Sasha stood there, cheesing at the two of them. Oh brother.

"Sasha, I meant to ask you. Would you be willing to help with volunteering for some fundraising for the museum? Harold hasn't quite worked out what we'd need, but we do need volunteers," Marcus said.

"Sure thing. I'll be glad to help. I'll let the committee know as well."

"Great. How's the wedding planning going?" he asked.

"We just started talking about it." Jaslene showed them the wedding planning spreadsheet. "I booked a florist and baker for you. We'll have to think about music next."

"Can I hire Imani to play the violin at my wedding?" Sasha asked.

"Ooh! That's a great idea. I'd have to ask her first. Her schedule is packed, but I'm pretty sure we could fit it in."

"I read the feature about her in the *Post and Courier*. She's doing big things."

"That she is. She's applying to conservatories out of state. I'm nervous about her possibly leaving."

"You don't have to worry about that. Imani is grown and responsible. She'll do great." Sasha smiled.

"I know. I'm more worried about myself than anything else." Jaslene made a note on her spreadsheet to ask Imani about playing at Sasha's wedding.

"What worries you?" Marcus asked.

She shouldn't have said that. "The usual things, I guess."

Marcus and Sasha waited for her to say more, but what more could she say without getting all emotional in front of them?

"Go on," Marcus said.

"Yeah, I want to know too, sis."

Her face heated. "Well . . . it's a lot to think about. She'll be gone next fall. It's been just me and Imani since her mother died. We've become very close-knit. When she leaves, it'll be lonely, to put it lightly. She's my only family left." Her voice cracked on the last part. *Gah. Embarrassing.*

"We're not blood relatives, but you're like family to me." Sasha hugged Jaslene, and another tear trickled down her cheek.

Jaslene returned the hug, and more tears wet her face. *Super embarrassing.* "That means a lot."

Sasha squeezed her tight. Jaslene realized that she was crying in Marcus's office, and she quickly shifted away and wiped her face. "It's nothing really. I'm just getting sentimental over here. That's all."

Marcus stood off to the side, compassion written all over his features. If things were different between them, he would probably hug Jaslene too, but that wasn't happening.

"When did you start feeling this way about Imani?" Sasha stepped away.

"I don't know. It just happened the closer we got to her senior year."

"Don't hold all of that inside." Sasha held Jaslene's hand, squeezed it tight. "It'll break you."

"I'm not holding it in."

"Well . . . you aren't now because you spoke about it.

If you ever need to talk, please call me. Text. Email. DM. Whatever you need. I'm here."

"Me too," Marcus said.

She felt the weight of Marcus's gaze, and it sent a wave of heat through her body. It took everything in her power not to look at him.

"When my little brother, Trey, went to summer camp, I was nervous for him too," he added.

Marcus rarely spoke of his brother. "You were?"

"Yes. I was supposed to be his protector. The person who beat up bullies on his behalf. I was worried that he wouldn't be able to stand up for himself without me there. I tried to give him boxing lessons before he left for camp, just in case." He chuckled.

Jaslene smiled. "I can picture that now."

"I know, right? I was all over the place." Marcus crossed his arms, his eyes filled with reminiscence. "Trey did good at camp, though. I had nothing to worry about."

"I bet you were a good big brother," Sasha said quietly.

"Nah. I wasn't."

Jaslene's heart pierced. Marcus was opening up, so she needed to listen. "I didn't know you back then, but I'm sure that you were."

Marcus lowered his gaze, silent.

"Do you keep any memories of Trey? Pictures or other things?" Sasha asked.

"No. All of that is at my grandparent's house."

Jaslene remembered seeing pictures of Trey hanging on the wall at his grandparent's house. She understood why Marcus didn't keep pictures too, given what had happened. "Have you set up a time for us to see them?"

"Not yet, but I will this afternoon."

"Y'all are going to Marcus's grandparents' house? Together?" Sasha said. "Ooh, I like the sound of that."

"What's that supposed to mean?" Jaslene asked.

"You know what it means." Sasha gave them both exaggerated winks.

Here we go again. Sasha poked and poked until she stirred up thoughts that Jaslene had stuffed in the cluttered closet of her mind. "Now, let's get back to your wedding. Did you have any ideas for caterers?"

"Changing the subject, I see," Sasha said. "I'll go along with this, I guess."

Sasha rattled off the names of caterers, but Jaslene was half listening to Sasha's words. Marcus discussed Trey. That was huge. Was Trey the reason why it was so hard for Marcus to talk about the downside of things? Could be.

A part of her wanted to know more about Trey, and a bigger part of her wanted Marcus to gain some sense of closure. Time was needed for both, and right now, she was willing to give it.

Chapter Six

*M*arcus couldn't stop thinking about Jaslene believing she wouldn't have any family in South Carolina after Imani left for school. It wasn't supposed to be that way. Marcus and Jaslene should've had a different ending.

How could he put her at ease about Imani's transition to adulthood? Unlike Sasha, Marcus couldn't tell Jaslene that he would be there for her. She had pushed him away once, and although they were talking again, Marcus wouldn't assume she wanted something more. Yeah, Jaslene had given him a vase with an orchid, but he'd look like an idiot if he took that as a signal that she wanted to take their relationship a step further. Marcus wasn't that kind of a guy.

No sense to spend more time than was good for him analyzing her actions of late. He needed to set up an appointment to see Grandpa Clark, not speculate about Jaslene.

He picked up his desk phone and dialed the number to

the church office. Lucinda, New Life's administrative assistant, worked until about two o'clock every day. Marcus still had time to catch her.

The phone picked up on the third ring. "New Life Church, how may I help you?"

Grandma's cheery voice answered the phone, and he smiled at her joyous greeting. "Hey, Grandma."

"Marcus! So lovely to hear from you."

"Lucinda took the day off?"

"Yep. She took her child to the dentist. I'm filling in for her."

That was Grandma Clark, always lending a hand whenever someone had a need, oftentimes without considering her own. As the pastor's wife, she had the unspoken task of attending to the needs of the church: making sick visits, presiding at the women's group meetings, and filling in wherever Grandpa Clark needed. What would she do if she weren't a pastor's wife? Did she have career interests or hobbies of her own? Marcus had asked her that question once, but she brushed him off. Grandma Clark needed a break from her activities, but whenever he brought up the possibility, she disregarded it.

"I asked your grandfather if he would help with fundraising at the museum. He said he wasn't interested."

"I expected that."

"Well, I don't. I'll just have to keep hoping and praying that he'll make a turnaround. What do you need, grandson?"

Maybe Marcus shouldn't set up an appointment. His

grandfather obviously wasn't interested in Marcus and his needs.

"You still there, Marcus?"

"Um . . . I'm still here."

"What do you need?" she asked again.

Then again, Jaslene was counting on Marcus to make this call. He should follow through. He needed to get this over and done with so that he could refocus on fundraising. Harold would be asking for a status update, and Marcus needed something to report. "Does Pastor Clark have any openings in his schedule?"

"Pastor Clark? Why so formal?" She chuckled. "You mean your grandfather?"

"Yes."

Grandpa wanted Marcus to call him pastor. It was another reason why Marcus thought it best to keep his distance, honor the request for formality. "I need to set up an appointment with him."

"An appointment? Child, it's a good thing you want to see him in person. But you don't have to make an appointment with your kin. Come on over now, if you'd like."

"Can't do that."

"Why not?"

Hoo-boy. Should he tell her the reason?

"I'm waiting for an answer, Marcus." All the humor left her voice.

"Grandpa told me that he only wanted to see me by appointment."

"What?" Her voice increased a few notches. "He said that to you?"

"Yes."

"Well, I'll be. Ain't that a hot mess. He's taking this grudge toward you too far. I'm gonna talk to him."

If Grandma confronted his grandfather, the meeting could be ruined before it began. "Please don't. I want to avoid stirring the pot."

"You're not doing the stirring. I am."

Marcus glanced at the closed blinds of his office. Sunlight streamed through the vinyl. "I don't want you to do any stirring either. Let me handle this. It's a delicate situation. I need things to go smoothly."

"All right. I won't say anything. But I'll be at this meeting, in case your grandfather acts up."

Marcus twisted his mouth. Jaslene would be there too. Once his grandmother saw the two of them together, she'd go straight into matchmaker mode. Marcus needed to brace himself for that too. "Jaslene will be coming along for support."

"Jaslene? Well, well, well. How'd that happen?"

"I . . . uh . . . She learned about the New Life Church exhibit, and she wants to get it off the ground too. She suggested this meeting with Pastor Clark."

"It's Grandpa Clark. And Jaslene is a smart gal. She and I think the same way. Wait a second. The two of you spoke about the exhibit. Does that mean that you're . . . *talking*, talking?"

Marcus laughed. She sounded like a nosy next-door neighbor. "No. We're just acquaintances."

"I see. Bring your girlfriend and her niece over to the house for Thanksgiving dinner on Thursday. We're gonna have a wonderful feast."

Thanksgiving dinner? If he brought Jaslene over for Thanksgiving dinner, then Jaslene could assume that he wanted to get serious. He wasn't ready for that. "Jaslene probably already made other plans for the holiday. How about this Saturday afternoon around one o'clock?"

"That works. We'll have plenty of leftovers, and I'll add in a little more food for the two of you. Can't wait to see you at home. You haven't been over for a home-cooked meal in the longest time. I'm tired of this disagreement between you and your grandfather. I want our family to be gathered around the table together."

Together. He hadn't sat down for lunch or dinner or anything at their house since the falling out with Grandpa Clark. Prior to that, while they were engaged, he and Jaslene visited their house for Sunday dinners, but Marcus stopped taking her to their house. When Jaslene questioned him about it, he brushed it off, not wanting to rehash that experience.

"Does Jaslene still like peach cobbler? I can make that too."

Grandma was tempting him a little too much. Peach cobbler was his favorite. "We both love peach cobbler. And you're right. Feels good to think about getting together again."

"Wonderful. See you soon, Marcus."

After they hung up, a sense of assuredness came over him. Jaslene was right when she'd said that time was short and he should mend the rift with Grandpa Clark. He would try his best to do so, if only to give Grandma Clark hope.

"You nervous about seeing your grandparents today?" Jaslene bounced her heel against the floorboard.

"A bit. I hope everything goes well. How about you?"

Should she tell him? "I'm nervous too. And I didn't think that I would be."

Marcus pulled his black Ford F-250 in front of his grandparents' ranch-style home and turned off the ignition. "I was thinking about the last time you and I were here. Remember that?"

"I do. I always enjoyed visiting them. I'm assuming we stopped going after what happened with your grandfather. Am I right?" She opened her purse and grabbed a tube of lip balm from her makeup pouch.

"You're right. But today's a new day." Marcus twirled his key ring on his index finger. "She asked if you still have a thing for peach cobbler. I told her you did. Hope you don't mind."

How sweet that his grandmother still remembered. "Don't mind at all. My stomach's rumbling just thinking about her cobbler."

They were quiet. It seemed like the two of them needed to settle into this moment, this slice of time where they sat in his truck, readying themselves to visit his grandparents like in the old days.

"Appreciate you coming along today. Maybe we'll get the bench this time. That peach cobbler might convince Grandpa Clark to change his mind."

She laughed. "Your grandmother's peach cobbler does that to people." Jaslene smoothed on her lip balm and checked herself in the visor mirror.

"You look beautiful," Marcus said.

Goose bumps prickled on her forearms. "Sounds like you're trying to appease me."

"Not at all. I'm telling the truth. Your hair looks nice."

Jaslene wrapped one of the curls around her index finger, and it bounced when she released it. "I co-washed my hair last night and put in a leave-in conditioner. Then I twisted it to set the curls."

"Natural looks good on you."

His words comforted Jaslene, and her body stilled. He was being sincere. She knew that for certain.

Marcus helped her out of the pickup truck, and they headed up the walkway. A line of chrysanthemums greeted them as they walked the winding cobblestone path to the bright yellow door. The rest of the lawn was unkempt, however, and a riot of dandelions sprouted in patches across their lawn.

"Wonder if the church groundskeeper has been maintaining things over here," Marcus said, apparently taking note of the same thing.

"Looks like he hasn't."

"Hmm." Marcus shaded his eyes and scanned the landscape. "The landscaping needs help."

Once they arrived at the entrance, Marcus rang the doorbell, and shuffling echoed in their direction. A moment later, Grandma Clark greeted them, smiling. "Why hello there, Marcus . . . and Jaslene. Pleasure to see the two of you together again."

All righty then. Grandma Clark wanted grandbabies. "Pleasure to see you again too, ma'am."

"No need to call me ma'am. Come on in. We have leftovers from Thanksgiving, and I made a little snack for the two of you, if you're hungry."

"I'm very hungry," Jaslene said.

"That's *very* good."

They made their way down the carpeted hall leading to the dining area. The house hadn't changed since Jaslene was last here. In the center of the dining room wall, a glass case showed off all the porcelain figurines and pictures of Marcus's childhood. Photos of Marcus's parents, and Trey, filled most of the wall space.

Her heart squeezed at the sight. It must be hard for Marcus to see those pictures of his little brother. That could be another reason why it was easy for Marcus to not return here after the disagreement with his grandfather.

Jaslene wasn't like that. She liked having pictures of Hope all over her living space and her office. Both places were practically shrines to her sister, but if Jaslene were honest with herself, the sister-shrines hemmed her in.

A quiet recognition filled her. She hadn't considered the notion until now.

Jaslene sat at the worn chair at the table and crossed her legs at her ankles. Directly across from her hung a holy trinity of portraits: Christ and his disciples at the Last Supper, a young Martin Luther King Jr., and a smiling President Barack Obama. All three were the cornerstone of Black American culture, especially for the older folks.

Maybe one day, there would be a photo of a notable woman added to their wall.

Grandma Clark set the Thanksgiving leftovers on the table before them. Fried turkey. Seafood salad. Collard greens. Baked chicken. Fried catfish. Hopping John. Sweet potato pie. And, of course, her famous peach cobbler.

"Grandma, that is a lot of food."

"Don't fuss at me." Grandma Clark swatted him playfully. "Get a plate and eat."

"Yes, ma'am," he said.

Jaslene laughed and did the same.

"I'll get your grandfather and let him know that you're here."

After Grandma Clark left, it was the two of them. Jaslene instinctively scooted her chair next to him, a preemptive measure for what was to come. "You'll be okay," Jaslene whispered.

"I hope so."

A few minutes later, Grandpa Clark entered the dining room, his wife behind him.

"There's plates over there." Grandma Clark pointed to a stack of paper plates on their Formica countertop.

When Jaslene waved hello to Pastor Clark, his steps slowed. "Nice to see you again, Jaslene."

"Likewise."

Pastor Clark shifted his focus to Marcus. For a long minute, the pastor appeared conflicted, as if trying to decide whether to speak to his grandson. "I didn't know Jaslene was coming. You two a couple again?"

OMG. "No," she said quickly. "We're not together as a couple. We're just . . ."

What were they? Friends? Enemies? Acquaintances? They were two people who wanted to borrow the mourners' bench for the museum. That's what they were.

"We're not dating," Marcus said, and he left it at that.

"I see." Pastor Clark looked back and forth between them. "That's the problem with you young people these days. You don't know nothing about commitment."

"Oh hush, Reginald. They didn't come here to hear all of that."

"It's true. If they respected commitment, they'd be married by now. There's nothing stopping them. I was ready to officiate their wedding before, and I'm ready to officiate it now. My ministerial license is still valid."

Marcus opened his mouth as if to object but soon closed it.

Jaslene's neck muscles tensed. This was embarrassing.

"Stop being rude, Reginald." Mrs. Clark swatted at her husband. "They're friends. Isn't that right?"

"Right," Jaslene and Marcus said in unison.

Friends. Was this how the rest of this dinner would fare? Because if that was the case, she wasn't ready.

After Pastor Clark made his plate and said grace, they ate in silence. Jaslene welcomed the reprieve from questions about their relationship status.

Pastor Clark appeared to wait to speak again until Marcus met his gaze. "Your grandmother told me that you wanted to discuss something important. What is it?"

Marcus set his fork on his plate. "As you know, I'm working on the New Life exhibit at the museum. And Jaslene and I got to discussing the mourners' bench. We wanted to ask if you could lend it to us for the exhibit."

Grandpa Clark's face grew grim. "I already discussed that with your grandmother."

Marcus nodded. "Yes, but—"

"I'm planning to get rid of the shed and its contents. Just haven't gotten around to it yet. But I will."

"I didn't know you were planning to do that," Mrs. Clark interjected. "Why didn't you tell me, Reginald?"

"I don't know." He shrugged. "Never crossed my mind."

She raised an eyebrow at Jaslene. "See how my husband treats me? Keeping secrets from his own wife. That should tell you a thing or two about what marriage is like after sixty-seven years. I think you and Marcus are the most precious young folks, but don't jump into any commitments until you know everything about your partner."

"Yes, ma'am," Jaslene said. "I agree completely." *Especially since I'm getting to know more about Marcus.*

"Oh hush, Effie. I'm not keeping any secrets from you."

"You kept this one from me," she said. "And if you're not keeping any secrets, then tell me more about when and how you came up with this plan to get rid of the shed and everything in it."

Pastor Clark was silent and so was Marcus. *Hmm. Interesting.* He didn't want to get in between his grandparents' spat. "My sister Hope took some notes on the exhibit when she volunteered there."

"Ah, yes. Hope. She was such a lovely woman. I was so grieved when she passed," Mrs. Clark said. "We were looking forward to welcoming you, Imani, and Hope into the family."

Her kindness moved Jaslene. "You were?"

"Of course, we were, honey. Why wouldn't we be?"

When Jaslene and Hope were orphaned as children, they had become their own family. They stuck together like glue too. After they were adopted, they still felt separate from their adoptive parents. Once Jaslene and Hope came of age, their assumptions proved true. Hope and Jaslene went to college in-state, and their adoptive parents visited them on campus a few times, but then the phone calls and visits dried up. The tuition money for their schooling dried up too. Hope and Jaslene fell out of contact with their adoptive parents, and that was when the idea for Fairytale Weddings began. The business, along with student loans, helped the sisters stay afloat. "I don't know. I guess I've been so used to having Hope and Imani as my only blood relatives that the idea of having an extended family hadn't hit me—"

"Until now," Mrs. Clark said, and reached over and patted the back of Jaslene's hand.

She nodded, unable to say more. Mrs. Clark's empathy toward her was like a warm blanket.

"I completely understand why the two of you decided not to get married," Mrs. Clark continued. "My husband understands too. He's . . . he's just being grumpy."

Pastor Clark wiped his mouth with a napkin, obviously choosing not to weigh in on this tender conversation.

Jaslene nodded. Did Marcus ever tell his grandparents that she was the one who broke things off? Jaslene had never told Marcus the reason until recently, but if his grandparents knew that Jaslene had ended the relationship, would Mrs. Clark be as empathetic to her today? The question bothered Jaslene.

"That mourners' bench is important," Mrs. Clark said to Jaslene.

"It is. Marcus and I were discussing its significance earlier." Jaslene shared about how the bench had been used during church services.

"I know all about it." Mrs. Clark had a faraway look. "We all need a place of refuge, a space to breathe."

"Exactly," Marcus said.

"I guess it's time for you to show us this bench, husband." Mrs. Clark adjusted her bifocals and aimed a look at him.

Pastor Clark shifted. "Can't. There's too much stuff in the shed. It'll be hard to get to."

"Too much stuff never stopped me before." Mrs. Clark stood. "Let's go."

"No," Pastor Clark said.

"Yes."

"No," he repeated.

"We don't have to see it," Marcus said, apparently uncomfortable with the direction of this conversation. "We'll finish our dinner and leave. No big deal."

Leave? Was Marcus giving up that easily? No way could she walk away now. She needed to see what Hope saw in the bench. "Let's go to the shed."

Pastor Clark set his fork down. "I haven't been in that shed since . . . since the mass shooting at New Life. Last thing I did before I got word of what happened was double lock the shed."

Jaslene shifted her focus to Marcus, and his expression softened.

"I didn't know that, Reginald."

"Now you do."

Silence filled the room. Jaslene recalled the day when that tragedy happened. She was at a wedding in Columbia when Marcus had called and told her the news. Horrible day.

"I think Marcus and Jaslene being here today is a sign of good providence. We'll see the bench today." Mrs. Clark placed her hand on her husband's forearm. "We're going to take this step, husband. Together."

Pastor Clark nodded. His eyes were filled with emotion. "Yes, we will."

The connection between Pastor and Mrs. Clark was palpable, warm and rich and deep. Jaslene sensed it in her bones. How blessed they were to share such a strong love. Jaslene wanted a love like theirs.

"I'll take you all to the shed but don't break anything," Pastor Clark said.

"Promise," Jaslene and Marcus said in unison.

While they finished eating in silence, a yearning took root within her. One day, she hoped to experience a love like that too.

Chapter Seven

*A*fter eating, they headed onto the front porch. Marcus couldn't help but feel empathy toward Grandpa Clark. If only Marcus had known what his grandfather was feeling, he would've reached out to him, regardless of their differences. Instead, a grudge kept them apart and for that, Marcus held remorse.

They filed out the front door, the clapboards creaking underneath their feet. Grandpa Clark slowly bent his knees, his face scrunching up. He placed his palms on the wood and felt around for something. "Getting too old for this."

"What are you doing, Reginald?"

"Getting the keys to the shed." His gnarled fingers lifted one of the clapboards, and he pulled out a rusted cashbox. After messing with the combination lock, it popped open.

"What's the box for?" Grandma asked.

"It's where I keep keys and other important items."

"I had no idea." Grandma shook her head.

"Now you know." He grabbed the keys from the box

and locked it quickly. The four of them walked across the dandelion-infested lawn and down a narrow walkway leading to the back. A gray shed came into view.

Grandpa Clark stopped a few feet away from the shed, sadness on his weathered face. Grandma stood next to him and held his hand.

"You can do this, baby," she said. "I'm right here with you."

His grandfather nodded and inserted the key into the lock, his fingers trembling as he tried to pry it open.

Marcus winced. "We don't have to do this."

"We're doing this. It's time," Grandpa said. "It's well past time."

The lock clicked open, and the door swung wide. Dust particles floated from the shed and into the daylight as they stood outside the doorway. Grandpa Clark nodded. "Yes. I'm walking inside."

His grandparents stepped into the shed first, still holding hands. Marcus and Jaslene glanced at each other, and he couldn't help but think about holding her hand. That wouldn't be right though. Instead, the two of them walked in separately.

Stepping over boxes and old pieces of furniture, he scanned the area but couldn't see much. He turned on the flashlight on his cell phone and swept the light over the room. An old bicycle, a sewing machine, a wooden ironing board, and a dollhouse were piled together in the center of the shed. He swept the light over the room and spotted a black chalkboard and some student desks too. "This place is a treasure trove of items."

Grandpa Clark nodded.

"You okay?" Marcus directed the question to him.

"Fine. Just fine."

"So many good things in here," Marcus said.

"And you're thinking of tossing it. I don't agree with your plan. You know the moisture and heat in this shed can ruin this stuff over time." Grandma Clark swiped a layer of dust from one of the school desks. "Marcus knows how to properly care for and maintain these things. You should hand them over to the museum."

Grandpa Clark didn't say a word. Not a good sign. Better change the subject before he kicked them out of the shed. "What were all of these school desks for?"

"New Life used to have a one-room schoolhouse. It was started shortly after the Civil War to educate the formerly enslaved." He lifted the blackboard from the dirty wooden floor and leaned it against the wall. "One of our great-greats was a teacher here. Her name was Sophronia Clark. She graduated from Xavier University in Louisiana and returned to South Carolina to teach Latin and grammar at our schoolhouse."

That knowledge moved him. He felt . . . a part of something much bigger than himself. "I didn't know," Marcus said.

"There's a lot of things that you don't know, grandson."

Grandpa Clark pulled up two metal stools and set them out for Jaslene and Grandma Clark.

"Sometimes I wish you would let me know. I went through all of this schooling to learn history, and the history is right here in this shed."

Grandpa Clark shook his head. "You might've known earlier if you helped out at the church more. But you had other plans for your life."

"Leave him alone." Grandma Clark stood and wagged her finger at her husband. "He didn't come here to get admonished."

"I'm not admonishing him. I'm stating the plain facts. If he would've helped, he would've learned. That's all."

Marcus resisted the urge to respond. His grandfather would never let him live that down. "It's okay, Grandma."

"No, it's not. Now I'm tired of seeing the two of you at odds with each other. It breaks my heart." Her voice held a tremor. "It's not right."

"Fine, dear," Grandpa Clark said. "I won't talk about that anymore."

"Good." Grandma wiped the corner of her eye.

Jaslene and Marcus exchanged a look. Oh, how he wished Jaslene wasn't here to see this back and forth. What did she think of all the rifts and grudges and disagreements between him and his grandfather? A part of him was embarrassed that she witnessed it, but Marcus *had* brought her here.

"I guess we better keep looking around," she said.

"Yes, let's keep looking." Marcus scooted behind a folding table to inspect the rear of the shed. He could spend hours in this space.

Marcus trailed his index finger along the edge of a hymnal and flipped it open. The date on the title page was 1942. He turned the page and scanned the words to "Be Thou My Vision."

"What do you have there?" Grandma Clark eyed the page. "Ah, that's one of my favorite hymns."

Grandma hummed the tune, and Marcus smiled. She used to sing church hymns every morning while making breakfast. Grandma Clark had a special way of hallowing the ordinary. That was why Marcus got along easier with her than with Grandpa. Still, his grandfather was reeling from that mass shooting. That explained things too.

"Is that the mourners' bench?" Jaslene pointed to a nondescript mahogany bench that was amidst a bunch of tables and chairs. The furniture was jumbled together in a haphazard mess. Nothing set the bench apart as something to treasure and preserve. It could be easily overlooked.

"That's it," Grandpa Clark said, his tone resigned. "Help me get it out from the rest of the things, Marcus." They picked up a stool and a blackboard that was on top of the bench and set it aside.

"Let's lift this together on three. One. Two. Three."

Marcus heaved, and his shoulder and neck muscles strained against the bench's weight. Good thing he had been lifting dumbbells three times a week or else he'd be in a world of hurt.

They placed the bench in the open space in the center of the shed. The bench was pretty banged up. He studied the etchings up close. The markings didn't look like haphazard nicks and scratches. They were more like carvings without a pattern or design. "Do you know anything about the marks on this bench?"

His grandfather paused as if weighing whether he should say anything. "I know a little something about it. Whenever folks came to the mourners' bench to air their grievances and the wrongs done to them, they'd leave a mark on the bench. Something like a signature so that their presence and their grievances could be remembered. Most couldn't write—or it was dangerous to show they knew how to write—so the mark was how they wished to be remembered."

"Interesting," Marcus said. "A way to release bad memories."

"Bad memories have a way of sneaking up on you," Grandpa Clark said. "No matter what you do to get rid of them."

Marcus thought of his grandfather and the mass shooting at New Life, of Hope and Trey too. "You're right. Bad memories tend to stick."

Grandpa Clark appeared to appraise him. "I tried to share these facts about the past with your father, but he was focused on being a high paid doctor. He didn't care."

"I care."

His grandmother stopped humming.

Grandpa Clark pinned Marcus with a look. "I promised your grandmother that I wouldn't fuss at you, and so I'm keeping quiet."

His grandmother resumed humming and walked to the opposite side of the shed. A heaviness settled inside of Marcus. He cared a whole lot. Why else would he be here?

Grandpa Clark translated caring as doing things his way, and his way meant Marcus needed to become the next pastor at New Life. Somehow, Marcus would have to prove that his work held value.

"Look at this."

Jaslene's voice pulled Marcus out of his thoughts. "Someone wrote their name on here. It says . . . Solomon and Janey. Is this the same Janey who had my . . . I mean, *the* engagement ring?"

My engagement ring. She'd almost said it. Was she having second thoughts? What would he do if she did?

No need to consider that now. Marcus knelt to get a better look at the marks on the bench. Tentatively, he and Jaslene ran their fingers over the etchings as if they were touching a sanctified object. In many ways, they were.

This place, the quiet, untouched shed—being surrounded by all of this history—it was like another kind of sanctuary. For Marcus, researching history was its own kind of prayer. Perhaps one day, Grandpa Clark—the pastor—could see that too. Marcus's fingertips felt every bump and curve of the bench. He shone a light on it, examining the bench up close.

Grandpa Clark walked to the bench and squinted at the marks. "Yep. That says Solomon and Janey, all right.

I never got up close to see their names before. Then again, I haven't been in this shed in a while."

Why were Janey's and Solomon's names etched onto the mahogany? What was their grievance?

It was something major enough to cause them to carve their identity onto this object. The copy of Janey's letter, which they'd read the other day held in Marcus's mind. Janey and Solomon wanted to run away together. Janey and Solomon were in love.

Love.

Jaslene placed her fingertips over the same places that Marcus touched. Watching her hands made his heart swirl into a flurry of leaves. The Jaslene of today was not the same Jaslene from two years ago. He wasn't the same Marcus either. His desire grew.

When Marcus was a teenager, Grandpa warned him of desire. He had said desire was deceitful, but that was his religion taking. If it were so deceitful, then why did this moment feel so very honest?

Marcus sighed and circled the mourners' bench. He needed to get back to Janey and Solomon, not speculate about himself and Jaslene. There had to be more information on Janey and Solomon elsewhere, something that told a fuller story than the one on this bench.

This could be a futile effort. It could be years before he found more information. Grandpa Clark could be right. Marcus could've made better use of his skills by going to seminary instead of studying old objects in the hopes of making connections and finding meaning.

Grandma Clark's humming stopped, and the only sound was the chirping of birds outside. Despite his doubts, the research thrilled him. Marcus studied the etchings, tried to look at them with fresh eyes. He would need more time to make sense of the peculiar curves and indentations in the lettering, and for that, he would need Grandpa Clark to lend him this bench.

Marcus shifted his focus to his grandfather, who was busy riffling through a toolbox. "Grandpa?" he said instinctively, forgetting Pastor Clark's formal title.

He glanced up, no objection in his eyes. "Yes."

"I'd like to analyze this bench more. There's only so much research that I can do in a shed. My resources are back at the office. I'll try to figure out why their names are on here. After all, Janey and Solomon are our ancestors. It'd be important to know, not for a public exhibit, but for us, for our family."

Frown lines formed on Grandpa Clark's forehead. "I know you mean well, but I can't do that. Everything is the way it needs to be—locked away in this shed. We don't need to go digging for answers or speculating on the past. It's bad enough that the past creeps up on us in other ways."

Dejection returned. Locking things away and hiding them wasn't healthy, not for Grandpa Clark, not for Marcus either. Yes, he had warned Jaslene that his grandfather would refuse, but hearing the refusal hurt.

Would Marcus ever be able to bridge this chasm with his grandfather?

He didn't know.

THE FOLLOWING MONDAY Jaslene worked from her office, and then she headed to the museum at five o'clock. During her walk, sparrows fluttered in the Lowcountry sky and settled on the branches of a magnolia. One bird soon flew from its branch and joined other sparrows gathered around a piece of bread.

A young, brown-skinned woman wearing a pale blue headscarf and an ankle-length white skirt tossed more pieces of bread their way. Jaslene stopped mid-walk and buttoned her ivory cardigan, watching the sparrows nibble on bread crumbs.

"Hi there." The young woman waved.

"Hello." Jaslene continued in the direction of the museum, and her thoughts traveled to the meeting with Marcus's grandfather. She'd been trying all morning to figure out a proper response to Grandpa Clark's refusal to lend the bench. Hearing him say no left her saddened, but she couldn't be surprised or shocked. Marcus had prepped her.

Still, a part of her hoped Grandpa Clark would say yes. After seeing Janey's and Solomon's names on that bench, she wanted to know more. After all, Jaslene wore Janey's ring at one point. Jaslene felt a connection to the woman, even though she was from another era. Their love story moved Jaslene, made her think of what could've been. In a way, Marcus and Jaslene had their own unfinished love story. That made her feel even more connected to Janey.

Janey glanced at her bare ring finger. Marcus had given her an irreplaceable gift when he placed that sapphire ring on her finger, and she returned it. A wave of regret washed over her. What was she thinking? Why did she do that?

No. She couldn't have any regrets. Jaslene knew exactly why she returned the ring, and she needed to stay confident in that decision. There wasn't any turning back or changing her mind.

The museum came into view, and she did a slow jog to cross the street and go inside. Moments later, she was in the W. E. B. Du Bois room. Jaslene needed to focus on Sasha's wedding, not on her old engagement ring.

She grabbed Sasha's wedding files from her tote—along with the trusty spreadsheet—and she pulled out a tape measure, unrolled it, and got to work by making measurements of the place. After she was done, she took out her notebook and circled the space, thinking of how she'd create a uniquely Filipino and African American look.

She could utilize batok shapes as an accent design on the reception's linen napkins. Their intersecting lines and shapes would give a clean, modern look. Peace lilies would look great for the centerpieces. The flower symbolized goodwill and positivity in the Philippines.

Jaslene tapped her chin. If she wrapped kente cloth around the vases that held the peace lilies, that might look good. It would depend on the color of the cloth. Or she could utilize weaved basket centerpieces and wrap the kente cloth around the basket's rim. Perhaps put a potted peace lily plant inside of the basket. She jotted down some notes. Before she settled on a design, she'd have to experiment with it first. A wave of contentment flowed through her. She hadn't done this type of brainstorming in a long time, and it felt good.

The sound of footsteps in the hallway broke her concentration. Marcus entered the Du Bois room. Today he had on a gray cable-knit sweater, and a white collared shirt peeked from underneath it. His khakis were navy instead of his usual tan. "How was your day?" he asked.

"Very productive. I was going through my checklist for Sasha's wedding when I remembered that I needed to get measurements of this space."

"What else do you have to finish for Sasha's wedding?"

"I've decided to create the aesthetic for her wedding." Sasha told him about the opportunity with *Southern Bride* too.

"Wow. I'm looking forward to seeing what you create." Marcus paused. "I've been thinking about you for the past few days."

Jaslene's heart fluttered. "You have?"

"Yes. I haven't been able to sleep well after what happened on Saturday. It's been on my mind a lot."

Did he remember when she accidentally said *my engagement ring*? She hoped he'd forgotten. Jaslene certainly wouldn't bring that up now. "No big deal. We tried. That's all that matters."

"I wish I could agree with you, but after being there, I

can't be comfortable with how it ended. Something else has to be done." Marcus clasped his hands. "I know how much it meant for you to see your sister's notes. I don't take that lightly."

"It's all right," she said.

"I'm sorry it turned out that way."

She sensed care in his tone. Did he care for her?

The question hung in her mind, but she released it. "To be honest, I couldn't help but keep thinking about Solomon and Janey. Their story is intriguing. Don't you think?"

"Most definitely." He unclasped his hands. "No matter how much I research, history will never tell me how the enslaved felt emotionally. Those feelings are lost to time. But that bench . . . that bench gave me a hint. It was surreal."

"Those two must've been deeply in love."

"I agree."

Silence filled the space between them. The unspoken thoughts, the electricity between them, hummed and buzzed and sent a sensation through her which she hadn't felt in the longest time.

Marcus kept his gaze on Jaslene, and expectation bloomed within her. She let it grow for a moment, but then she pushed it aside. She had a "to-do" list to attend to. "I better get back to work. Wedding planning duties call."

"Right," he said softly.

A tap on the door broke their moment. Harold stepped

into the room. "Afternoon, Marcus. Jaslene. Nice to see you both. How are things going?"

"Pretty good. Prepping for Sasha's wedding and trying to get an accurate gauge on how many people will fit in this space." She held up the measuring tape. "I meant to ask you. Is it okay if I bring in extra lighting for Sasha's wedding?"

"Sure. I have some extension cords if you need those."

"I probably will," Jaslene said. "I also need to figure out the seating arrangements."

"You can fit about one hundred to two hundred guests. We have tables in storage if you need them. They fit into this place perfectly."

"Oh, good. I was wondering about tables too. Thank you," Jaslene said.

Harold kept looking at the two of them, as if trying to figure them out. Suddenly self-conscious, Jaslene moved her focus back to the measurements she'd written down and her design ideas.

"How are things going with the foundation?" Marcus asked Harold.

"I haven't spoken to them since they communicated their requirements to us. And right now, we don't have much time to meet their benchmarks."

Curious, Jaslene stopped what she was doing and listened in on their discussion. "What's this about benchmarks?"

Marcus and Harold explained the situation to her. "We won't be funded for this fiscal year, and we'll have to close down," Harold finished.

"What? I didn't know this," Jaslene said, looking at Marcus.

"Now you know," Harold said.

"Didn't you say before that one of the board members for the Lee Ray Foundation was related to one of the members of the Confederate group that's applying for the grant money?" Marcus asked Harold.

'That's a true statement."

"Isn't that a conflict of interest?"

Harold was quiet for a moment. "It would be a conflict if the member of the Confederate group was on the foundation's board. But I know what you're saying, and yes, I'm pretty sure that relative has influence over the decisions the board makes. I can't do much about that."

"What about Heather Gates?" Marcus asked Harold.

"What about her?"

"Do you think you can reach out to her and explain our situation? She might be able to ask her father if he can comment publicly about our situation, especially since he ordered those Confederate statues to be removed."

"Hmm. I hadn't thought of that. Good idea, Marcus. I'll see what I can do. Might give her a call today. So how's the fundraising and all going?"

"Um . . . I haven't made as much progress on it as I wanted. I got sidetracked, but I'll get back to work."

Marcus hadn't made much progress because Jaslene convinced him to visit his grandparents. She shouldn't have done that. Marcus had more important things to deal with, and now he really could lose his job.

Harold raised an eyebrow. "What did you get side-tracked with? It wasn't a personal emergency or anything, was it?"

Should Jaslene mention to Harold that it was all her fault? If she did, Harold might start seeing her as a distraction to Marcus's work.

If she didn't say anything, then Marcus would have to fend for himself with Harold. He could start thinking that Marcus was incompetent, and he could end up losing his job anyway. That wouldn't be fair to him.

"It's my fault," Jaslene said quickly.

"Your fault about what?" Harold asked.

Jaslene fiddled with the file that she held. *Just say it.* "I'm the reason why Marcus hasn't started working on fundraising yet. I saw the unfinished exhibit on New Life Church, and I thought it'd be a good idea to get the mourners' bench from his grandparents. If we get the exhibit finished in time, then it'd be a great opportunity to bring in more visitors to the exhibit. You'd be able to meet one of your benchmarks for the grant."

"Did you get the bench?" Harold looked at her, curious.

Was Harold getting a change of heart about the exhibit? "No, we didn't. I'm sorry. But we can still work on bringing the exhibit to fruition. It doesn't have to be an either-or situation, especially since it'll draw more visitors."

Harold looked between them again. "Do you still think the exhibit will bring more visitors, Marcus?"

Great. She'd made things worse. Marcus couldn't oppose his boss. That would be awful. Jaslene should've kept her mouth shut.

"What do you think?" Harold repeated.

"I agree with Jaslene."

Oh, lordy. This was not good. Jaslene took a deep breath.

"I'm glad to see that the two of you are so passionate about the exhibit, and I do see the value in it, but there are other ways to bring in visitors without having to put up an entirely new exhibit."

Another disappointment. Jaslene was really hoping that Harold would agree, but that wasn't happening. Marcus probably didn't know a thing about fundraising. Neither did she, but she did know how to put on an event. "If it's any consolation, I can help with the fundraising."

"You can?" Harold said.

"Most definitely."

Marcus appeared surprised. "That's nice of you . . . especially given that you're busy with your own work."

"We could plan some type of fundraising event. Working on events is my forte, after all. It'll be great."

"I hadn't thought of a fundraising event. Sounds like a good idea. How about we set up a meeting for the three of us later this week? I'll send out a calendar invite," Harold said.

"Sure," Jaslene and Marcus said in unison.

Harold walked out the door, his steps sounding in the hallway. After Harold left, a sense of assuredness had overtaken her.

"Thank you, Jaslene. You didn't have to do that."

"I know, but I want to. I wish you would've told me that the museum is in danger of getting shut down."

"I should've mentioned it to you." Marcus sighed. "We can still work on the exhibit on our downtime, if you don't mind."

She smiled at his comment. "I don't mind at all."

"I'll email Sasha and the committee today and see if they can help with gathering information for the exhibit. They can get more information on Denmark Vesey's influence while we focus on the bench. I still want to convince my grandfather to loan it to the museum. I don't know how though."

"Don't worry. Something will come up. We'll shift most of our focus to the fundraiser, and we'll keep our fingers crossed that your grandfather will change his mind."

"It's a plan," Marcus said.

A sense of assuredness filled her. She was going to help keep this museum in existence. No matter what.

Chapter Eight

Marcus clicked Send on the email to Sasha and the committee. "Do you want to brainstorm ideas for the fundraiser now?" Marcus asked, encouraged at the prospect of Jaslene helping with the event.

"Most definitely."

"First we need to send invitations. The museum has a mailing list. We can send e-invites and paper ones. And we need to continuously post on social media."

She jotted this down. "When do you plan to have the event?"

"The sooner the better. But I don't want it to get in the way of Sasha's wedding."

"True." She pulled up her calendar on her phone and scrolled through the dates. "We can do this before the wedding, since raising funds needs to happen soon."

"Agreed." This moment reminded him of when they used to have weekly planning sessions for their upcoming nuptials. He had looked forward to those sessions because they not only planned for the wedding, but they daydreamed about life after their wedding. That wasn't happening anymore, of course, but the more Marcus spent time with her, the more they melded.

"You should make in-person or phone contact with those folks on the museum's mailing list. People link faces with names. The connection will make folks amenable to donating."

Talk to people? It was one thing to muster up the courage to contact Grandpa Clark again, but it was quite another to talk to complete strangers. "I'll ask Harold if he wants to do that instead. He should be up for it."

The light from Jaslene's eyes dimmed. "Why not you? You're capable."

Marcus didn't want to get into all the reasons why, if he had the choice, he preferred to keep to himself. Best to shift the focus away from himself. "There's a reason why I chose to be a museum archivist and not an event planner."

"Hmm." Jaslene rested her chin in her hands. "You never told me why you chose your profession. I'd like to know."

Hoo-boy. So Jaslene was asking the hard question. Might as well give her the tough answer. "I won't hurt anyone doing this type of work . . . for the most part. I deal with the old and with events that have already taken place. Events that don't involve me at all."

A slight frown formed at Jaslene's lips. Pity. She had pity on him. "Does your choice have to do with your feelings about Trey?"

A lump formed in his throat. Marcus nodded. "And also Hope."

"I get it." Jaslene's expression went from pity to understanding. "I can't tell you to get over it because I know where you're coming from. I've done the same thing by not contacting Sasha after all that happened."

"Glad that you see my perspective."

"But you know what? We're going to do this, you and I. And we're doing this together," Jaslene said. "So that's a win."

Hearing her say those words brought sunshine to his heart. Grandma Clark had said similar things to her husband the other day. Perhaps there was hope for Jaslene and Marcus after all. "It's a very big win."

A curl fell loose from Jaslene's bun and graced her cheek. She was stunning, inside and out. After everything that happened between them, being around Jaslene was turning out to be a small miracle, a beautiful, tiny miracle, and he treasured it.

"Back to brainstorming. I wish we could have the exhibit ready in time for the fundraiser, but if we don't, we can talk about it during the event. That might motivate donors too."

"Good point."

"We'll need to draw a big crowd since visitor count was one of the benchmarks. I wonder how we can draw people to the fundraiser, given that the exhibit won't be up and running. We'll have to think of something else." She tapped her chin. "Ooh! I have an idea. Imani. She can play at the fundraiser too, in addition to playing at Sasha's wedding. I'll have to check her schedule. Let me text her, since I have to ask her about Sasha's wedding too."

Jaslene sent a text and waited for a response. "She said it's fine. She needs to check out the sound in the museum too. Is it okay if I bring her here tomorrow to check that out?"

"Of course. I haven't seen her in ages. It'll be good to catch up with her again."

"We can also ask businesses if they'd like to donate items to raffle." Jaslene set her phone aside and took more notes. "There's a photography business around here that also sells vintage prints. It's named Avila's Lens. They could donate a print to the museum."

"I like that idea."

"You know who would be great for a donation? That bridal shop down the street. Trying to think of the name of the owner."

"Derek?"

"Oh yes. Derek," Jaslene said. "He got married recently. Some of my clients get their wedding gowns from his wife. I'll ask them if they have a vintage looking dress or accessory that they can donate." She scribbled something on her notepad. "And tours. You can offer exclusive walking tours of the museum. That might increase foot traffic if we emphasize some feature that they can't get anywhere else."

"We could have our museum docents do that during the event," Marcus said.

"We need to think of a theme for the fundraiser. Any ideas?"

"That's out of my league. I have no idea."

Jaslene flipped to a new page in her notepad. "We could have a theme that features an era in Black history. Like the Harlem Renaissance. We can dress like we're from the 1920s."

"Oh yes," Marcus said. "And you could do the center-pieces for the event too."

"Hmm. Between you and Sasha, I'm going to be in event designer mode again." She laughed.

"That'll be a good thing. I remember when you and Hope were planning to add design to your wedding planning business."

Her expression shuttered.

"Something the matter?"

Jaslene shifted. "These design projects are just one-off things. I'm not planning to do anything more after Sasha's wedding or the fundraiser."

"Why not? You're good at it. Even the little touches that you added to my office did wonders for that space. You should pursue it full force again."

She shrugged.

When they were engaged, he had prepaid her tuition at a local community college so that she could get her professional certification as an interior designer. It was supposed to be a wedding present, but Marcus never got the chance to surprise her with the gift. When he tried to get a tuition refund, they said there weren't any refunds on non-degree programs. So he took the loss. "It was just an idea. I know it's tough to get back to the way things were. We're taking it one day at a time."

"One day at a time." Jaslene glanced away from him, and he studied her profile, the softness of her cheek, the shape of her lips, the tension in her jaw. "Do you think it'll ever happen? Do you think things will be back to the way they were? I mean, not in a perfect sense, but do you think we'll ever return to some semblance of normalcy?"

Could they? He wasn't sure. "I hope so."

She didn't say anything.

"You know," he said, "if we had gotten married two years ago, our married life would've been far from perfect. We're still human. We would've had a few spats between then and now."

"Kind of like your grandparents and their spats."

"Something like that, but love is bigger than disagreements. Their love is bigger. Probably why they've been married for sixty-seven years."

"And our love . . . or at least the love we used to have for each other, isn't big enough," Jaslene said, facing him again. "Is that right?"

Her question pierced. What could he say? From the looks of it, their love wasn't big enough. When times grew dim, their relationship ended. Nevertheless, Marcus still cared for her today, despite the ocean between them. "I don't know."

Jaslene took a deep breath. "We were supposed to be planning for the fundraiser. How'd we get on this topic?"

Because we love each other.

Doubt crept in. Did he still love Jaslene? Or was he merely nostalgic about their old relationship? He couldn't tell. With Jaslene, the past and present intertwined in beautiful, unending threads. For now, Marcus would be content with simply weaving it.

MARCUS DEFINITELY KNEW how to rattle a woman. His gaze spoke loudly. He still wanted Jaslene.

Did she want him too?

Jaslene didn't *not* want him. He made her smile when nothing else brought joy. In response, she placed that orchid on his desk. Yet attraction was an emotional privilege that she couldn't afford to indulge in. She had other things to focus on: weddings and fundraisers and Imani.

Once she was done at the office, she picked up Imani from school and drove to the museum so that Imani could test the sound. When Jaslene came to a stop near the bridal shop on the corner, she made a mental note to call or email the bridal shop to ask them about donating a dress for the raffle.

Moments later, her mind hummed with Marcus's words. No matter how hard Jaslene tried to not think of him, she did. Marcus opened her soul to the world around her. Jaslene used to live in drudgery. Life used to be a neutral gray, but with him, she experienced golds and reds and shades of blue. He lit a living flame inside of her.

But she feared the fire it would create.

As an orphan, Jaslene trained herself to keep the world at bay. The world could hurt her, and when Hope died, her fears solidified. Since meeting Marcus—again, she was learning how to be alive—again. Their lives were meant to be knit together, the good parts and the bad. They were branches of the same tree, feeding on a rich soil of disappointments, tenderness, and love. That's what scared her the most.

What if Marcus wasn't around anymore? Would she be uprooted?

"You okay, Auntie?"

Jaslene turned on the signal and made another left turn. "Yes. Why'd you ask?"

"You seem deep in thought. That's all." Imani shifted the violin case in her lap.

Jaslene didn't want to talk about what was on her mind. "I hope that the sound at the museum works for you."

"I hope so too. When you told me about the funding issues, I got worried for Marcus." She paused. "So, I'm assuming that you and Marcus are on good terms again?"

"We're talking. I even went with him to see his grandparents."

"Now that's a very big deal. Looks like the two of you are on more than good terms."

Jaslene kept her eyes on the road and didn't say a word.

"Your silence tells me that I'm right," Imani said matter-of-factly.

"Ha-ha. You assume too much." Jaslene pulled up in front of the museum and turned off the ignition.

"Does Marcus know I'm coming here today?"

"Of course. He's looking forward to seeing you."

"That's a sign, Auntie." Imani's brown eyes widened for a split second.

"What?"

"Hello?" Imani snapped her fingers in Jaslene's face. "You don't see it, but I do. You visited his grandparents. He wants to see me again. You two are getting serious."

Jaslene smiled, remembering Marcus's words from yesterday. "He seems interested."

"And you're most definitely very interested."

Jaslene chuckled at Imani's adverb-filled insistence. "Let's go inside and stop talking about this." They exited the Toyota and headed to the museum.

Inside, the foyer appeared brighter. Jaslene glanced up to see additional light bulbs in the fixtures. Nice. They headed to Marcus's office. He was at his desk looking very handsome, as usual. His Caesar haircut accentuated his jawline and cheekbones. If he wasn't a museum archivist, he could be an actor on television.

He glanced up from his work and waved. "You two are right on time. How's it going, Imani?"

"Amazing! I'm so happy to see you again . . . to see the two of you together."

Oh brother. Jaslene gave Imani a tight smile.

Marcus pointed to an empty music stand in the corner of his office. "I got that for you this morning. I found it in the storage. I'll take you to where you'll perform. It's spacious."

After picking up the music stand, Marcus led them to the Du Bois room. Imani gave Jaslene a thumbs-up, winked at her several times, and mouthed the words, *He really likes you.* Jaslene held back a laugh.

"Here we are," Marcus said.

"You got new light bulbs, I see," Jaslene said.

"Yes. The maintenance folks put them in a few days ago."

Imani circled the space and looked up. "Nice high ceilings. That's a good thing."

Jaslene set up Imani's music stand while her niece tuned her violin. Marcus pushed the rectangular table against the wall. "I want to give you all the space you need, Imani," he said.

"Cool." She tuned her violin and rosined her bow.

Marcus set up two empty chairs near the music stand, and he gestured for Jaslene to sit next to him. When she did, Marcus scooted his chair close. She inhaled his sandalwood scent.

"When Auntie told me about the fundraiser, I searched for the perfect piece of music." Imani placed her sheet music on the stand. "Have you heard of Florence Price?"

Marcus squinted as if trying to recall. "I have, actually. I learned about her a few months ago."

"Not many know about Ms. Price," Imani said. "They discovered her full body of work nine years ago, hidden in the walls of an old house."

"Wow," Jaslene said.

"I know, right? She was brilliant and prolific, but she never got her rightful place in the musical canon. Should be up there right next to Gershwin, but we know how that goes," Imani said. "Anyway, she's my musical inspiration. I wanted to play her piece Violin Concerto no. 2.

Her stylistic choices in this composition demonstrate how Black spirituals can engage with the classical art form in innovative ways."

Jaslene smiled. Her niece was brilliant.

Imani tucked her violin in the crook of her neck and played.

The gentle tune pulsed through Jaslene, and the tension in her shoulders relaxed. The melody reawakened confidence in her, a confidence that Jaslene had figured was long gone.

Imani's bow danced across her violin. She brought energy and her signature virtuosity to the composition. Imani would be a blessing to any conservatory in the country, the globe even.

The intensity in Imani's expression while she played always inspired Jaslene, but seeing her play now reminded Jaslene of all that she had lost in herself. That drive to overcome any obstacle tossed her way. That feeling of becoming so enveloped in her work that she forgot everything else. That's why it was like whenever Jaslene had designed weddings for clients back in the day.

Marcus shifted in his chair, and his arm brushed against hers. She became acutely aware of his presence. They hadn't been this close to each other in a long, long time. She savored his nearness but resisted the urge to rest her head on his shoulder.

Imani's song came to a close, and Jaslene and Marcus gave a hearty applause. "That was amazing, hon," Jaslene said.

"I agree," Marcus said. "I'm not an expert in classical music, but from what I heard, you'll be at one of the top conservatories in no time."

"That's kind of you to say." Imani tucked her violin underneath her arm. "I'm going to put my stuff in the car. I'll see you outside, Auntie."

"Okay, love. I'll be there in a minute."

After Imani left, Jaslene and Marcus stood alone in the museum. Jaslene glanced at the empty music stand. "I hope Imani gets all that she desires."

"She will. But what about you?"

His question caught her off guard. "What about me?"

"What do you desire?"

Her pulse ramped up. She stood and walked over to the empty music stand, running her fingertips over its edge. "Simplicity."

"In what way?"

"Life got complicated after my sister died. So many decisions to make. So many responsibilities to juggle. So many feelings to sort through. I want to be able to sit on the front porch of my house and people watch. That's it. Simple."

A small light shone in his eyes. "I remember us talking about that."

"I'm glad you remember," she said, gently grasping the edge of the music stand. They held eye contact for what seemed like infinity, and an energy pulsed between them. Marcus got up from his seat and stood close to her. Her heart flipped, and she fixated on his thick, dark lashes.

Any woman in the world would pay good money for those lashes.

"When we were engaged," he said, his voice soft, "I wanted to give you a simple life, one where you were free to pursue your interests apart from any obligations."

She smiled. "We were so optimistic, weren't we?"

Marcus studied her for a moment. He retrieved his phone from his back pocket, opened the email app, and showed her the screen. "This is an email from the local community college. I paid the full fee for you to get certified in interior design."

"You did?"

"Yes. It was supposed to be a wedding present, but we never got married so I never got the chance to give this to you. I'm giving this to you now."

Was there an ulterior motive to this? "Why?"

As if registering the real meaning of her question, he added: "No strings attached. I'm giving this to you in friendship. Regardless of what happened between us, you deserve to get that certification."

She stared at the email on his phone, unsure whether she should accept this or not. Perhaps this was her second chance. "There's no time limit on when I can register?"

"No. The credit is on your account, and they don't give refunds." He laughed. "Believe me. I checked."

Jaslene took the phone in her hand, and then she looked at the date on the email. It was two weeks before their wedding. "Now I'm thinking about what if I decided to not be Sasha's wedding planner? Would I have missed this second chance?"

"I wouldn't worry about what-ifs. So . . . does that mean you're going to enroll in the class?"

"I'll give it some serious consideration." She shook her head, disbelief and hope tumbling in her heart. "I'll have to attend to Imani's needs first, but if there aren't any conflicts with her schedule and the local college's class schedule, then I might enroll."

"I hope you do."

Life was coming together. Not in the way that she envisioned, but in the little things: Imani playing for the fundraiser and Sasha's wedding, helping Marcus, getting this opportunity to get a certification. A brighter future glimmered on the horizon, and she reveled in it.

Chapter Nine

On Saturday afternoon, Marcus drove to Grandpa Clark's house with a lawn mower in the cab of his Ford F-250. It was sixty-eight degrees outside. That was autumn in the Lowcountry.

He didn't make an appointment or notify his grandparents that he was on his way. Marcus didn't want to be prescreened by them. He simply wanted to be a grandson making a visit to see his elders. He had grown tired of the tensions with Grandpa Clark. Hopefully this impromptu visit would disrupt, or even erase, that feeling.

The back road to their home was narrow, unpaved, and very difficult to navigate, but he preferred it to the wider, more traveled highway. Marcus drove over gravel and grass to get to the tiny parsonage. Rural homes lined both sides of the road. After driving for about twenty minutes, he approached the lake where Trey had drowned all those years ago. Marcus's body tensed, and he blinked back the threat of tears. That was one of the hardest days of his life. He should've been able to save Trey.

As he drew nearer to the lake, something bright caught his periphery. A patch of sword lilies grew near the calm body of water. "Jaslene had a thing for those flowers," he said quietly. Marcus slowed his truck and pulled over to the side of the road. He drew a deep breath and reveled in the silence. Although he drove by the place, he rarely stopped near the lake. Could he do this?

"Yes, I can," he said to himself. After turning off the ignition, he headed in the direction of the flowers, their vibrant colors dotting freshly cut grass. The closer he got, the more the tension in his shoulders relaxed. Once there, Marcus bent and touched the petals of one of the lilies. They exuded beauty with their rich shades of pinks and whites and yellows. He traced his finger over the edge of one petal, imagining times when Jaslene had voiced her sorrows to these flowers.

"Can I help you, sir?"

An attractive young woman wearing a pale blue head-scarf, faded jeans, and a white T-shirt stood before him. Her skin was a chestnut brown and almost flawless—except for two faint scars on her left cheek. She must've lived in one of the houses around here.

"Sorry," Marcus said. "I was driving by, and these flowers caught my attention. I had to see them up close."

"You have a good eye if you noticed them from the road. Most people drive by without seeing. Others don't travel this road at all." She gestured to the sword lilies. "They're beautiful, aren't they?"

"Very beautiful."

"My son planted this garden before he died," she said. "I maintain it for him."

Her son? She looked young to be a mother.

"You can take some if you'd like," she continued. "Take all that you need. Share them with your loved ones. Flowers make the best gifts."

"I know just the person who would love these. Very kind of you." He plucked a few sword lilies from the ground.

"I'll get you a vase. Be right back." She left, and he surveyed the garden.

A bird fluttered and stopped near the edge of the lake. Tiny ripples skimmed the placid body of water. Tough to imagine that over twenty years ago, this place was complete chaos. Ambulance. Police. Worried onlookers. And a young Marcus, helpless and unable to save his younger brother.

Footsteps crunching underneath the grass interrupted his thoughts. "Here you go." The lady handed him a blue vase.

"Thank you, ma'am. Really so very kind." He placed the sword lilies in the vase. "I'm Marcus, by the way. What's your name?"

"Mary." Her scars gleamed in the sunlight.

Marcus studied her skin for a moment, wondering how she got her scars.

"Something the matter?" she asked.

"Nothing. Nothing at all." He glanced away, embarrassed.

"Stop by anytime." She smiled at him. "You're always welcome."

Marcus nodded, absorbing the calm and simplicity around him. "I might do that. Thank you again."

After waving goodbye, he returned to the pickup and carefully set the vase in his passenger seat. The sword lilies were vibrant, their leaves gently bending in the slant of sunlight that streamed through the window. He would give Jaslene the lilies the next time that he saw her, but first, he'd have to see his grandfather. Marcus continued his drive down the unpaved road. From his rearview mirror, he caught sight of the garden, but Mary was gone.

Ten minutes later, Marcus pulled in front of his grandparents' home. The dandelions were about to seed and random patches of grass created an indistinct maze of greenery. He hopped out of the car and headed to the front porch. A trickle of sweat trailed Marcus's brow, and he wiped it away. Nervousness didn't do well for him. If Grandpa Clark didn't let Marcus in the house, perhaps he'd at least improve his lawn. Marcus rang the doorbell.

"Who is it?" Grandpa Clark's gruff voice sounded from the other side of the door.

"Marcus. Your grandson."

"Effie didn't tell me you were coming by," Grandpa said, the door still closed.

His brain scrambled to find the words. "I didn't call her. I figured . . . Last time I was here, I noticed your lawn wasn't looking too good. Figured I'd stop by and work on it. You don't have to let me inside if you don't want to. Just wanted to let you know what I was gonna do."

Footsteps could be heard on the other side. The door-knob jangled open. A five-o'clock shadow covered his grandfather's face. Bushy gray brows scrunched into a V. "You fixing my lawn?" His tone was gruff, suspicious.

"Yes."

"You're not here to bug me about the stuff in the shed, are you?" Grandpa Clark's brow furrowed even deeper. "Because I said what I said."

"No, sir. Just working on the lawn. That's all." He gestured to his pickup truck. "See? I brought my lawn mower and fertilizer with me."

Grandpa Clark didn't take his focus from Marcus, as if weighing whether to believe him.

"I promise," Marcus continued.

"All right then. You work on it. I'll be inside."

For the next hour, Marcus edged the sides and ran his lawn mower over the entire quarter acre. By the time he finished, his muscles ached. He put the lawn mower and fertilizer in his pickup truck. As he was about to leave, Grandpa Clark walked onto the front stoop. "Come on in for some sweet tea."

This was a change. "You sure?"

"Positive." Grandpa Clark waved him over.

Mowing the lawn was the right thing to do, after all. As soon as Marcus entered the house, he spotted the plastic-covered couch in the living room but waited. Moments later, Grandpa Clark brought in a pitcher of sweet tea and an extra chair for Marcus to sit. Then Grandpa Clark got two drinking glasses. "Lawn looks good."

"Glad you like it." Marcus poured himself a glass of sweet tea. "What happened to your groundskeeper?"

"He got a job doing building maintenance at the elementary school. The pay is better, and so he quit. I don't blame him. He has a wife and two children to care for. Still attends New Life, though. Good man."

"Haven't been able to find another person?"

"No. I will, though." Grandpa Clark folded his paper napkin in half.

"Until you do, I'll help maintain your lawn. That is, if you want me to." Marcus sipped his sweet tea.

His grandfather squinted, as if trying to decide whether that would be a good thing. "Aren't you busy with work?"

"Yes. But I'd hate to see the lawn get bad."

The lines around Grandpa's eyes smoothed, and he nodded. "All right. You can come by so long as it doesn't take up too much of your time. I know you're busy with work and all."

He was actually concerned about Marcus's work schedule? "It won't take up time. I won't need to mow the lawn again for a while since winter starts in a few weeks. But I'll stop by on the weekends to rake the leaves."

Grandpa Clark nodded his assent. The ticking of the wall clock punctuated their silence. Marcus took hold of that silence and rested in it. Grandpa Clark was actually letting him stop by on a regular basis. This was a tiny miracle.

"Jaslene doing okay?" Grandpa Clark asked.

"Yep."

"I hope she wasn't too disappointed about me not lending the bench. I could tell that she was."

"Don't worry about it. We discussed it afterward, and we're fine with what you decided."

"Glad to hear." He paused, apparently assessing Marcus. "So . . . things are still on the mend between the two of you?"

Good question. When he encouraged Jaslene to sign up for the class at the community college, he wasn't expecting her to actually consider doing so. "We're talking, but it's nothing serious like it was before. That's good enough for me."

"I see." His grandfather's eyes pierced, and Marcus shifted underneath his gaze.

"Mind if I give you a little advice about you and Jaslene?" Grandpa Clark asked.

"Not at all."

"When I left for the war, I wasn't sure if I'd ever see your grandmother again." He sighed. "I wanted to marry her, but who knew if I would return to the States? So I left for my duty station without proposing to her."

"I didn't know that."

"Of course, you didn't," Grandpa Clark said matter-of-factly. "The older I get, the more I see that I'm getting too old to keep secrets. At least that's what your grandmother tells me."

Marcus crossed his arms and chuckled. "She's right, you know."

"Yeah, she is. When I was overseas, I couldn't help but

think about how she was doing," Grandpa Clark continued. "I wondered whether she found someone else to love. When I returned, I heard through the grapevine that someone was courting her."

"What'd you do?"

"Nothing. Never told her that I was back in town."

"You just let her go?" Marcus said.

"I did. She continued courting the other guy. Then I heard that they were engaged. I knew that there wasn't any chance for me. I needed to move on."

Marcus sensed the defeat in Grandpa Clark's voice. "How'd the two of you end up together?"

"A week before her wedding, she caught her fiancé kissing on someone else. I heard about that through the grapevine too. But I didn't reach out to your grandmother or anything. I didn't want to seem opportunistic. I just went about my business."

"Honorable." Marcus smiled.

"Perhaps. A few months later I went to a social at the rec center in downtown Charleston, and she was there. She didn't have a date, and so I asked her to dance. The rest is history," Grandpa Clark said. "A year later, we were married."

"A happy ending."

"Yes. But it wasn't a perfect ending. Our life together has had its share of ups and downs. Despite all of the hard times, I'm glad I asked her to dance that day." Grandpa Clark refocused his attention on Marcus.

"Me too. I wouldn't be born if you hadn't asked her to dance."

"You're right about that." Grandpa Clark chuckled and then his expression turned serious. "If you still have any inkling of a feeling toward Jaslene, don't give up on her. Don't give up on what could be between the two of you. Life could change in a moment, and you'll wish you made a different choice."

The more time he spent with Jaslene, the more he thought about what could be. Yet making a different choice was a risk he wasn't ready to take. There were too many variables involved. Too many fluke things could happen, just like what happened with Trey and Hope. His heart wasn't ready to absorb another blow. "I'm not so sure. Life has changed in so many ways for me, and I don't like it, to be honest."

"I know what you mean, grandson. But I wouldn't let that stop you." Grandpa Clark tapped his fingers on his knee. "Although things turned out well for me and your grandmother, there are still many things I wish I would've done differently in my life. Many things I regret."

"Like what?"

"That doesn't matter now." His expression flickered. "Anyway, it would be nice if the two of you came to church service tomorrow. Consider this my invitation."

Jaslene and Marcus at New Life? They hadn't been there since the day of their non-wedding. On top of that, Marcus stopped attending regular services after his falling-out with Grandpa Clark. "I don't know."

"You don't have to be there this Sunday, but whenever you two are ready. We'd love to see you both."

Could he return to that church? Could Jaslene? The questions pulsed through him. Grandpa Clark was reaching out to him, and Marcus didn't want to let him down. Then again, what if Marcus asked Jaslene if she'd like to go to New Life together, and she said no?

Decisions. Decisions.

Yet Grandpa Clark had taken a chance all those years ago when he asked Grandma Clark to dance, and that changed their lives for the better. Perhaps it was time for Marcus to do the same. "I'll ask Jaslene, but I can't guarantee that she'll say yes."

"All you need to do is ask, grandson. That's always the first step." Grandpa Clark took another sip of his sweet tea, the ticking clock punctuating the silence.

WHAT IF SHE couldn't do it?

What if she couldn't get her brain together to design an event worth having?

What if she signed up for that certification program and ended up flunking the class?

The fear. The doubts. The questions. All of it piled on now, and Jaslene couldn't find her way out from the darts attacking her mind. Part of the reason why she had decided to only focus on wedding planning was because she was afraid of her own creativity, afraid to let it thrive and grow. Now that she was taking steps into that arena again, worries returned. On top of that, Marcus issued this new challenge: get certified as an interior designer.

After they discussed the possibility, Marcus had forwarded the email about the program. She opened the email on her phone and stared at the message. She would have to make a decision on whether to take up his offer or not. What to do? Too much to think about at the moment. She needed to brainstorm for the fundraiser anyway.

Jaslene got a fresh, blank notebook and jotted down ideas. The Harlem Renaissance theme. Cab Calloway and the great poets of the time came to mind. Music and writing. Words set to music.

The faint sound of music from the living room captured Jaslene's attention. That must be Imani. She left the tiny desk in her bedroom to hear the music more clearly.

Imani was seated in a chair in front of her smartphone, which was positioned in a ring light. And she was playing her violin directly in front of the camera. It was the same, lovely piece that she played at the museum the other day. After a few minutes, Imani stopped the recording and glanced up. "Hey, Auntie."

"Hello, love."

"I was just recording a piece for my applications. I need to send off all of the applications by Wednesday, but I want Mrs. Carlisle to watch the recording first."

Her heart pricked. Imani was moving forward. "That song is one of my favorites. It sounded so lovely at the Du Bois room, too. I think you'll do well with that composition."

"I hope so." Imani rosined her violin bow. After finishing, she sat on the love seat and pulled a throw pillow close to her. "It was nice seeing you and Marcus together at the museum the other day. I saw the two of you holding hands."

"Holding hands? I didn't hold his hand."

"Uh-huh, you did." Imani nodded. "Saw it with my own eyes."

Jaslene thought long about that moment when she got close to Marcus. They were very near to each other, so near that she inhaled the scent of his cologne. Jaslene was most definitely not holding his hand. That did not happen. At all. "We didn't hold hands. I would've remembered if we did. Marcus and I were simply moved by your performance. There's nothing happening between us."

"I wish I would've taken a photo of the moment so that I could show it to you myself. Y'all were holding hands."

Jaslene was about to squelch Imani's assumptions when her cell phone buzzed. She glanced at the screen, and her tummy flipped. "That's Marcus."

"Aha! See, y'all got a thing going on." Imani giggled. "I knew it."

"He's probably calling about the fundraiser, that's all." Jaslene rolled her eyes and clicked the Talk button. "Hello, Marcus?"

"Hey. Do you have time to talk?"

His voice hit a low note that sent a zing through Jaslene's body. "Sure. Is something the matter?"

"Nothing's the matter. I wanted to ask you something."

Imani sat at the kitchen table, and her attention was apparently fixated on this conversation between them. "What's he saying?" she whispered.

Jaslene tried to wave her off, but it wasn't working. "Keep going, Marcus."

"I stopped by Grandpa Clark's house today. I mowed his lawn and everything."

"Wow. How'd it go?" Jaslene nodded, impressed.

"He invited me to a Sunday service at New Life."

"That's a big deal. What'd you say?"

"I said I'd think about it." Marcus paused. "Grandpa Clark invited you too. He wants us to be there together."

Her pulse stopped for a millisecond. Together? She was invited to the place where they were supposed to get married. There was no way that she could step foot in there again. That might be well and good for Marcus to do, but not her. "That's asking a lot."

"I know. It seemed like it really mattered to him to see us there together. I told him I'd ask you, but of course, you don't have to agree."

She didn't have to agree, but Jaslene also didn't want to disappoint Grandpa Clark. Even though he denied them the bench, she still didn't want to let him down. "Returning to New Life would be hard for me. I mean, I'd have to sit there and look at the spot where you and I almost got married and . . ."

Her voice broke. Even discussing it was hard. That day was fresh in her mind. She had just finished getting dressed for the ceremony, wearing her pale pink wedding gown and holding a bouquet of pink and white tulips. Excitement and anticipation had flowed through her, and she'd headed to the vestibule to get ready to walk down the aisle. Then the news had arrived.

A groomsman whispered something to Pastor Clark, and the lines in his forehead deepened. Pastor Clark pulled her over to the side and delivered the news.

"Your sister's been in an accident. She's at the emergency room."

Jaslene's chest turned cold. She had tossed her bouquet of tulips aside and rushed out of the church, tears streaming down her face. Marcus drove her to the ER, but it was too late. Hope had died.

Jaslene hadn't stepped foot in New Life since then.

"Jaslene?" Marcus's voice pulled her to the present.

"I can't do it," she said. "I can't return. Did he say why he wanted us to be there?"

"No. But he discussed how he almost didn't get married to Grandma Clark. I think a part of him feels bad that he never got to officiate our wedding."

"I wonder why. It wasn't his fault." Jaslene glanced over at Imani. Her eyes were fixed on Jaslene's conversation. "How do you feel about going back to New Life, Marcus?"

"My first instinct was to say no, but I think there could be some benefit in returning."

"What benefit?" she asked, surprised by the sarcasm in her tone.

"That's the thing. I won't know unless I go there . . . with you."

It took a lot out of her to start designing again. Going to New Life was too big of an ask. "I'll need to mull this over a bit. Is that okay?"

"Of course. Take all the time you need."

She hung up, and her brain buzzed.

"What'd he say?" Imani asked.

"A whole lot." Jaslene summarized the conversation.

"Oh."

"I know. That's exactly what I thought." Jaslene headed to the kitchen and poured herself a glass of apple juice. "I can't go back there. That would be the worst. The absolute worst."

Imani rested her chin in her hand, apparently deep in thought. Imani was one of Jaslene's bridesmaids on that day, and her niece had rushed out of the church right after Jaslene. Jaslene had told Imani what happened, and she rode with Marcus and Jaslene to the ER.

"I know it might be hard, Auntie. But it might be a good thing for you to go to New Life."

Did she just hear her niece correctly? "Are you serious?"

"Yes. Mom loved New Life. Perhaps going there with Marcus will help you see why."

"No. No. No." Jaslene shook her head. "Can't do that."

"You can." Imani reached over and gently squeezed Jaslene's hand. "I believe in you."

Jaslene's vision grew blurry, and she blinked back the urge to cry. "I can't. When your mother and I started Fairytale Weddings, I never thought that there'd be a day when I'd have to take care of this business alone. Never thought there'd be a day when she wouldn't be at my side. She was always the leader."

Imani was silent; her expression, kind.

"I always figured that the love department was your mother's domain," Jaslene continued. "She started the wedding planning business. I was just tagging along. Part of me is scared to return there, you know?"

Imani sat close, and she wrapped her arms around Jaslene.

"I'm scared of messing up," Jaslene said. "Messing up at being your guardian. Messing up with the business. Your mother and I were supposed to do everything together."

"I know. I feel the same way sometimes. Well . . . all the time, to be honest."

"I never told you this, but sometimes when you play the violin, I sense Hope in the melody," Jaslene said, wiping her tears.

"Me too. That's part of the reason why I haven't quit," Imani said. "I sense her every time I play. Gives me chills thinking about it. You know what?"

"What?"

"If Mama were here, I think she'd want you to go back to New Life too. I really think she'd want you and Marcus to get back together, but I'm willing to accept baby steps on that one."

Jaslene smiled.

"So what will you decide? Will you go to New Life?"

If Jaslene said yes to Marcus's invitation, then she would be saying no to a whole bunch of other things. No to her reservations. No to what she thought her future would look like after Hope.

Yet her sister once said that the best gift that they could give to themselves was the gift of moving forward. Jaslene could at least try. A flood of memories came to mind: the joy she found in paging through a magazine for design inspiration, the excitement of starting her business as a teenager. Those moments had provided a blessed solace for Jaslene. Designing events for people had been her refuge, especially during bouts of loneliness. There was this void inside of her, this hole, and design filled it—or at least design filled it temporarily.

Although Jaslene couldn't change the past, she could give herself another chance. "I'll go to New Life with Marcus."

Imani smiled. "Good for you. You won't regret it."

Chapter Ten

*E*arly on Sunday morning, Jaslene dropped Imani off at the performing arts center for an all-day music rehearsal. Afterward, she returned home to get ready for church and prepare for Sasha's arrival too. When Jaslene had told Sasha the samples were ready for *Southern Bride*, she said she would arrive on Sunday to pick them up. Since Jaslene was also designing centerpieces for the fundraiser, she created an extra sample. *Southern Bride* would receive two of Jaslene's creations after all.

As Jaslene was entering her condo, the clickety clack of heels coming up the stairs startled her. Soon, Sasha's signature hair came into view, followed by her smile. "Hey, Jaslene!"

"Morning. I wasn't expecting you this early." Jaslene unlocked her door and stepped inside of her condo. Sasha followed. They plopped down on the couch. "I can't wait to see the centerpieces. Where are they?"

"Be right back." Jaslene headed to her living room to get the centerpieces. One was filled with peace lilies, and the other had violet and red asters. The one with the peace lilies would be used for Sasha's wedding, while the deeper colored flowers were for the fundraiser. Jaslene had wrapped gold and black ribbon around its vase and included photos of some of the great artists of the era: Langston and Zora and Cab. Jaslene carefully set both pieces on the coffee table.

"Ooh! These are gorgeous. I knew you could do it!"

Jaslene smiled. "Thank you for encouraging me."

"No problem, sis! What do you have planned for the rest of the day?"

Jaslene told Sasha about her plans to go to New Life today with Marcus.

"That's great." Sasha applauded. She could be so dramatic, but Jaslene loved it.

Sasha helped Jaslene pick out an outfit for church: a cream-colored blouse with a Peter Pan collar, cream dress pants, and tan flats. After trying on the outfit, Jaslene studied herself in the full-length mirror in the living room.

"How do I look?" Jaslene twirled, showing off her outfit.

"Fabulous! Now all you need is an ivory hat, and you'd look like a styling church lady."

Jaslene laughed. "That wasn't my aim, but it's an interesting take." She smoothed the front of her blouse. "I don't know why I'm so nervous."

"You're nervous because it matters to you," Sasha said, smiling. "I could see how much it matters to you, just by the look on your face."

"You're right. It matters a lot." Jaslene sat on the couch and reached for her black purse.

A knock sounded. "That must be Marcus." Jaslene opened the front door.

"Morning, ladies," Marcus said, stepping into her home. He wore a tan suit jacket and pants, along with a white collared shirt. Marcus could've easily just arrived from a photo shoot for *GQ*. He held something behind his back, but Jaslene couldn't see it from her vantage point. "Where's Imani?"

"I dropped her off at a rehearsal this morning. They started at seven o'clock," Jaslene said, still curious about what he held behind him.

"You two are practically wearing matching outfits. This is so cute. I have to take a picture." Sasha got up and grabbed her phone from the coffee table.

"You don't have to do that," Jaslene said. "And we didn't plan it this way."

"We may not have planned it this way, but it looks as if you and I were thinking the same thing," Marcus said to Jaslene.

He was right. They shared the same mind . . . at least in the clothes department. "What's behind your back?"

Marcus showed her the blue vase with sword lilies. "For you."

Jaslene held back a gasp. "Oh my. Those look exactly like the lilies Hope had given me. Same exact colors and everything. Where'd you find them?"

"At a small garden on the way to my grandparents'

house, and the lady there said I could have some. I immediately thought of you, especially after the conversation we had." Marcus handed her the vase.

Jaslene studied the petals and leaves of the lilies, and a sense of serenity gathered within. They appeared alive, as if they were willing to listen to anything that she had to share with it. "This is so precious."

"I'm glad you like them."

His voice was gentle and kind. Why did she assume that being apart from him was better than being together?

"You ready for the picture?" Sasha asked, holding up her phone.

"Yes." Jaslene stood close to Marcus, holding the blue vase of lilies.

"One. Two. Three." Sasha snapped the photo. "Awesome. I'll text this to you right now."

Jaslene set the vase of flowers on the coffee table, and the sunlight from the window shone on them.

"Oh, Marcus. I got your email about doing research for the unfinished exhibit. The volunteers and I will definitely get started on looking for information on Janey, Solomon, and Denmark," Sasha said.

"Cool." Marcus sat at the couch.

"I registered for an interior design class at the community college," Jaslene said.

"You did?" A look of surprise colored Marcus's expression.

Jaslene nodded. "I start in the summer."

"Good for you. I was hoping that you would."

The three of them left Jaslene's condo. After saying a quick goodbye to Sasha, Jaslene and Marcus got into the pickup truck. They rode to New Life in silence. Marcus took the back roads to the church.

"That's where the garden is located," Marcus said, pointing to his right. "Church service starts soon, and I don't want us to be late. But would you like to return sometime later and see it up close?"

"Definitely." Jaslene pictured the sword lilies in her mind. What should she do with them? Should she talk to them, as she did with the other sword lilies? Hmm. Not sure if she was ready to do so, but they were lovely to have in her home.

Her thoughts went to Imani. Jaslene couldn't believe that her niece was sending in her applications soon. If Jaslene were honest with herself, she still felt conflicted about the possibility of Imani leaving South Carolina.

"You okay?" he asked.

She kept looking out of the window. Should she say anything? "Yes and no," she finally said. "Imani is putting her applications together for conservatory. She was up late recording an audition piece."

His eyes widened while still remaining on the road. "Oh, really? Hardworking, lady."

"Yes . . . she is. I'm so very proud of her, you know. But I'm also a little sad too."

"You're still worried about her leaving?" he asked.

She cleared her throat. "Seeing her record an audition piece . . . I don't know. It rattled me, and I don't know what to do. I guess I'm just being overprotective." She sat up straighter in the passenger seat.

"You and Imani have been through a lot together. Your feelings are understandable."

"I'm helping her apply to these schools, and now that she's actually applying, I don't know. I'm facing that fact. I feel so strange now."

"It's a natural feeling to not want to let go of the people we love."

"True." She bit her bottom lip. "Do you think that this is a phase that I'll get over?"

"Perhaps."

"This has been the hardest thing for me to process, to be honest. I told Imani that living on her own was going to be way different than living with me or her mom. There's a huge wide world out there, and this world is fun and joyful and so many good things can happen, but also . . . it can be cruel. She'd need to protect herself from the cruel. I don't want her to get hurt. That's all. When Imani was born, I promised Hope that I'd look out for her."

He paused. "She's grown. I'm pretty sure that she can manage for herself."

"I'm still her guardian. That's my one responsibility that I can't mess up."

"And you haven't. In fact, I think you're doing a wonderful job. But she'll have to learn some things on her own. You'll have to let go."

Why'd he have to sound so sensible? "Yes, I know. But . . . whose side are you on, Marcus?"

"There's no sides here. I just think it's important for you to know, that's all."

Maybe he was right. Or maybe not.

"You mad at me now?" he asked.

She shook her head. "Bothered. But not mad."

"It'll be okay. Just trust," Marcus said. "Here we are." He parked his pickup truck near the white steepled church and turned off the ignition. "Good thing we're here early. We'll get a good seat."

"True," Jaslene said.

Marcus drummed his fingers on the steering wheel. "You ready for this?"

Jaslene placed her purse in her lap. "Yes and no."

"I feel the same way. But we'll be fine. We have each other." He stepped out of the truck, went around to the passenger side, and extended his hand to help her get down.

Jaslene savored holding his hand. She almost didn't want to let go, but she did. "I can't believe I'm back at the place where I was ready to say 'I do.'"

"I know, right? It's surreal in a way."

They walked to the church's entrance and stood at the bottom steps, staring at the old building. She could do this. Just put one foot in front of the other.

Marcus smiled at her. "Ready to go inside?"

Imani's encouraging words came to mind. "As ready as I'll ever be."

MARCUS'S AND JASLENE'S steps were in sync as they headed up the brick stairs. Moments later, they were inside of the sanctuary. The familiarity of the place brought a feeling of comfort, a feeling of home. Bright red carpet covered every inch of the floor. Cushioned pews lined the left and right sides of the sanctuary.

A gold chandelier hung from the ceiling, shining its golden light. Marcus used to sit in that front pew, right near the organ. As a child and teen, he had listened to many a sermon and sung many a hymn, Sunday after Sunday, year after year. When he was young, he thought church was boring and repetitive, but looking back, coming here provided a steady rhythm to his life, a rhythm that anchored him for the coming storms.

"Where'd you want to sit?" he asked.

"Wherever you like. I don't have a preference."

He slid into the front pew.

Jaslene set down her purse, and a swath of her dark hair swished forward. The light from the stained-glass windows sent streams of color over her cream outfit. Marcus scooted close to her. The scent of her rose perfume enveloped him. Marcus used to love holding her close and inhaling the scent of her. If they had said their vows at New Life and if Marcus and his grandfather had been on good terms, this would've been their regular Sunday routine: attending church; enjoying a brunch of French toast, orange juice, and bacon; and then spending the afternoon reading or napping or kissing . . .

He glanced away, not wanting to desire a life that may never be. Marcus shifted his focus to the altar, the place where they were supposed to exchange vows. His heart pierced at the sight. Being here was harder than he envisioned.

A dark object caught in his periphery, and he glanced to the right. The mourners' bench. "Look." He tapped on Jaslene's shoulder.

"Whoa. Pastor Clark brought the bench from the shed."

Marcus stood and headed toward the artifact, spotting the place where Janey's and Solomon's names were carved. The etchings shone with clarity now that the bench was polished. "I wonder why my grandfather changed his mind about keeping this in the shed."

"Your last visit must've had a strong influence on him," Jaslene said.

"I can't believe he brought this out for view."

"Why can't you believe it? You're still his grandson. He listens to you, regardless of your disagreements." Jaslene smiled.

Seeing the bench again brought a flurry of memories to the surface, and they were all about the sapphire ring which Solomon had stolen. If only Marcus knew the reason why Solomon stole it, then Marcus could piece together Janey and Solomon's story.

Moments later, the door near the exit sign opened and Grandpa Clark entered. "Marcus. Jaslene! So great to see the two of you here." He gave each of them a huge hug.

Grandpa Clark rarely gave hugs. Jaslene was right. Perhaps he and his grandfather were making good progress in their relationship after all.

"We decided to take you up on your invitation," Marcus said.

"And I'm glad you did." Grandpa Clark appeared to study them. "You two are a good team."

Yesterday's talk came to mind. "I agree."

"Is that my handsome grandson and his girlfriend?"

His grandmother's familiar voice brought a smile to Marcus's lips. Grandma Clark headed up the aisle, dressed in all white: a huge white hat, a white knee-length dress, and white shoes. Shiny gold sequins bordered the hem and the cuffs of her outfit.

"My goodness. This is a miracle. So glad you're here." She kissed Marcus on the cheek and gave Jaslene a hug.

"I see the mourners' bench over there." Marcus pointed to the artifact. "What made you bring it out?"

"After talking with you yesterday, I figured it shouldn't be in hiding anymore. I also decided to keep the shed and its contents."

"That's so good to hear," Jaslene said.

"I'm glad you approve, Ms. Simmons." The lines around Grandpa Clark's eyes crinkled, and his brown eyes shone. "I have to get ready. We're starting in a few minutes. See you in a bit."

"I'm going to sit on the opposite pew because I might need to say the announcements if Sheila doesn't show up." Grandma Clark winked at them. "You two lovebirds make yourselves at home."

"We will," Marcus said.

If his grandfather was keeping the items, would he be willing to lend them to the museum? Marcus would have to wait and see.

More congregants entered the sanctuary and seated themselves in the pews. The choir gathered in the loft, wearing their deep blue robes that were accented with black velvet down the center. Grandpa Clark returned, sitting at the minister's chair behind the podium. The service began with the hymn, "Lord, You Woke Me Up This Morning," and the congregation joined in.

Chill bumps pricked his forearms at the resonant melody. Back in the old days, whenever the choir sung, his grandmother used to nudge him and Trey to clap and sing along. The two brothers didn't join in all of that whooping and shouting and running around the church. Best to leave that to the older folks.

Today, he clapped to the tune. Each note was a balm that soothed the parts of him that he had hidden, the parts of him that he thought were beyond fixing.

After the music and the announcements, Grandpa Clark took his place at the podium. "I'm so happy to welcome two special people today. My grandson, Marcus, and . . . Jaslene. They're not strangers to us. Let's give them a warm welcome home."

A chorus of welcomes and hellos surrounded them. "Lovely to see two young people here."

A lady with smooth, deep brown skin and silver hair hugged the two of them.

He had forgotten how friendly everyone was at New

Life. Being a recluse had cut him off from the warmth of a stranger's smile or the hello of a congregant. Who knew harmonious music and hugs could do such a thing?

When the welcomes and hellos were finished, Grandpa Clark began his sermon. Marcus shifted closer to Jaslene and the back of his hand touched hers. A smile formed on Jaslene's lips. "Can I hold your hand?" he said to her in a whisper.

She nodded yes, so he did. Her hand felt like the rose petals at the garden, soft to the touch.

"We have to give ourselves mercy as we traverse this thing called life. The older I get, the more I need mercy and love. Love never fails," Grandpa Clark said from the pulpit.

Marcus smiled at the conviction in his grandfather's voice. Love never failed, but it was certainly messier than Marcus had wanted it to be. He studied Jaslene for a moment. The love they shared was a flame that had been snuffed out by circumstance, but the flame still smoldered. It simply needed some rekindling. He glanced over at the mourners' bench and spotted the place where Janey's and Solomon's names were carved.

When Marcus and Jaslene broke up, she returned the ring to Marcus, and he, in turn, gave it to his grandmother to return to her husband. What was Grandpa Clark's reaction when his wife gave him the ring? Did he think that Marcus was rejecting their shared history? Was that the reason why Grandpa Clark was so reluctant to lend the bench to the museum in the first place?

Or was Grandpa Clark disappointed for Jaslene and Marcus? Grandpa Clark must've been sad for them on some level.

And where was the ring today? Was it hidden in the shed too? Marcus wanted to find out.

The sermon continued for a long time. Grandpa Clark's call-and-response style of preaching always moved the congregation, and today wasn't any different.

"Preach on, preacher!"

"Speak, pastor!"

"Well!"

An elderly woman dressed in a pale pink dress and a matching pink hat took up the tambourine and shook it after each natural pause in Grandpa's sermon. The sound resonated in his soul. The organist joined in by playing a series of notes, each one accenting a word or a phrase that Grandpa Clark said.

More shouts and claps filled the old sanctuary. One middle-aged woman took a run around the church, tears streaming down her face. So many people came here every week with quiet burdens.

A man who looked to be in his eighties or nineties made his way up the aisle. He wore a brown suit that hung loose on his slim frame. A stray thread hung from the hem of his suit jacket. The man's face was weathered but resolute. He headed toward the mourners' bench, looked at it for a long second, and then knelt at one side of the bench, his hands clasped in prayer. His lips moved in a quiet mur-

mur. The woman in pink knelt at the bench and joined him in prayer.

Marcus's heart stopped for a millisecond. The elders still knew of the significance of the bench. They not only knew it, but they lived it.

The church erupted in a chorus of clapping and praising. The voices of the congregants joined in with Grandpa Clark's preaching. Jaslene was also standing, listening intently to Grandpa Clark's words. It seemed like everyone was experiencing a breakthrough this morning. After the sermon, Grandpa Clark invited more folks to the bench, and people approached it. All joined in a symphony of petition to an unseen force. The sight moved Marcus.

When the service was finished, people started socializing with each other while others lingered at the bench or in the pews.

"That was something," Jaslene said to Marcus.

"It was."

After Grandpa Clark finished greeting people, he waved at them. "I hope you were edified by today's service."

"Oh, yes. This was powerful," Marcus said.

"I thoroughly enjoyed it," Jaslene added.

"You're welcome to return any time," Grandpa Clark said.

"We might do that," Marcus said, glancing over at the bench again. Should he ask Grandpa Clark where he kept the sapphire ring?

Nah. Jaslene might assume that Marcus wanted to get

more serious about their relationship. He wanted to figure out the answers to his other question though. Why did Solomon steal the ring? "You know, I got to thinking. Would it be okay if I poked around and did more research on Janey and Solomon? It wouldn't be for the museum exhibit, since that's not happening right now, but I'd like to do so for you."

"Me?" Grandpa Clark raised an eyebrow.

Marcus nodded. "I can't guarantee that I'll find anything, of course, and my work on the fundraiser will take precedence. But I can look in my downtime. What do you think?"

Silence. Marcus soon regretted even asking. He should've never asked. He pushed too much.

"That'll be fine," Grandpa Clark said, directing his attention to Jaslene. "You two should work on that together, especially since you were talking about how much that exhibit meant to your sister."

Jaslene's eyes widened for a moment. "I could do that. I'm interested in learning more about them anyway."

"Good. That's very good." Grandpa Clark smiled.

Chapter Eleven

On Monday evening, Jaslene had grown nervous about seeing Imani. Earlier that morning, Imani had mentioned that she was interviewing with some admissions representatives from conservatories who were visiting musicians in the state. Jaslene felt a mixture of excitement and anxiety about the opportunities being presented to Imani, but now the anxiety outweighed the excitement.

She glanced at the vase of sword lilies on her coffee table, but she couldn't muster the energy to talk to them.

Even though Jaslene wanted by-the-minute texts on how Imani was doing, Jaslene kept herself busy by vacuuming her carpet a bazillion times and dusting every crevice of her condo. Stress cleaning kept her mind occupied. A teeny, tiny part of her acknowledged that it was important for Imani to do this on her own.

Just as she was about to clean the baseboards, the doorknob jiggled. Her heart stuttered. She headed to the front entrance, then halted.

"No need to look super anxious," Jaslene said to herself.

Jaslene did an about-face, grabbed the microfiber towel, and resumed wiping off dust bunnies in the living room.

The front door creaked open, and the sound of approaching footsteps grew louder. Imani's figure loomed in Jaslene's periphery.

"Hey there, niece," she said, feigning interest in a newly cleaned baseboard. "How were the in-person interviews?"

"Cool." Imani sat on the plush brown couch and pushed it into a reclining position.

"Just cool? That's it?" She stood and tossed the towel in her bucket of cleaning supplies.

Imani nodded. "It was more than cool. It was amazing, but I figured you wouldn't want to know."

Ouch. How could Jaslene respond to that? She couldn't. "I do want to know, Imani. I admit that I'm just being an overprotective person about this phase of your life. I care too much, basically."

Imani bit her bottom lip. "I know that you care."

The sound of the ceiling fan punctuated their silence. Jaslene grabbed a chair from the dining table and scooted it next to her. "Tell me the exciting parts."

Imani's expression softened, and a warm light emanated from her eyes. "There are so many incredible programs at The New School's Mannes School of Music. They even have exchange programs, but they're not like your typical exchange programs. With this, you get to travel and play in concert halls around the globe."

"Oh, really?" She kept her voice even.

"Yes, really! I've always wanted to travel the world and play for audiences everywhere."

"That sounds exciting."

"It is. The admissions officer gave me her business card. And she said that I could email her if I have any other questions." Her eyes beamed. "I think that she knows that I'm looking into Juilliard, and so she's looking at me as a valuable addition to the student body. At least that's what I'm assuming." Imani's voice teetered toward a squeal.

"That's fantastic, love. I'm happy for you."

Her niece's eyes squinted for a moment, as if to assess whether Jaslene was, in fact, happy for her. Jaslene held mixed feelings. It was wonderful that Imani had all these opportunities available for her. She deserved every single one of them.

Imani grabbed her canvas backpack and unzipped it. "Meeting the admissions reps in person was perfect timing. Because look." She reached inside her bag and pulled out a stack of mail. "An envelope came in from the Virginia Symphony. It's from the music director of the South Carolina Philharmonic."

Jaslene's breath caught. Imani had been wanting to perform with them. She auditioned with them last month. "Oh my! Did you open it yet?"

"Nope. I wanted you to be with me when I opened it."

"You're too sweet."

Imani carefully unsealed the envelope, hands shaking, and she read, "'Dear Imani, We are pleased to inform you that we'd like you to perform in one show in the spring.'"

"They want you to perform with them!" Jaslene said, thrilled.

"Yes! This is going to look so good on my applications to conservatory."

"You've been working hard." She hugged Imani. "I'm so proud of you. You've accomplished so much. And you persevered, despite the setbacks. You deserve this."

"Thank you." Jaslene paused, as if weighing whether she should say more. "You know what?"

"What?"

"After talking with the admissions reps, I was thinking that if I get into a New York conservatory, then I'd get an apartment out in the city, instead of living on the school grounds."

Jaslene's neck tensed. "You sure about that?"

"Of course. What's the problem?"

How should Jaslene word this? "I mean you'll be so busy with classes. On campus classes. Practices. Performances. If you're traveling back and forth from one location to another, that would wear you out."

"I'll adjust," Imani said, her voice tight. "I just want to try living on my own."

"But you'll already be living on your own when you leave me."

There was a silence that stretched between them.

"This is a new phase of life for me, and I want to explore every aspect of it."

"But you will, and you won't have to pay New York City rent to do so."

"I plan to get roommates and split the rent," Imani said.

Oh brother. She had a solution to everything. "You'll want to stay near campus as much as possible. Don't put yourself out there. New York City is a huge adjustment. Take things in baby steps."

"I wish you would trust me on this, Auntie."

Jaslene didn't answer right away. She remembered Marcus's advice to her the other day. How could she respond in a way that didn't push Imani away? "We're not even at that point yet. Let's not talk about this anymore."

"I want to talk about it though," Imani said. "It seems like you're not on board with the idea. But I need to take this step."

Jaslene was quiet. There was only one other way to handle this situation. "If you insist on living in an apartment out in New York, then I'll move up there with you."

Imani's long lashes fluttered. "What?"

"I'll move up there with you. There's no way that I'm going to stand by and risk your safety."

"Auntie, you can't move to New York with me. You have an entire life here in South Carolina. You're getting close to Marcus again. You can't do that."

"Why not? It makes perfect sense. I won't be on campus. I'll find a studio apartment nearby and I can resume my business from there." The more she spoke, the more everything seemed to make more and more sense. "If anything happens to you, then I'll be there to . . . to protect you. Yes, that's what I'll do. I promised your mother that I would."

Imani set the mail from the Philharmonic on her lap. "If I got accepted into a New York conservatory, I wouldn't want you to go to New York with me."

Those words kicked Jaslene in the gut. "Excuse me?"

"I wouldn't want you to come to New York with me. I'd go there alone. If any difficulties arise, I'll figure it out on my own."

Imani's expression was set. There was no changing her mind. Jaslene's pulse kicked up a notch. "Figuring things out on your own is hard. I'm here for you so that you don't have to learn some lessons the hard way."

Imani shook her head. "I need you to trust me, Auntie."

"If I let you go there and something happens to you, then it will be my fault. I won't be able to forgive myself for that."

Imani paused. "I'm grown now. You've done so much for me, and I'll be forever grateful. But this is my time to move on to the next stage . . . and it's your time to let go."

The conversation that Jaslene had with Marcus yesterday resurrected itself. *She'll have to learn some things on her own. You'll have to let go.* The two of them were speaking the same language apparently. Let go. Could she let go? Was that even possible? The prospect scared her to the core.

Perhaps that was what living fully was all about: dealing with losses and disappointments and learning to live fully, despite them.

The notion unsettled Jaslene, but she leaned into the feeling. Her eyes blurred and she blinked rapidly. "Letting go is hard," she said softly.

"I know."

The more she leaned into the idea, the more she understood that this was about more than her niece. It was about her. Could Jaslene release the grief from losing Hope? Could she fill the emptiness with something different, with something new? If she did, she would leap into unknown territory, and that was terrifying. If she didn't, then she would stay in the endless loop of silent sorrow.

We have to give ourselves mercy as we traverse this thing called life. The older I get, the more I need mercy.

Pastor Clark's words pulsed in her heart. And they sounded right. She would take that leap. "I'll try to let go," Jaslene said. "Do what you need to do . . . but if you ever need me—if you ever need anything—know that you have me always."

Imani hugged her. "I know, and I thank you so very much."

Jaslene hugged her niece back, and she pressed her cheek to Imani's hair. The scent of shea butter sent sensations of comfort and safety and home. The longer she held Imani, the more those worrisome feelings drifted away. She would learn to let go. Jaslene didn't know how this story would end, but she was growing more certain that if she released her grip on this grief, it would open a multitude of pathways into a brighter future.

JASLENE AND MARCUS agreed to meet up at the university library on Thursday to see if there was anything else they could find about Janey and Solomon. Marcus had reserved a room at the library in advance and was supposed to arrive close to noon.

She headed inside the library, and the warm space was a welcome reprieve from the cold outside. The library had a cute holiday theme going on. A wreath hung at the entrance, and a lit and decorated Christmas tree stood proud near the checkout desk. An animated snowman and reindeer rotated their heads, providing laughter to the children and parents gathered around it.

Jaslene checked the Notes app on her phone. They would be working in a study room at the library. Room 209.

After checking around, she found the room. Marcus was setting up the space for them. He looked adorable with his black-rimmed glasses. This time he wore an olive V-neck sweater vest with a white collared shirt and jeans. She peeked at his feet to check out his shoes: black loafers. A nice touch. Jaslene tapped on the glass door and waved.

Marcus did a double take and answered the door. "Hey there."

"Hey, yourself." Upon stepping inside, a backpack overflowing with books came into view. It was on a chair against the wall. "Looks like you brought your entire home library with you."

"Yep. I did."

Jaslene scrunched her nose. "Are we going through all of these books today?"

"Not at all." Marcus laughed. "I brought them in case."

"In case of what? A fire at your house or something?" Jaslene picked one up and flipped through the pages.

"Oh, I see you've got jokes today."

"Something like that." Jaslene sat next to him. "What'd you want me to do?"

"We need to try to fill in the pieces. We know that Janey and Solomon were in love with each other and that they wanted to get married."

"Or at least Janey wanted to get married. Solomon could've changed his mind."

Marcus's gaze seemed to probe hers when she mentioned the last part. "True. For some reason, their plans didn't happen. We have yet to know why. I know you think that Solomon fell out of love with her, but I disagree. Anything could've happened." He opened a red folder stuffed with papers.

"I can see your point," Jaslene said.

"You can?"

"Of course. You look surprised," she said.

"Completely surprised. I mean . . ." He rubbed the back of his neck. "Before you were convinced he ditched her."

"I know. But people also get caught up in situations that are outside of their control. It has ripple effects in other areas." She glanced at the pages in his red folder. "When I saw the bench again at church last Sunday, it got me thinking. There's more to their relationship than my own assumptions."

"And what were your assumptions?"

Marcus asked the question casually, but underneath she sensed something more. "I assumed Solomon was unreliable."

"What do you think of him now?"

A swirl of questions arose in her mind. "I don't have the answer yet, but I know that I can't make assumptions. That's all."

"Wise." Marcus didn't take his gaze away from her and her eyes didn't waver either. The more time she spent with Marcus, the more she wanted to spend even more moments with him. Although they had dated all through college, they only tapped the surface of who they could be together.

Marcus refocused on the paper in front of him. "From the date of Janey's letter, I know that Janey and Solomon were alive in 1822, which is the same year that Denmark Vesey was accused of planning a revolt, but somehow there was a disconnect between Janey and Solomon. Things didn't go for them as planned."

"Just like there was a disconnect with us," she said without thinking.

"Excuse me?"

"I, uh, I was just thinking out loud." Jaslene cleared her throat, embarrassed.

"I heard you. What's up?"

Oh gosh. She didn't want to delve into this now. "You really want to know?"

"I really, really, want to know."

"We had our separate views on how we should go into a marriage together. I didn't want to go into it grieving, and you thought that we could."

"Yes, and I still think that we could bear those griefs together."

Could bear? Was he having second thoughts about them? "What are you saying?"

"I'm not saying we should get married or anything, but I want a friendship. Good friends talk about these things openly. Good friends help each other when they're down. I want to be that friend to you, and I'd like you to be that friend for me."

Jaslene considered his offer. "How'd we miss this about each other?"

"Miss what?"

"This . . . friendship. These discussions. Your learning about me and sword lilies, and my learning about you and your feelings about Trey and your grandfather. We should've known these things about each other the first time around."

"As for Trey, I didn't feel comfortable talking about him or about what happened with my grandfather. That's my bad. Not yours."

"I know," she said. "I just wish we would've known. Perhaps it would've kept us together when Hope died."

Silence. What would they have done differently? Did that even matter now? Marcus cleared his throat. "I'd like to ask you something. I'd also like an honest answer."

"Yes?"

"If I asked you to marry me today, what would you say?"

The question caught her off guard. "You intending to propose?"

"No. Just wanted to get a gauge on where I stand with you, that's all."

So now he was trying a different, bolder approach. Well, bold as far as her heart was concerned, because if she said yes, then she would be admitting that her feelings had changed toward him. If she said no, then she would probably end up hurting his feelings. "I don't feel as put off by being around you as I once did."

Marcus chuckled. "That's a start."

"I definitely like you, Marcus. But I couldn't say yes to you if you proposed to me today."

He bit his bottom lip. She could sense the unease forming within him even as she spoke. "But friends? I think we can definitely be friends to each other. I'd love that."

Marcus didn't respond to her straightaway. "What do you think?"

"Friends works. It is the best thing, if you ask me." Marcus took the papers from his folder and set them before her. One of them was a picture of the engagement ring he had given her. Janey's ring.

"Where'd you get that photo?" she asked.

"I took it a while ago. When Grandpa Clark had told me how the ring came into his family. I thought I'd keep a photo for posterity."

"Does he have it now?" Jaslene asked.

"To the best of my knowledge, yes. I gave it to my grandmother, and she should've given it to him."

An awkward silence returned, given that they both knew why the ring was back in his grandfather's possession. She studied the photo of the pear-shaped sapphire ring.

He tapped his chin. "Pieces like this are pretty rare.

And so only a few, wealthier families would own something like this. I was hoping to see if there are any personal property inventories in the public records for Charleston. I want to see if we can find the original owner of this ring. If we do, then perhaps it can lead us to get more information on Janey or Solomon."

"That's smart."

"When you get into this line of work, you end up trying to think of all kinds of creative ways to get the information that you need." Marcus shrugged. "Here's a record of a local jeweler who has been in business in downtown Charleston since the 1820s. I called them and told them about the work I was doing, and they were enthused to help, especially after I told them about the potential exhibit. I have an appointment to meet with them next Tuesday at two o'clock. They're on Chalmers Street."

She studied the photo up close. When Marcus had proposed to Jaslene with that ring, she had felt honored that he would give her something that held such significance. She wanted to know more about Janey when they were engaged, but he had only known a little.

"I also went to the university library and made copies of their old personal property records from the coastal South Carolina region. That's where Solomon or Janey would've most likely lived. I'm hoping to find their names listed in the property records. I thought we could spend some time going through them."

Her heart pricked. He gestured to the papers. The names of Janey and Solomon in *property* records. "Oh."

"If you're not up for reading the documents, then I'll do it. There's a lot of names to go through. It might take me forever, but—"

"I can look through the names. It's fine with me."

They spent the next few moments in silence, reading all of the information on the pages. Marcus toggled between looking at that information and reading documents on his laptop.

Jupiter. Sallie. Elias. John. Names of enslaved folks who lived long before her. People who had dreams and hopes that extended beyond the life they were given. "Seeing these names makes it more real."

"I know," Marcus said, his tone turned grave. "The first time I pored through a document like this was when I was a grad student. Felt so many kinds of feelings. I had to put the pages down. Couldn't do anything else for days afterward."

She glanced up from the pages and leaned back in her chair. "What made you continue?"

"I care for the people listed in the records. Whenever I look at their names, I remember that these are real people." He paused as if deep in thought. "You may not have noticed it, but I have a framed copy of a list like this in my office."

She twisted her mouth. "I don't recall seeing it."

"It's small. But it's there." He sighed. "I look at it every day as a reminder as to why I'm doing this work."

"I'm glad that you've found your purpose."

"I have."

They stared at each other for a long moment. Her purpose should've been with Marcus. The longer they spent time together, the more the notion grew. Uncomfortable, she glanced away and scanned through the documents. "Look at this. This property record lists someone by the name of Solomon."

"Really?" He leaned closer to her, and she could feel his soft breathing on the crook of her neck. "The property record of Odysseus Finch III. That must be the name of Solomon's enslaver." Marcus jotted down a note.

"What should we do now?"

"We need to check out more newspapers from this time period and see if there's anything else we can find about Odysseus. Otherwise, we'll just be at another dead end. I'll send a note to the volunteers with some links to online newspaper records." He seemed deep in thought, and then he refocused on her. "Would you want to make a trip with me next week to the jeweler on Chalmers Street?"

He lifted his chin and gave her another look that said, *I want you to be there with me.*

Despite her hesitations, she wanted to be there with him too. "I'd love to. There's a craft store in that area. I wanted to browse there to get ideas for the fundraiser. Do you think we can stop by the craft store after meeting with the jeweler?"

"Of course."

Chapter Twelve

Marcus arrived at Orion Jewelry Store at two o'clock. He peeked inside the shop, but he didn't spot Jaslene. Marcus waited outside of the store so that they could walk inside, together. December's chilly air made his cheeks cool. Marcus shoved his hands in the pockets of his bomber jacket.

It was like they were ring shopping . . . That was too hopeful of a thought, but for a few brief moments, he relished in the idea.

He wanted this meeting with the jeweler to provide some connections, connections that he could share with Grandpa Clark. They already made great strides in their relationship, so much so that his grandfather put the bench in the church. If he could fill in some gaps in Grandpa's family history, perhaps that would cement their relationship. Family history meant a lot.

Seconds later, Jaslene's Corolla eased into an empty parking spot in front of the jewelry store, and his heart skipped. It reminded him of the anticipation he'd felt when they went on their date at a local barbecue restaurant. Marcus spent extra time trying to figure out what to eat on the menu, just to prolong their time together. That was when Marcus had known that Jaslene was someone special.

He headed in her direction, and she exited her car. As she did, a gentle breeze rustled through the curls in her hair, and some of them brushed against the soft curve of her neck. He used to love kissing her collarbone, her neck, and her lips . . .

Whew. Yes, Marcus had said that he wasn't planning on proposing to her, but he had to admit that the idea of doing so had crossed his mind a couple of times lately. And the notion wasn't just hypothetical, even though he had told Jaslene that it was in theory only.

"Afternoon."

"Afternoon." She closed her car door and pressed the autolock button on her key fob. "Ready to investigate?"

"I am," he said. "We'll see what we find today."

"I'm confident we'll find something good." She smiled and headed toward the entrance. Marcus followed. Jaslene wore a navy pantsuit that hugged her curvy, petite shape. He couldn't help but let his gaze linger for a moment.

As Marcus opened the door for her, a gentle chime sounded, indicating their arrival. An elderly man with salt-and-pepper hair was standing at the opposite end of a glass jewelry case. From Marcus's vantage point, it looked as if he was sizing rings.

"Are you my two o'clock appointment?" the man said, not looking up from inspecting rings.

"Yes. I'm Marcus Clark, and this is my . . . friend. Jaslene Simmons."

"Pleased to meet you both. I'm Theodore." He shook their hands. "You mentioned on the phone that you have a photo of the ring."

"I do." Marcus produced the photo for him. "I figured that I'd ask you about the piece because you're the only jeweler that was in business during that time."

"Ah yes. We had humble beginnings." Theodore looked at the photo. "Very lovely design. Unique too. Where's the ring now?"

"My grandfather owns it."

"Too bad you didn't bring it along," Theodore said.

"Bringing it here would be complicated. He's protective of the piece."

"I can see why. This ring was definitely created by one of our jewelers. I can tell because it has our signature insignia on the band. Nice that you were able to capture such detail in this photo."

"Thanks," Marcus said. "The insignia drew my attention when I first saw the ring."

"We kept an inventory of every ring that was ever designed and sold from our shop."

"Every single ring?" Jaslene said.

"Yes," he said. "I'm going to check and see if this ring is in our records. It should be. Give me a few moments."

The man went to the back of the store, and Jaslene smiled at Marcus. "I'm keeping my fingers crossed that he'll turn up with something good."

"Me too."

Jaslene started browsing the other jewelry in the store. "They have the most unique pieces here. If I had more discretionary funds, I'd probably splurge on one of their pieces."

He smiled at Jaslene. If they were dating, he'd probably buy her a necklace or a bracelet from here. He wanted to give Jaslene whatever kind of jewelry she desired. "See anything that you like?"

"I like it all." She scanned the case. "Oh! Look at that." She pointed to a gold chain that featured a sapphire pendant. "That pendant is the same shape as Janey's ring."

Marcus looked at it closely. "You're right."

"It makes sense that it would be the same style, given that the ring came from this store."

"True." A wanting filled Marcus. If Jaslene ever wore that engagement ring again, he would want to give her this necklace to match it.

"I found a record." Theodore emerged from the back room. "I had to search way back, but we have something. Kimberly, my assistant, spent about two years taking paper records of acquisitions and sales and making electronic copies of them. Grateful for her, because I'm not a tech person. It made the search easy." He smiled. "Anyway, this is what I have. Looks like the ring was sold on June 21, 1821." He squinted at the paper and looked at it up close. "There's an annotation that the ring went missing a year later. The owner must've made the report in case someone tried to sell it back to us."

1821. That was a year before Denmark Vesey was accused and convicted. "Interesting. And what was the name of the original owner?"

"Odysseus Finch."

Marcus and Jaslene looked at each other. That was the same Odysseus who enslaved Solomon. "Could I have a copy of that record?"

"Sure thing. Give me a second and I'll get that to you."

"Wow," Jaslene said.

"Wow is my thought exactly. Maybe Odysseus caught wind that Solomon had taken the ring and he was punished."

"Might be."

"Here you go, Mr. Clark." Theodore handed him a copy of the record of sale. "If you ever have any questions, feel free to reach out and ask."

"I do have one question," Marcus said, pausing. "Do you know if the Finch family is still in Charleston?"

"I have no idea. We just keep the sales records."

"Figured I'd ask. Thank you again, sir."

Jaslene and Marcus left the jewelry store. Marcus couldn't get the discovery out of his mind.

"That connection is uncanny. Why'd you ask the jeweler if the Finch family was still in Charleston?"

Marcus leaned against the parking meter. "I figured if we could locate them, then perhaps I could ask them what they knew about their ancestors. It might help us figure out why Janey and Solomon never got together."

Her expression stilled. "If I were you, I'd stay far away

from them. I wouldn't want to have anything to do with the Finches."

"I get that, but my family and theirs were linked together in a sad relationship. Might be good to unpack that."

Jaslene was silent. Had he said something wrong?

"I disagree," she said. "Better to leave them alone, even if they had all the answers you were searching for."

"Why?"

"Talking to them would be too much to deal with. At least it would be for me. Perhaps that's why Hope was working on our family tree and I wasn't. Too complicated."

Marcus was silent. She was right, but at the same time, he didn't want to avoid talking to them, if he could locate them. "I'm a historian. I gather information from all sources."

Jaslene shrugged. "Then you're a rarity. Most historians only tell one side of the story, the side that benefits them."

"Very true. I don't want to jeopardize the integrity of the museum's work though."

"You wouldn't be. Any answers you need can be found by other means."

"I want to know why Solomon took the ring. If I could ask the Finches, then they might have the answer."

"Isn't it obvious why Solomon stole the ring?" Jaslene said, facing him. "He took it for love."

Love. The word reverberated within him. "We have no

idea whether the ring is linked to Janey and Solomon's relationship personally. Solomon could've taken it for another reason."

"We can ask your grandfather," Jaslene said, her voice matter-of-fact.

"Last time I asked, he didn't know the answer. I'd like to know. Our museum is known for its meticulous research, and I want us to maintain that reputation. Or else we won't have any credibility with the community."

"I want to ask you something," Jaslene said.

"What is it?"

She let out a slow exhale. "At one point, you used that engagement ring to propose to me. Doesn't it hold some personal value to you, apart from your work?"

Was this a trick question? "It . . . does. But I'm not using the ring to propose to you anymore."

Jaslene twisted her mouth, apparently disappointed.

"You told me that if I proposed to you, that you'd say no. So why does it even matter?"

"It doesn't matter. I was just . . . just wondering."

Was she having second thoughts about their relation-ship? Did she want to be more than friends? "And what is your point?"

"When it comes to this ring, how can you separate the personal from the professional?"

Her question struck a nerve. He couldn't. When they were in the jewelry store, he speculated about giving her a pendant that matched the ring. That was far from a professional desire. Marcus wanted to tell her as much, but he couldn't. "I just do."

Disappointment colored her expression. Time to change the subject. "How about we see my grandfather again and let him know what we discovered?"

That look of disappointment didn't leave her face. "Sure."

"Do you want to go to the craft store now?"

Her eyes shifted and she checked the time on her phone. "Um, no. I don't. Some other things came up. Text me when you're ready to meet with your grandfather."

She walked to the driver side of her car and got inside. Minutes later, Jaslene drove away. A flurry of dry leaves kicked up behind her vehicle, leaving him behind.

JASLENE COULDN'T SLEEP. The conversation with Marcus played over and over in her mind all evening. Marcus held no personal attachments to the ring, and that bothered her—even though it shouldn't.

The fact that it upset her only proved that her feelings for him increased. What could she do about it? Nothing. At three o'clock in the morning, Jaslene got out of bed and headed to the kitchen. There was no way that she was getting any sleep tonight, so she might as well stay up. She poked her head in the refrigerator, grabbed the carton of orange juice, and poured a glass. That was when she caught sight of her notes for the centerpieces.

Marcus was instrumental in helping her delve into wedding decorating again. She wouldn't have been able to complete the centerpieces for the fundraiser and the samples for *Southern Bride* without his encouragement, but all of that talk about personal versus professional upset her.

Jaslene took a sip of juice and sat at the table, studying the notes she had made a little over a week ago. She spotted Marcus's block-lettered handwriting on one of the pages.

I like this one the best. But it's up to you, of course.

His comment was followed by a smiley face. Jaslene studied the sketch in question. It was a centerpiece made of sword lilies, and there was a placard attached to the base. The placard featured a line of poetry from a poet of the Harlem Renaissance. She had gotten the idea to make this particular centerpiece after she considered two things: the mourners' bench, where folks carved their names to be remembered, and the vase of sword lilies, flowers she used to speak to whenever she felt down.

Jaslene studied the vase of sword lilies that Marcus had given her. These flowers were more decorative than therapeutic. She had lost all desire to talk to plants a long time ago. Nonetheless, their presence brightened up her space, and looking at them gave her comfort, despite the questions she held within. She gazed at the vase of flowers. Should she try talking to them again?

"What should I do?" she blurted out.

The flowers didn't answer. She continued to focus on their leaves and petals. The glow from the lamp shone on the lilies. In that moment, the flower seemed to breathe. Inhale. Exhale. Inhale. Exhale. She breathed along with it, and a sense of peace washed over her.

All would be well.

The thought comforted her. Jaslene took another sip of orange juice. The fundraiser was in a little less than two weeks, and the centerpieces were ready to go. All she needed to do was find a few more lines of poetry for the placards. She pulled her phone from its charger and searched for other lines of poetry. Jaslene found the poem "Lament over Love" by Langston Hughes and read it. The poem was about a person who regretted ever falling in love because love hurt more than anything else. The lines were so true. Love hurt.

But something else was true too. Jaslene loved Marcus. She knew it the moment he had said that he could separate the personal from the professional. Her reaction to his comment was surprising, to say the least. The upset that surged within her was enough to make her rethink her feelings toward him. What should she do? She didn't know.

The vase of flowers stood proudly underneath the kitchen light, the petals perfectly curved, reminding her of the outstretched arms of a mother who was ready to embrace and comfort. "Thank you," she said to the lilies.

Jaslene had to find more lines of poetry for her finished centerpieces. The website with the Langston Hughes poem on her screen also showed links to other love poems by Black writers. She read each and every one. Should she allow herself to feel this love for Marcus again? Such a huge risk, but it was getting harder to suppress her feelings.

Her phone beeped, indicating a new text message. She read it:

> OMG. Jaslene. I have the best news. I know it's late, I just checked my email. Southern Bride wants to feature your centerpieces in the Spring issue.

> What?! That's great.

> I know, right? They're also going to be at my wedding taking photos. They're going to showcase my wedding in the same article where they discuss your centerpieces. They just need a short bio of you. I'll send you the email of the editor, and you can send all of that to her.

> Thank you so much, Sasha. This is a blessing.

> No problem, sis. I love you.

> Love you too. Now go to sleep. It's almost four in the morning.

Sasha signed off with a string of smiling emojis. Jaslene giggled and put her phone back in its charger.

Seconds later, the soft sound of footsteps coming from the living room interrupted her thoughts. The kitchen door swung open, and Imani entered. Her hands were filled with sheet music, and she appeared exuberant. That was a feat for someone at four o'clock in the morning. "Hey, love. What are you doing up?"

"I could ask the same of you." She set her papers on the table. "I was looking through sheet music."

"This late at night?"

"Yes. I'm nervous that I won't get accepted into any school."

"No need to worry. You'll get accepted into a conservatory. Remember that you're choosing them just as much as they're choosing you."

"You're right." She glanced over at the lines of poetry on Jaslene's notepad. "What's that for?"

Jaslene told her how the lines of poetry would be used in the centerpieces for the fundraiser.

"Nice! How are you and Marcus doing, by the way?" Imani asked.

The enthusiasm in Imani's eyes made Jaslene wince. Should she just give a general *all is good* answer, or should she say what's really on her mind? Imani would probably be able to read her mind anyway.

"We made a lot of headway with planning for the fundraiser. And we did some research on Marcus's family background." She then explained everything about the exhibit and the engagement ring.

"Super interesting."

"I know," she said flatly.

"What's the matter?" Imani asked.

"I asked him if he felt any personal connection to what used to be my engagement ring, and he basically said that it didn't matter. His response shouldn't have bothered me, but it did."

Imani nodded. "I see your point. Does he know how you feel?"

"No, he doesn't. I'm scared to even feel this for him, scared that it won't work out."

"I can see why. You know what? I'm scared too. I'm always trying to put on this confident face for you, for Mrs. Carlisle, for the people who are watching me perform." Imani scratched at the nick in the table's surface. "It's a lot of pressure. I feel like I have to deliver. That I have to not let Mama down. You're not alone in how you feel, Auntie."

The concern in Imani's voice moved Jaslene. "Oh, niece. I don't think that you'll ever let your mom down, no matter the result. I bet she's smiling down on you right now, proud."

"Could be." Imani appeared to focus on her sheet music. The overhead lights shone on her dark curls. If Jaslene were only thinking of herself, then she'd tell Imani to give in to her worries and stay in the state for school, but Jaslene didn't want to do that. Imani had so much beautiful potential, and it would be a shame for her to not pursue it.

Jaslene reached over and place her hand over Imani's. "If you ever feel like this is too overwhelming for you, then you can take a break. Get some time to refocus and regroup. But don't quit. Don't ever quit."

"Are you going to quit on Marcus again?"

Imani's words stung. Hearing her niece turn the table on her was tough. "You really know how to tell it straight."

"After the funeral, we all needed time to get our bearings. I know that I did. But if you ask me, I don't think that Mama would've wanted you to not get married. Especially since she was going to be the maid of honor. She was looking forward to seeing you say 'I do.'"

Jaslene pondered Imani's words. "You think I shouldn't quit on him?"

"Nope. I don't. If the love between the two of you is real, then it'll last."

Imani was right. The love that Jaslene had for her sister would never end, and as Jaslene spent more and more time with Marcus, she was realizing that the love she had for him wouldn't end either.

If Jaslene could turn back time, she didn't know if she'd do things differently with Marcus. From the day her sister died, everything had become one big haze. Perhaps her love for Marcus never dissipated, but it simply grew dim in light of all the events.

Should she have gone on and gotten married anyway? Jaslene wasn't sure. But in this time of knowing and being around Marcus, she realized that love was still there.

However, she had built all these roadblocks to love in the past two years, and she would need time to learn how to unblock every barrier that she had built. Would Marcus be willing to wait on her? To wait until she found the space to freely love him again, without fears or reservations?

"After the disagreement that we had yesterday, I'm not certain as to whether Marcus would even want to be open to the possibility of a relationship again. He doesn't seem as invested in his feelings as I am. He probably doesn't have any feelings at all toward me."

"He might not. That would suck."

"It would." Jaslene groaned.

Thunder rumbled outside, and the window reverberated.

"Regardless, you'll have to tell him your true feelings for him. He might feel that same way."

Jaslene pondered actually telling Marcus how she felt for him. Would he be willing to hear her out? She hoped so. "I'll do that."

Chapter Thirteen

*T*he following week, anticipation filled Marcus as he made his way to his grandparents' parsonage. He was looking forward to sharing his discoveries with Grandpa Clark and Jaslene. Most important, he was looking forward to seeing what Grandpa Clark would say about those discoveries.

When Marcus pulled his pickup truck in front of his grandparents' house, he turned off the ignition and glanced over at Jaslene, seated next to him. "Appreciate you accompanying me today to see my grandparents, especially after the talk we had."

"Happy to do so. The more we learned about Janey and Solomon, the more attached I got to their story. But you know that already," she said.

"I do." He studied her as she gazed outside the window. There was a calmness about her that he hadn't seen when they had spoken about the ring before.

"You did a great job on your grandparents' lawn," Jaslene said.

"Thanks. I put some work into it. But I only had to mow the lawn once since winter starts tomorrow. I came by a few more times to rake the leaves. I don't need to mow his lawn again until April or so," he said.

"Well, your efforts paid off." Jaslene paused. "Hey, before we go in there, I just want to say that I apologize for arguing about the ring the other day. I didn't mean to make assumptions about your work and all that. I know it's important to you."

"No need for an apology. I get where you're coming from. I've got a little more info I'll share with you and Grandpa together."

They climbed out of his pickup truck and headed to the front door. Grandma Clark's champagne-colored Buick LeSabre was in the driveway. After ringing the doorbell, Grandma Clark greeted them.

"Hey, it's my two favorite people." She gave them each a hug. "Come on in. You want some sweet tea?"

"Sounds great," Marcus said.

She went into the kitchen and called out. "Reginald, Marcus and Jaslene are here."

"Be down in a minute."

They sat on the chairs in the living room. Jaslene scooted closer to him, and he relished the nearness of her.

Moments later, Grandpa Clark arrived and sat in the armchair across from them. "Nice to see you two again. Together."

Marcus laughed. "The feeling is mutual."

"You find anything new about Solomon or Janey?"

Marcus relayed their findings about the ring.

"You said that the enslaver's name was Finch?" Grandpa Clark asked.

Marcus nodded. "You heard of him?"

"No, I haven't." Grandpa Clark crossed his arms. "I knew that Solomon took the ring from his enslaver, but I never knew their name. Now I do."

Marcus weighed whether he should ask to see the ring up close, but it might bring back too many other memories, especially since Jaslene was here.

"Solomon risked his life to get that ring. To me, that means it was for something very important. We just don't know what it was for."

"After we went to the library and spoke to the jeweler, I asked Sasha and the volunteers to help me find whatever they could about Denmark and the alleged revolt. Last Friday, Sasha emailed me an article from a local newspaper that was published at the time. Solomon is named in the article."

"Really?" Jaslene said.

"Yes. Most articles only focus on Denmark. They rarely name the enslaved that were also accused. According to the newspaper, Solomon was accused of stealing a sapphire ring from his enslaver, Finch, in order to exchange the ring for munitions to aid an alleged revolt led by Denmark Vesey."

"Solomon took a huge risk," Jaslene said.

"I know. The news headlines say that after the plot was discovered, Denmark and a group of enslaved men were called to trial and executed in early July. Solomon was one of the executed."

They all sat in silence with that piece of news. It was still hard for Marcus to absorb that discovery. Knowing that Solomon had possibly taken the ring to free himself and others made him not want to find the Finches. Even though Jaslene apologized to him, her sentiments were right after all.

"So that's why Janey and Solomon didn't get married," Jaslene said. "He was killed."

"Janey must've been pregnant with his child at the time that he died." Marcus took a deep breath.

"Yes, pregnant and alone."

Grandpa Clark's expression was serious. "You said Solomon died in the month of July?"

"Yes."

"And my church members died in that mass shooting three years ago in June. Both died in the same season. Summer." The wrinkles in Grandpa Clark's forehead deepened.

Empathy filled Marcus. He needed to listen to his grandfather.

"The day of that mass shooting was one of the hardest days in my life." Grandpa Clark wrung his hands. "I often think: What if I would've made another decision that day? My church members would still be alive."

Hearing Grandpa Clark sound so broken unraveled something in Marcus. "It was never your fault. You're not to blame."

"I disagree. New Life is my responsibility, and every member of the church is my responsibility too."

Marcus kept blaming himself for Trey's death, just like Grandpa Clark blamed himself for the passing of his congregants. Was that why Marcus and Grandpa Clark were at odds before? Because they were too alike—carrying burdens they couldn't shoulder?

"When I took up the call to ministry over forty years ago, I promised to care for every soul that joined New Life." Grandpa Clark glanced outside the living room window, and the afternoon sun shone on his weathered face. "It was a promise I made to myself."

"And you kept your promise," Marcus said. "You're keeping your promise today too. You're leading New Life well."

"I'm not. After that happened, I realized that it was time for me to step aside."

"Was that the reason why you wanted me to be the next pastor?" Marcus asked.

"Would it have made any difference if I told you?"

That was a big question. Marcus needed to think through his response. "I don't know. I do know that I love my job. But I can't reach back into the past and say what I would've done. The past is the past. We can only learn from it. We can't change it."

"You're right about that," Grandpa Clark said. "And . . . I'm glad that you found work that you enjoy."

"That means a lot coming from you." Marcus clasped his hands, stunned.

Grandpa Clark nodded. Marcus wanted to convince his grandfather of all the ways that he was doing a good job at New Life, but no amount of convincing could change his grandfather's mind. Marcus wanted to help him gain that closure. "I bet some of those people who were executed in July 1822 may have stepped foot in New Life at one point, especially if Denmark Vesey preached there. Their lives were touched by New Life in some way. We know Solomon was at the church."

"True," Grandpa Clark said.

"Even if Denmark wasn't able to protect Solomon's life or the lives of the other enslaved who were accused of planning a revolt, I'm sure Denmark inspired them," Marcus said. "I know for certain that you inspired the church members who died that day. Maybe not in the way Denmark did, but you inspired them nonetheless."

"Very kind to say that," Grandpa Clark said.

"Just stating the facts."

"I agree with Marcus," Jaslene added. "You've done great work at the church, and you'll continue to do so."

Marcus turned his gaze on Jaslene and studied her with a gentle eye. Jaslene tucked a curl behind her ear. Right now, Marcus would give anything to embrace her.

"Seems like you two have it all figured out. That's what happens with couples." Grandpa Clark focused on Marcus. "Don't let her get away from you this time. You have a gem here."

His grandfather was right. Jaslene was a gem that shone brighter and brighter with each passing day. What was going to happen with the two of them? Would Jaslene ever get to the point where she would want to be more than friends with him? He hoped so.

Marcus needed to set his reservations aside and ask about the ring. "Could we see the ring that Solomon had stolen?"

"You want to see the ring? Today?" Jaslene asked, surprise in her voice.

"Yes."

A knowing look colored Grandpa Clark's features. "I put it up in the safe-deposit box at the bank. I'd have to drive over there to retrieve it."

"Oh . . . well, don't worry about it then. I thought it'd be here, that's all," Marcus said.

"Why'd you want to see it?" Grandpa Clark gave Marcus the googly eyes.

Oh, brother. "For research. Yes. I wanted to see it for research. But it's okay if you don't have it with you."

"Ah. Okay then. I'll leave it at the bank." Grandpa Clark scratched his chin.

A part of Marcus wanted to tell his grandfather to get the ring from the safe-deposit box, but he didn't want to look too eager to see it, especially in front of Jaslene. He needed to change the subject. "We're having a fundraiser at the museum on Saturday. We're trying to raise money so that we can remain open."

"Remain open? What's going on?" Grandpa Clark asked.

Marcus told him everything.

Grandpa Clark paused, apparently weighing his next words. "What will you do for work if the museum closes?"

"I don't know. There aren't that many jobs for museum archivists out there. And even if I got a job somewhere else, I most likely wouldn't get to specialize in Black history like I do now."

"That would be a shame if that happened," Grandpa Clark said. "I'll keep you in prayer that it'll all work out for you."

Did his grandfather just say that he'll pray for Marcus to keep his current job? That was a huge change. "Appreciate it."

"I'll have to see if I have anything scheduled. If I don't, your grandmother and I will be there to support."

Grandpa Clark's words were gold. He was really being sincere.

Jaslene's phone rang, and she checked it. "Oh, that's Sasha's florist. I have to take this call."

After Jaslene left, Marcus gave his grandfather information on the fundraiser, just in case he could be there.

"And if I want to make a donation to the museum, how can I do that?"

Marcus did a double take. "You actually want to donate to this cause?"

"Of course I do. You know, I wasn't too keen on your endeavors because all I could see was having you as a pastor at the church, and I didn't think I was a good enough pastor after all that happened. But I'm thinking about what you said today. About how I shouldn't feel guilt over what happened on that horrific day. I'm not fully there yet, but you've given me something to ponder."

Marcus smiled. 'That's good to hear."

"And I also see that you don't have to be a preacher to move people's hearts. There are many ways to reach the world and touch hearts and minds. And your way of accomplishing that is important—very, very important."

Surprised filtered through Marcus. He couldn't believe what he was hearing. "That . . . is a game changer. Thank you for supporting. Where's Grandma? I wanted to say goodbye."

"Oh, she's probably working on some project or something. I'll find her in a second. Before you leave, grandson, I wanted to emphasize that I meant what I said about Jaslene. I'm glad to see the two of you together. And I am also going to be praying that I get to officiate your and Jaslene's nuptials. Are you sure you don't want me to get the ring?"

Marcus laughed. "I'm fine. We have no plans to get married. We're friends."

"Don't wait too long on love."

Love. What if Marcus brought up dating again but she rejected him? Jaslene wasn't holding resentments toward him, but not holding resentments and being in a committed relationship were two different things. How in the world would he start a conversation like that?

IF HIS GRANDFATHER could have a change of heart, then Jaslene could have one too. Assurance. That's what she felt. She just had to figure out *how* she would tell Marcus she loved him.

He drove her home, and the drive back felt easy—the familiar quiet between good friends. Jaslene missed these moments with Marcus, and now she was going to let him know how much it meant to share them again. Jaslene used that quiet drive back to rehearse ways to reveal her love. Should she be straightforward and to the point? Or should she bring it up in a more roundabout way?

As Marcus neared her condo complex, she was running out of time for anything roundabout.

"Thank you again for being there with me, Jaslene."

"You're welcome." She pursed her lips and tried to figure out how she would say what she needed to say.

"So I guess I'll see you at the fundraiser on Saturday." He put his truck in park.

"That's right. The fundraiser." Jaslene placed her hand on the door handle, but she didn't budge. She had to say this now. How did the adage go? Speak now or forever hold your peace?

"Something the matter?" Marcus asked.

A rush of heat trickled down her neck. Could he look any more intently? "I wanted to talk to you."

"About what?"

"About us."

His gaze flickered. "Sure. What's up?"

Whew. This was going to be harder than she had imagined. *Be direct and to the point.* "I got to thinking the other day about why I had gotten so upset when you mentioned that you can easily separate your personal versus your professional feelings toward the engagement ring . . . I mean, the ring. That was when I realized that . . . I still love you."

"You do?" His eyes widened, and his lips parted subtly.

"Yes, I do."

There. She said it. No hesitating.

"I still love you too," Marcus said. "And to be honest, when I think of Janey's ring, I think of us. I just wasn't sure how to voice my feelings at the jewelers."

Sunshine flowed through her. All this time, she had been protecting herself from feeling love because she couldn't bear to get hurt. "Can we . . . test our relationship? See if we can do this again?"

"You're serious?"

"I am." She tugged gently on the gold-and-silver bracelet on her wrist. "What do you say?"

"I'd love to. I was waiting for you to come around," he said, a teasing note in his voice.

Her shoulders—everything about her—relaxed into those words.

"So it was the engagement ring that convinced you to take a chance, huh?"

"Yes," she said softly. "But I'm not thinking about marriage or anything. I want to take things slow."

"That sounds divine. It'll give us both the time and space that we need."

The soft rise and fall of his chest captured her attention. Saying goodbye at this moment felt too abrupt. The only thing left was to . . .

Calm down, Jaslene. Take this one day at a time.

They walked to the front door of her condo with the afternoon sun on their backs. Her mind was a melody of ideas. They were actually going to date each other. She was taking a step in the right direction, at least that was what she hoped. "Where should our first date be?"

"Good question, and one that I can't answer right off the top of my head. I'll have to think on that one. I want it to be somewhere special."

She studied him. His brown eyes captured hers. "Well . . . I don't know how special you think this is, but I was thinking that we could be each other's dates for the fundraising event. It's going to be a formal occasion, and so I figured that could be a good start for us."

"Hmm. I like the idea of that. The fundraiser it is." Marcus leaned against the doorjamb to her condo. "But I would also like to do something with you that doesn't feel like part of my day job. I'll try to think of other unique places where we can go."

Jaslene smiled. She always enjoyed that about Marcus. He used to find the best outings for them. Once he took her to a winery in Myrtle Beach. Another time, he took her parasailing. "Great. We'll take it one date at a time. Just don't have me do any daredevil things for our date after the fundraiser."

"Why'd you think that I'd do that?"

"Because you've done it before," she said matter-of-factly. "Remember the parasailing?"

Marcus gave her a fake shocked look. "Wait a second. I didn't know that you didn't enjoy parasailing."

"I enjoyed it until it was time for me to ascend into the air. Then it was literally downhill from there."

Marcus laughed. "Why didn't you tell me that you were afraid of parasailing?"

"I wasn't afraid," she said. "I mean . . . I was cool with it until it was time to actually be supported by nothing but the wind."

His brown eyes shone. "Now I know. I'll keep this in my mental files. Don't take Jaslene parasailing."

"And don't take me on anything else that could be dangerous."

"Agreed."

Marcus kept looking at her, and she became very self-conscious. "What is it?" Jaslene said.

"You're beautiful."

Her heart did a backflip. The sunlight filtered through the branches of a nearby magnolia, and a new sense of hope dawned. She could do this. She could at least try.

"I'm excited about how this could turn out," he added.

"I'm not going to say all of that and jinx it."

Marcus shook his head. "I don't believe in jinxes. I have faith that all will be well with us. No matter what."

She loved his confidence, his steadiness. Marcus always won her trust. "You know, even when everything happened with Hope, I was very grateful for how you stood by me during that time. I'm just sorry that I wasn't able to do the same for you."

Her words must've struck a nerve, because Marcus was super quiet. "We're human. I don't hold that against you at all."

An ocean of compassion filled Marcus's eyes. "You're incredible. I hope you know that."

"And so are you." Marcus stepped closer to her, and the hair on the backs of her arms stood at attention. The nearness of him almost made her float.

"I've been wanting to ask you a question," he said.

"What is it?"

"Can I call you 'Jazz' again?"

The word sounded like honey from his lips. "Yes, you can."

Marcus gently placed his hand on her shoulder. The last time he touched her like this was during their rehearsal dinner. Marcus had leaned over and whispered how he was looking forward to that evening. A broad smile came across her face when he'd said that, because she was looking forward to the same.

He lifted his hand from her shoulder, and Jaslene found herself longing for his touch. She made one step toward him, and a curl fell forward. Marcus reached over and tucked it behind her ear, and then he touched her hair for a moment. Jaslene disregarded every objection that tried to rear its face. She couldn't fight her draw to him—a draw that grew stronger with every single moment.

"You have the loveliest lips," she said.

Marcus gently caressed the back of her neck, sending a tingle down her spine. There was anticipation in his eyes, and it fed hers. She closed her eyes, allowing herself to be close to him, to fully feel this moment.

Marcus planted a kiss on her lips—soft, gentle, kind. Her lips tingled with the cocoa butter scent of his lip balm and her expectancy. A rush of emotion flooded her, and she soon remembered not only why she loved Marcus, but why she could no longer bear to be apart from him ever again.

Marcus was the man for her. She wanted to stay in this moment forever. Only she couldn't. Because there were other things to attend to in life. But in these particular seconds of her particular life, Jaslene felt fully alive again.

Chapter Fourteen

𝒯he day of the fundraiser finally arrived, and Marcus was nervous. Everything had to go without a hitch tonight. Harold had basically put him in charge of ensuring everything went smoothly. On top of that, Marcus wanted to ensure that his date with Jaslene would be as normal as they could possibly make it, given the circumstances.

As soon as everything was settled with the program and the guests, he would sit at one of the tables with Jaslene and enjoy their dinner.

Marcus headed to the general atrium where the main fundraiser activities were being held. Spotlights were strategically placed around the circular area, each one highlighting a miniature display of an aspect of the Harlem Renaissance. One display featured photos of musicians of the era: Cab Calloway, Louis Armstrong, Duke Ellington, and more. Another display showed writers of the era: Zora Neale Hurston, Nella Larsen, Countee Cullen, and Claude McKay.

Jaslene had arranged for music from the era to be

played in the background during the social hour. Louis Armstrong's "Savoy Blues" reverberated through the speakers. A mock-up of the infamous Apollo Theater sign hung over the main area where the speakers and performers would make their presentations this evening.

Each table featured Jaslene's unique centerpiece. It was his favorite of the two she had designed: a sword lily with lines of poetry inscribed on a placard that was pasted to the pot of each plant. He never asked Jaslene whether she had "chatted" with the vase of sword lilies he had given her, but from the looks of it, Jaslene still held an appreciation for them.

People started trickling into the atrium, and Marcus's pulse quickened. These were the people who could potentially donate to the museum, which in turn would help the museum get the funding from the Lee Ray Foundation. He took a deep breath. Marcus was not the socializing type, but he would need to schmooze tonight.

He headed toward the crowd of people at the ticket line so that he could greet them. That was when he spotted Heather Gates at the entrance. "Ms. Gates," he said, walking in her direction.

Heather gave her coat over to the coat check and waved at Marcus. "Great to see you this evening. This looks like it's gonna be a fabulous event."

"We're confident that it will be a success. Thank you for coming out tonight." They exchanged pleasantries, and then she joined the rest of the crowd.

"Grandson!"

The sound of Grandma Clark's voice startled him. She looked elegant in her black sequined dress. Grandpa Clark looked spiffy in his black suit and red tie too.

"You made it." Marcus hugged them.

"Of course we made it," Grandma Clark said. "We wouldn't miss it for the world."

"How long have you been here?"

"Not long," Grandpa Clark said. "Only for about fifteen minutes. The line was long outside. You have a lot of people coming tonight."

"That's good. Hopefully they'll be very generous donors and spread the word about this place in their circles of influence."

"Speaking of donations, the church made a check out to the museum for five thousand dollars. It's not much, but I wanted us to show our full support." Grandpa Clark winked at him.

Marcus gaped. "Five thousand dollars? That's a lot of money. Thank you so much."

"If it weren't for your persistence, I would've missed out on the good that you're doing here."

If Marcus weren't surrounded by a growing crowd of people, he would've gotten teary-eyed. Instead, he shook Grandpa Clark's hand.

"When you get the chance, grandson, I'd like for you to show me around this place."

"Will do."

"Where's Jaslene?" Grandma Clark asked.

"Good question. I was just wondering that myself. It doesn't look like she's arrived yet, but she and Imani should be here at any moment. She decorated the space for this evening. Isn't it great?"

Grandma Clark nodded her head, impressed. "Very lovely."

"Is that you, Reginald?" Harold waved to the three of them and extended his hand to Marcus's grandparents. "Long time no see."

"Likewise." Grandpa Clark shook Harold's hand. "I've been busy as of late. But I promised my grandson that I would be here, and so I am."

"We're honored to have you."

"Marcus has been telling me all of the good things that have been happening here." Grandpa Clark gestured to the open space. "He especially mentioned an exhibit on my church that the museum is putting on."

Marcus inwardly winced. He didn't want to give the impression that he had been working on the exhibit when he should've been focused on the fundraiser.

Harold gave him a side glance. "Yes, we were working on it at one point. But it was put on hold for some high-priority tasks."

Grandpa Clark's countenance changed. "What sort of high-priority tasks?"

Harold explained everything to him.

"Oh yes. Marcus had mentioned that there was a funding emergency, but he never told me that the New Life exhibit was on hold because of it."

Oh brother. Now his grandfather was putting all of his business out there.

"That wasn't something you needed to worry about, Grandpa. That's just politics and the ins and outs of the job."

Harold gave him a nod and said, "I've got to do some politicking myself, Reginald. We'll catch up later."

"If you ever want to put on the exhibit," Grandpa Clark said, "let me know. I'd be willing to lend some of the items I have in stock for it."

Marcus's eyes must've bugged out. "What?"

"You heard me right, grandson. That bench that you were asking me about and that ring that Solomon stole from the Finches. I'm willing to lend them to the museum if you ever need them."

Harold looked at Marcus, curious. "The Finches?"

Something was up. Marcus nodded yes.

"That was the well-known family that enslaved people in the Walterboro area." Harold redirected his attention to Grandpa Clark. "You said that you have a ring of theirs?"

"Yes. It's been in *our* family for generations," Grandpa Clark said turning to his wife. "We better find our seats since the crowd is increasing. Talk soon."

His grandparents filtered through the crowd while Marcus stood there, waiting to hear it from Harold.

"You know that's a problem, right?"

Marcus shook his head no. "What's the problem?"

"Robert Finch, a descendant of the Finches, sits on the board of the Lee Ray Foundation. If they knew that a relative of one of our staff members had that ring in their possession, it wouldn't be a good thing."

A knot formed in Marcus's stomach. "But there's also a story about how that ring came into my family's possession. The mourners' bench, the ring, and the letter written by Janey tell a compelling story about Janey and Solomon."

"I know they do." Harold tugged on the lapels of his suit jacket. "But we can't jeopardize our funding, or else we won't be able to tell any story at all."

Be *able* to tell? Since when did the museum seek permission to share this history with the public? "What are you saying?" Marcus asked, worry in his voice.

"We can talk about it later," Harold said. "Let's get on with tonight's program. Imani is playing the violin in twenty minutes, right?"

"That's correct. I'll try to see where they're at." Marcus shifted his focus to finding Jaslene and Imani. He surveyed the crowd and walked the full area of the atrium, but they weren't there. Then he spotted them from across the room. Jaslene was wearing a black and gold dress suit. The shade of her outfit matched the color scheme of the centerpieces. Imani stood next to her, wearing all black and holding her violin case.

"Jaslene. Imani," Marcus said, waving to them.

"Hey!" Jaslene waved in return. "Sorry we're running late. There's traffic down here today. Lots of people are trying to get to this event. I saw people in line trying to get tickets earlier today."

"Really? That's great."

"Yes. The marketing efforts paid off."

"Thanks to your assistance," Marcus said.

They stood there, in the middle of the crowd, staring at each other for a long, long time.

"Earth to Auntie and Marcus." Imani snapped her fingers to get their attention. "You know that you guys are in public, right?"

Marcus laughed. "Oh yes. That's right. We're in public. And you, my dear, are scheduled to perform very soon. Let me show you to the platform where you'll play." He led them to the front of the space. "There's the microphone, a speaker, and, of course, your music stand. You can do a quick sound check if needed, and then I'll introduce you."

Imani smiled. "Sounds great."

While Imani was getting her violin set up, he and Jaslene found their reserved round table near the stage. They both sat next to their place cards.

"I'm glad I set up the night before. I would've been so stressed out to see these crowds."

"Me too," he said. "Let's call this first date of ours a test run, since we're both juggling multiple hats tonight."

"Agreed. How are things going for you?" she asked. "Is everything running smoothly?"

The brief conversation with Harold came to mind. "Kind of. My grandparents are here, so that's a good thing."

"That's wonderful." She set the napkin in her lap and smoothed it out. "I knew they'd be here."

"And there's more. He made a donation, and he's willing to lend the bench and the ring for the exhibit . . . if we ever get that exhibit off the ground, that is."

"What? He actually changed his mind?"

"Yep. I was kind of shocked myself."

Jaslene looked at him intently. "You seem bothered by something. What is it?"

Marcus relayed what Harold had told him about the Finches.

"Oh. That's an awkward position to be in." Jaslene twisted her mouth, apparently deep in thought. "But it's not certain that the exhibit will even happen, right?"

"Correct. But I'd like to see it happen."

"If I were you, I wouldn't worry, especially since the exhibit isn't official. Just focus on today," she said.

"You're right." But a part of him was concerned about what would happen if they were able to have the New Life exhibit. What would Harold say about featuring the ring? "I better get started. We'll talk later."

The crowd was filing up. Folks gathered around the tables and were chatting with each other. Some guests went full tilt with the Harlem Renaissance theme. Some ladies donned flapper dresses and wore their hair in French waves while the gentlemen wore tuxedoes and spats.

Marcus stepped to the podium. "Good evening, everyone. Thank you for coming out tonight to support us, especially as we're in the holiday season. Tonight is a special

night. Everyone here has showed up to support the pres-
ervation of the history of African American people in this
country. At the Lowcountry African American Heritage
Museum, our mission is to ensure that we give a voice
to forgotten stories from the past. Stories that have the
power to affect change in the present."

Some folks in the crowd applauded at his words.

Marcus continued, "But it hasn't been without a strug-
gle. Our museum is in danger of losing its funding, and
so with your generous support, we'll be able to keep this
place open. Right now we're at fifty percent of our fundraising goal for individual donations, but you can turn that
around tonight. At your tables, you will find many ways
to donate to the museum. We're opening tonight with a
performance by Imani Simmons. You probably heard of
Imani in the local news. I'll hand it over to her."

"Thank you, Marcus. I'm playing two pieces tonight.
The first song is from Florence Price, an African American composer."

Imani played the violin concerto beautifully while Marcus stood off to the side in awe. After her performance,
the crowd applauded. Some even started filling out the
donation cards. Hopefully, they'd get enough donations
to stay in operation.

AFTER IMANI FINISHED her performance, Marcus and
Jaslene sat at their reserved table. The woman sitting across
from them focused her attention on the centerpiece on the
table. That made Jaslene nervous.

The woman leaned over to inspect it up close. "These centerpieces are absolutely beautiful. I wonder who made them."

"I did," Jaslene said.

The woman looked at her. "You know what? I thought that you looked familiar."

They studied each other for a moment, and then the woman's eyes widened.

"Does your last name start with an *S*?"

How did she know that? "Yes. Simmons."

"Small world. When I was twenty-four years old, you designed my wedding ceremony and reception. I recognized the trademark style right away. I was so sad when you told me you were closing your business. You had such a great eye."

Jaslene tried to recall her old clients. She had worked with so many people back then that it was hard to remember them decades after the fact. Then she recalled the woman. "Oh yes. I remember you. Kelly, right?"

"Correct. Kelly Nielsen. Can we exchange contact information? I'd love to recommend you to others."

"Definitely."

"Ha! I told you not to give up. See?" Marcus said, smiling. "You've got more potential gigs now."

"True." Jaslene opened her clutch and handed Kelly a couple of business cards.

The rest of the evening was spent in relative ease. Marcus spent most of his time talking to the attendees, and she answered questions from folks about her centerpieces.

Every time someone complimented her on them, she got a little boost of confidence. Once this event was over, she was definitely going to make plans to formally add event design to Fairytale Weddings again.

After Harold made a speech to the guests, there was time for more socializing. Jaslene spotted Marcus and waved at him.

"I know that we haven't had much of a date this evening," Marcus said. "I'm going to have to make this up to you."

"Don't worry about it," she said. "The museum is important, and you needed to make sure that every single person knew how to donate and revisit the museum. Do you know where the museum stands financially yet?"

"Nope. I won't know that until January. Harold takes two to three weeks off during the holiday season. He'll hold a meeting in the new year to discuss how we did and the next steps that we can take."

"If I were in your shoes, I'd be a nervous wreck," Jaslene said. "Who am I kidding? I'm nervous for you already."

Marcus smiled at her. "I love that you care about this as much as I do."

"Of course, I do. I've spent a lot of time here in the past month or so. It's become like a second work home for me."

When she first walked into the Lowcountry African American Heritage Museum, she was so anxious, but her concerns eased with time.

After dinner was served, a DJ started playing more upbeat music. The song "Let's Do It, Let's Fall in Love," made famous by Ella Fitzgerald, played over the loud-speaker.

"Do you want to dance?" Marcus said. "I've done all the talking I can do to other people, and hopefully, more will be moved to make onetime or regular donations."

"We can dance."

Jaslene placed her hand in his, and they walked together to the dance floor. "This is the part where I wish I'd taken dance lessons."

"I thought you had signed up for lessons when we were engaged."

"Never got around to registering for a class," Jaslene said. "But that's neither here nor there."

Marcus's body was familiar and perfect. She placed her cheek on his chest and savored his embrace.

"This feels nice," he said.

"Mm-hmm. Remember when we were practicing our vows that day while we were on the bus together?"

"Yes," he said. "We were going to love each other to infinity."

"This feels like infinity." Jaslene glanced up at him.

"It does." Marcus gently brushed his lips against hers, and she kissed him, slowly, softly, gently. Jaslene remembered every curve of his mouth and drew him closer. A lightness filled her. They were one. Jaslene wanted to have more dances with him. Forever.

When the song was finished, they stepped away from the dance floor. Jaslene and Marcus headed to the dessert table.

After getting a slice of cheesecake, Jaslene spotted two empty seats near the coat check, and they cozied up to each other there.

"I saw more people talking about your centerpieces," Marcus said.

"Oh yes. They were. It was kind of neat. If it weren't for your encouragement, I would've never thought to try this out again. So thank you. I finished the prototype center-pieces for Sasha's wedding. Now all I have to do is create the rest of the aesthetic. I plan to update my website to indicate that I'll offer those services, in addition to wedding planning."

"Nice." Marcus loosened his bow tie and leaned back, content.

"What is it?"

"Can a man smile at his girlfriend?" he asked.

That was the first time that Marcus had called her his girlfriend since they agreed to date each other again.

"The kiss sealed the deal, if you ask me," Marcus added.

Jaslene laughed. He had a point.

"There are the two lovebirds." Grandma Clark waved at them and headed their way. "Look at the two of you. So cute both on and off the dance floor."

Jaslene's eyes widened. Grandma Clark saw them kissing. "Sorry about that, ma'am."

"No need to apologize to me! Young love is so ador-able. You know, Marcus, I always used to love to hold hands with your grandfather in public. I would've kissed him too, but the times were different back then. A woman couldn't do anything of the sort without other people gossiping about her." Grandma Clark shrugged. "I'm so glad that the two of you are free to love."

Grandma Clark had a way of making everything seem like a gift, even what Jaslene saw as mishaps. One day, Jaslene wanted to be just like her. That kind of perspective came with time and wisdom.

"We had such a wonderful time this evening," Grandpa Clark said. "And please let me know how and when I can lend those items to the museum. I'd love to see that exhibit come to fruition."

"We better get going now." Grandma Clark gave them a hug. "Give us a call. Or stop by. You're always welcome."

After they left, Marcus turned to Jaslene. "Thank you for encouraging me to keep reaching out to my grandfather. My restored relationship with him would've never happened without you."

"I'd love to know the secret to their happy marriage. They've had their share of problems and ups and downs, but they never let it separate them. That's a blessing."

"I think that the secret is their commitment to each other, in the good times and the bad. They're far from perfect, but that keeps them going."

His words rooted deep within her. "Sometimes I feel like you and I, we never even got to have a honeymoon period."

"We didn't have one."

Jaslene nodded. "Life is so haphazard that way. We can make all of these plans—all of the things to ensure that weddings happen without a hitch—and then . . . I got to the point after my sister's death where I thought that it wasn't worth it to try anymore. But after seeing your grandparents and being around you, I have a different perspective."

"I'm glad you did."

The laughter and chatter of the people filled the space. The lights in the atrium were a bit brighter than before, indicating that the fundraiser was almost over. A part of her didn't want this night to end. This was the first event where she had tried her hand at event design again, and it turned out to be pretty decent. When it came to trusting her design instincts, Jaslene realized that she had been her own naysayer. She resolved to never get in her own way again.

"Do you think that we'll ever get to be like my grandparents?"

"So we're going from girlfriend and boyfriend to talks of wedded bliss?" she said, teasing.

"I was just speculating," he said. "Nothing serious."

They were both quiet again, and that gave her room to truly ponder his question. "You know, I can't be certain of much in my life anymore. But perhaps one day I'll get to a place where I'll be able to share the same perspective as your grandparents." Jaslene sighed. "If I'm honest with myself, I think that I was logistically ready to get married two years ago. I had all of the boxes checked off. Everything was in order, and I knew how to put on a beautiful wedding. But the marriage part eluded me."

Resignation colored his features. "I would have to say the same for myself."

"In what way?"

Marcus crossed his arms and looked up, as if trying to formulate a response. "Because I blamed myself for things that were outside of my control."

She nodded. "Talking about this is helping us. At least I think it's helping us."

"It is," Marcus said. "You know, I want to give you an early Christmas present."

Jaslene's eyes widened. "A present? For me?"

"Of course, for you." Marcus reached in his suit jacket and produced the jewelry box.

Jaslene's heart pitter-pattered. Was he proposing to her? She carefully opened the box and gasped. "The pendant from Orion Jewelry Store."

The pear-shaped sapphire pendant sparkled, and it hung from a lovely gold chain. The jewel shone even more in the jewelry box than when she'd seen it in the store that day. "Marcus . . . I'm . . . I'm speechless."

"I saw you eyeing the pendant when we were at the jewelers and I said to myself, 'I want to get that for Jaslene one day.'" Marcus removed the necklace from its holder. "Then my second thought was, 'We only live once,' so I purchased it from Theodore at the jewelry store yesterday. And I just couldn't wait until Christmas. Can I put this on your neck?"

She nodded yes. He clasped the gold chain around her neck, brushing his fingertips against her shoulders.

"I love you, Jaslene."

"I love you too." She cozied up next to him. This night was perfect, and she wanted to remain in Marcus's arms for eternity.

Chapter Fifteen

*A*fter the first week of the new year, Harold called a meeting in his office to discuss the financial results of the fundraising gala. Marcus tried to gauge whether the results were positive or negative, but Harold was quiet on that part, stating that he didn't want to talk about the meeting before the meeting.

That caused concern. His career was on the line here, and if the numbers weren't good, he wouldn't know what to do. The only place where Marcus could get a job would be at a larger research university or at a museum in a larger metropolitan area. He'd have to move away from Charleston, and away from Jaslene. Their relationship status could be up in the air, and his heart couldn't bear to have that happen again. He loved her too much.

On top of that, his field of work was very specific. He didn't have a transferrable skill set. His background was best suited for a museum or university, and all those positions were competitive. He had lucked out when Harold made Marcus's internship into a full-time position.

Marcus checked the time on his cell phone. The meeting would begin in twenty minutes. He was about to leave his office and turn off the lights when he took note of the lamp that Jaslene had brought for him back in November. It was still on, and he had grown accustomed to its gentle light. He liked to always keep it on, even if the main lights in his office were off, but this time another idea came to mind.

He shut off all the lights in the office, including the desk lamp, and he slowly opened the blinds. Natural sunlight streamed through the windows, leaving an amber glow on the red rug in his office.

"Much better," he said to himself. Marcus looked out the window. He would no longer live in hiding.

Marcus stayed there for a few more moments, allowing the sunshine to warm his face. As he did so, it felt as if something inside of him was shifting. There was no longer a stoniness inside of him. That stoniness first formed when he had resolved to never forgive himself for what happened to his brother. That same stoniness hardened even more when he had told Grandpa Clark that he was going to follow his own career path, knowing that by doing so, his grandfather would never want to speak to him again. That stoniness turned into a boulder when Hope passed away and Jaslene had broken up with him.

But no more. Today Marcus resolved to live in a new day. He glanced outside his office window, and a mourning dove appeared. This time, it was on the sidewalk and stood in the full rays of the sun. Marcus smiled at the little bird. "You and I are finally figuring it out."

The bird tilted its head to the side as if to allow the sunrays to shine on it.

The alarm on his phone beeped, indicating that it was time for him to get to Harold's office. He headed down the hall, and he whispered a silent wish that all turned out well.

Harold's office was much tidier. There were no longer stacks of paper covering every inch of his desk. Instead, Marcus could actually see the top of his desk for once. It was gleaming too.

There was a line of chairs against the wall. Some of the other museum employees were already gathered inside of his office, and Harold motioned for Marcus to have a seat in one of the empty spots.

At the top of the hour, Harold began.

"Happy New Year, everyone. I called this meeting today because this museum affects all of us. Each of you has played an integral part in ensuring that this museum remains true to its mission, and so I want to thank you for working here, for showing up, despite our challenges."

Marcus braced himself. Harold sounded like he was making a farewell speech for the museum. Marcus would have to figure out another path for himself. And he'd have to tell Jaslene that their relationship would be compromised by a potential move.

Calm down. Calm down. It will all work out.

"We've raised enough money from the fundraiser and from individual donations to meet the requirements for the grant."

"Woo-hoo!"

"Yay!"

"Great news!"

Cheers and applause filled the room. A feeling of relief overwhelmed Marcus. He would get to stay.

"However, as you may know, there were two requirements that we needed to fulfill for this grant. The other one was visitor count. We are just below our goal mark for this."

"How many people do we need?" Marcus asked.

"We need to bring in about three thousand visitors a month, and right now we're at two thousand visitors a month, on average. We have to do a push to bring folks in. And this would be good to do, not just for this grant, but in general. It's been tougher to bring in folks after all of the challenges we've been facing. But we have a good team here, and I believe that we can do it."

"Will Sasha's wedding count for visitors?" Marcus asked.

"Yes. Her guests will receive museum admission tickets to attend her ceremony and reception here. I think she's having about two hundred guests. And those guests will get to tour the museum and walk around, so they can see the rest of the exhibits."

If Harold was doing a big push for visitors, having a brand-new exhibit would be a great draw. The New Life exhibit would be perfect.

"There's a quandary with getting in more visitors. I've already exhausted the resources that we had toward gain-ing more donors. It'll be a challenge to market and publicize this place again."

"Those who recently attended the fundraiser and those who have donated will be great helps in spreading the word," one staff member noted.

"Yes. We can definitely count on them."

Should Marcus bring up the possibility of putting together the New Life exhibit? Harold already expressed his reservations about getting the bench and ring from Grandpa Clark, but that didn't mean that other aspects of the exhibit couldn't be featured. He would ask. "How about putting on the New Life exhibit?"

The rest of the staffers turned their attention to Marcus. "Sounds like a great idea," one said.

Harold sighed. He appeared hesitant. "I'm not so sure about that."

"You told me that once we got enough funding that we could work on the exhibit. This is the perfect time. It would draw the repeat visitors as well as brand-new ones."

Harold crossed his arms. "I have my reservations."

His words were terse, but Marcus knew exactly what he meant. "Yes, and I'd like to discuss that with you."

"We can talk after this meeting."

Harold continued with the agenda, but all Marcus could think about was how to convince Harold. Although Marcus had said they could put on the exhibit without the ring and the mourners' bench, if he were honest with himself, both items would be great additions to the exhibit. Somehow, he'd have to convince Harold of this too.

Once the meeting was over, Marcus waited in Harold's office.

"Look, I know that I promised that the exhibit would happen after we got enough financial funding, but I don't know if now is the right time."

Marcus drummed his fingers on the armrest of the chair. "You promised."

"I know, but there are a lot of variables involved here too."

"I know those variables. I can see the potential controversy with featuring the ring in the exhibit, but like I said, those items have great meaning and significance. People should know about them."

Harold tapped his pen on the table, quiet and apparently deep in thought. "I'll have to tell you what happened while I was off from work."

Marcus sat up straighter, ready to listen to Harold.

"You already know that Robert Finch, a direct descendant of the Finches, sits on the board of the Lee Ray Foundation. Well . . . someone from Orion Jewelers contacted Robert and said you visited the store twice. They told the board member that your grandfather has that sapphire ring."

Theodore! "Do you know the name of the person who told him?"

"No, I don't."

Marcus stood and paced Harold's office. "When I was at the jewelry store, I asked the jeweler if he knew if the Finches lived in the area, and he told me no. He said no during both of my visits there. I can't believe this."

"Believe it." Harold grabbed a pack of cigarettes from the side drawer of his desk and opened it. "I've been working at this museum for decades. I've seen and been through a lot. Can't trust everyone."

A sense of dread formed in the pit of his gut. He had purchased Jaslene's pendant there too. He spent a whole lot of money on that necklace. Now his gift to Jaslene felt tainted.

"Mr. Finch called me up last week. Wanted to confirm if the information he received was true. I said yes. He said that if the ring wasn't returned, then we'd lose our chance at grant money."

"They. Said. What?"

"They said—"

"I know what they said. Can one board member make that kind of decision?" Marcus asked.

"Yes and no. They're a private organization. They make the rules. I wasn't being wishy-washy when I was worried about your grandfather owning that ring. Like I said earlier, I want to keep this museum in operation, not jeopardize it."

Marcus nodded, and guilt set in. He shouldn't have gone to the jewelers. He shouldn't have gotten that pendant. He shouldn't have been so interested in knowing more about Solomon and Janey. He should've left everything alone "This is all my fault."

"No. You were doing what you thought was best. And I would've done the same thing if I were in your shoes. The point of our existence is to help folks know the past. You wanted to know about your ancestors' past."

"And now it's come at a cost."

Harold nodded his assent.

"What'll we do?"

After lighting his cigarette, Harold said, "We can have the New Life exhibit, but your grandfather will have to return the ring to Mr. Finch as a show of goodwill."

Goodwill? Defeat filled Marcus. This was hard. "According to one newspaper account, my ancestor Solomon had allegedly hoped to exchange the ring for munitions in support of an alleged revolt led by Denmark Vesey. If we return the ring, then we're giving in. I don't think my grandfather will agree to that. It'll be like erasing Solomon's story and admitting defeat."

Harold's eyes shifted. "We're not admitting defeat. Returning the ring will ensure that the museum doesn't seem biased. And we're not erasing your ancestor either. You know the truth. Your grandfather knows the truth. Just because he returns it, doesn't mean that the story is erased."

Marcus squinted, not agreeing with Harold.

The smoke from Harold's cigarette trailed to the ceiling. "We can't risk our funding. That's where I stand."

That seed of defeat quickly bloomed into something more: a despondency, a sadness, a sense of loss. Why do this work if Harold would compromise? It didn't make any sense.

The look on Harold's face said that he didn't want to discuss the ring anymore. No point in trying. "All right, then. If we're going to do the New Life exhibit, then when can we have the grand opening to the public?"

"I'd like it to be sooner rather than later since this will

draw visitors. Sasha's wedding is this weekend. So I'd say two to three weeks after that."

"I'll see what I can do," he said, getting up to leave.

"And, Marcus?"

"Yes?"

"I know that this news about returning the ring is hard. But please trust me on this one. I only have our best interests in mind."

Harold had financial interests in mind. Marcus was right when he'd said that Harold needed to think of ways to make this museum financially independent. Now Harold had to choose between money and Solomon, and he chose money.

But funding from the Lee Ray Foundation was not guaranteed. If Mr. Finch was willing to withhold funding over something that happened a century ago, then that organization could change their mind on a whim and the museum would end up closing anyway.

When all was said and done, it was best to keep the ring, regardless.

Marcus said a quick goodbye to Harold and left.

How would he deliver this news to Grandpa Clark? He wouldn't take it well. Jaslene wouldn't take it well either. She'd probably stop wearing the pendant after hearing how the jeweler lied to him.

All that effort to show his love for Jaslene would be for nothing. His heart broke.

SASHA'S WEDDING REHEARSAL arrived sooner than Jaslene thought. She'd been preparing for it all along, but now it was finally here. She headed to the W. E. B. Du Bois room and surveyed the space. It looked even brighter than on the day that Imani had tested out the sound here a few months ago. When she arrived there, Grandpa Clark was ready to go. "Morning, sir."

"Nice to see you, Ms. Simmons. You ready for the big day?"

"I'm always ready for a wedding. And tomorrow is Sasha's birthday too. I have something planned for it. It's a surprise," Jaslene said.

"Two celebrations in one day. That'll be fun," Pastor Clark said.

"I'm going to see if the rest of the wedding party is here. I told everyone to be early, but you know how that goes."

Jaslene headed to the entrance of the museum. Outside, the sun was shining brightly overhead, and the branches of a nearby magnolia shivered in the cool air. Jaslene couldn't wait to see the trees bloom in spring.

It was so peaceful this morning. Jaslene was used to seeing more cars and passersby, but it was after the holiday season. Everyone was probably in recovery mode.

She scanned the parking lot for any indication of Sasha's red Nissan Z, but Jaslene didn't spot it. Making sure everyone was on time had become a key part of her job description, and it was one of the most stressful parts of being a wedding planner.

"They'll be here any minute now," she said to herself, walking to the museum's entrance.

Moments later, Marcus's black Ford F-250 pulled into

the parking lot. At least he was on time. He was the only member of the wedding party who was here.

After parking, he stepped out, looking handsome in his burgundy polo shirt and khakis. She might've been biased since he was her boyfriend and all.

"Hey, have you seen Sasha, Greg, and the wedding party?" Jaslene hated hearing the anxiety in her voice.

"And hello to you too." Marcus gave her a quick kiss on the cheek.

"Sorry. And hello." She tapped her clipboard. "I haven't seen them. Your grandfather is here. You're here, but that's it."

"They'll all be here soon. No need to worry."

Jaslene checked her watch.

"You're worrying," he said.

"I'm not worrying."

"Oh yes, you are. You have that line on your forehead. It always crinkles whenever you're worried."

Jaslene twisted her mouth. Marcus knew her way too well. She touched the pendant that Marcus had given her, and a look of sadness colored Marcus's features. "Are you okay?" she asked.

"I'm fine. I'm fine . . . Good that my grandfather is here. I wanted to speak with him about something before we started the wedding rehearsal."

"Oh, yeah? What about?" Jaslene snuck another look at her watch.

"Um . . . I'll let you know in good time. I need to run this by him first."

Hmm. Interesting. Guess she'd find out soon enough. Jaslene grabbed her phone from her back pocket to text Sasha, and a shock of red caught in Jaslene's periphery. Greg parallel parked Sasha's car in an empty space right in front of the museum. Other cars filled with the wedding party followed. They drove to the museum parking lot which was located in the rear. Jaslene waved to Sasha and Greg. "Thank goodness they're here. I'm gonna have to tell them to be more punctual."

"I'll be inside," Marcus said, smiling. "See you soon."

Jaslene refocused her attention on Sasha and Greg. "You all have to get here on time!"

"Sorry, sis. It won't happen again." Sasha gave her a hug.

"Hey, Jaslene." Greg hugged her. "Long time no see."

"It's great to see you again. How was your submarine tour?"

"Stressful. Glad to be home." Greg shoved his keys in his back pocket.

Minutes later, the rest of her bridesmaids and groomsmen gathered around the engaged couple in a semicircle. Like Sasha and Greg, they wore denim jeans and white button-down shirts.

"You all look so cute." Jaslene nodded, impressed. "Makes me think I should've worn denim and a white shirt too."

"I didn't want to ask you because I didn't want you to stress. You already have enough on your plate."

"True."

"Carla's sister called me," Sasha said. "Carla was diagnosed with meningitis yesterday, and she has to stay in the hospital for six weeks. She won't be able to be a bridesmaid."

"Oh no!" one bridesmaid said.

"What?" another said.

"That's horrible. I hope she feels better soon. Maybe we can make a care package for her." Jaslene made a note. "What do you think?"

Everyone nodded their agreement.

"Good," Jaslene said. "I'll put together an online sign-up list and send it out after the wedding."

"We'll have to find a fill-in for the bridal party," Sasha said.

Jaslene sensed her stress levels increasing. "Let's not think about that right now. We'll do a run-through and hopefully that'll give you and me time to brainstorm."

"Sounds like a good plan," Greg said.

Everyone headed into the museum. Inside, Marcus and Grandpa Clark seemed to be in a serious conversation with each other. "You two okay?" Jaslene asked.

Marcus looked up. "Yes, we're good. Just talking."

"We'll discuss that more after the rehearsal, grandson." Pastor Clark shook his head. "I can't believe he'd say something like that."

"I know."

Who were they talking about? Jaslene was more curious now, but she didn't have time to speculate. She refocused on the wedding party. "I'm glad everyone is here today.

We've met over the past few months, and I'm pretty sure that you've all been to weddings, and so our rehearsal should be simple. We'll have a few special tweaks, however." Jaslene grabbed a cardboard box filled with the eternity cord, the arras, and the wedding veil. She also got the straw broom that was propped against the wall. "We'll incorporate the cultural rituals after Sasha and Greg exchange vows. I'll cue everyone on what'll happen."

"This is exciting!" Sasha beamed. "Where do you want me to stand?"

"You'll stand near the entrance, and then you can walk to the front where Pastor Clark and Greg will meet you."

"Easy enough." Sasha headed to her spot.

After she did so, Jaslene then directed the bridesmaids and the flower girl to line up in front of Sasha. She positioned the groomsmen next to Greg on his left side. Then she motioned for Marcus to stand next to Greg. He did. "Thank you, ma'am," he said, winking.

She smiled. "You're welcome. Okay, folks, let's get started." Jaslene nodded to the cellist while Imani was putting rosin on the hairs of her violin bow. When she finished, they played.

The soft notes of Pachelbel's "Canon" played through the Du Bois room, and those notes sent a sense of comfort through her. When Marcus and Jaslene were supposed to get married, they had picked out Pachelbel's "Canon" too. Jaslene nodded to the first bridesmaid, and she walked down the aisle. The other bridesmaids followed in a straight line.

"Make sure you pace yourself, folks. Don't rush. This is a big moment for Sasha and Greg, and they need to savor every single moment."

The bridal party slowed down at Jaslene's instruction, and she slowly clapped her hands to the beat of the music. The gentle strains of Imani's violin, along with the cello, complemented each other. Jaslene smiled at the sight. This would be the most beautiful wedding ever—after they figured out what to do about Carla not being here.

Sasha and Greg practiced exchanging their vows. When they finished, Jaslene handed Marcus the cord while she held the eternity veil and the arras. "This is when your maid of honor and your best man would place the cord across your shoulders, the veil over Sasha's head and Greg's shoulder, and give you the arras. Then the maid of honor and Marcus would take turns stating what each represents. But . . . Carla isn't here. Have you thought about who you'd like to take her place?"

"You can walk down the aisle in Carla's place," Sasha said to Jaslene.

"Me?"

"Yes, you." Sasha smiled. "I'm pretty sure you can fit in Carla's dress, and you'll be paired up with Marcus. It'll be perfect."

Jaslene's eyes widened, and then she glanced at Marcus. He seemed happy with the idea, but the notion gave her pause. Being paired up with Marcus as if they were . . . a married couple or a couple getting married? That would be interesting . . .

"You look like I just asked you to walk into a hornet's nest," Sasha said, laughing. "You two are dating anyway. What would the problem be with walking down the aisle together?"

"It's not a problem with me," Marcus said, winking at Jaslene.

It shouldn't be a problem for her either, but now that they were actually talking about it, well, a flit of hesitation coursed through her. Dating Marcus was one thing, but walking down the aisle with him? That was quite another, even if it was only as part of a bridal party.

"Are you up for it?" Sasha asked.

Jaslene twisted her mouth, uncertain. What if she did this and she started getting all of her old, horrible feelings back with regard to her own wedding day. "I'm not sure."

Compassion colored Marcus's expression. "I know how you're feeling, Jazz. You won't have to worry, though, because I'll be next to you. Remember the promise we made to each other?"

She remembered it very well. "Yes, I do."

Marcus kissed her forehead. "I'll be next to you the entire time."

"All right. I'll be the stand-in bridesmaid. I'll just need to try on that dress today. We'll have to stop by Carla's house and get it."

"That will be no problem. She and her sister live together, and so I'm sure we can stop by sometime tonight or tomorrow morning." Sasha hugged her. "This will be perfect."

Chapter Sixteen

*T*he next day, Jaslene awakened early, because on top of her usual nervousness for a wedding, she had walking-down-the-aisle-with-Marcus nervousness as well. She rubbed her brow, stressed. All the emotions from her wedding day resurfaced. How would she deal?

She got up, and after getting ready for the day, she drove to the museum. Imani was in the passenger seat, and they rode there in silence. Peaceful.

Jaslene had sectioned off a dressing area for Sasha and another one for the bridesmaids. The groom and grooms-men would be arriving already dressed. She walked to where the bridesmaids were located, and she eyed Carla's dress hanging on the back of the dressing room door. Sasha and Jaslene picked it up last night, but she didn't get to try it on until now.

She quickly changed into the dress, and it was snug over her bottom. Jaslene tried to move and swish around, but it was very hard. *Eep.* Nothing she could do about that now. She sucked in her stomach and hoped there wouldn't be any dress problems during the wedding. Then she went looking for Sasha.

The faint sound of chatting and laughter could be heard behind a closed door at the end of the hallway. She lightly tapped on the door.

"Who is it?"

"Jaslene."

"Come on in!"

Jaslene gasped at the sight of Sasha. She looked divine in her princess-cut gown with a long train of tulle. Her normally straightened hair was in waves. "You look amazing!"

"Thanks!" Sasha twirled around in her dress. "I'm so nervous."

"You're going to be great. Just great."

Sasha looked her up and down. "How's the dress fit?"

Jaslene twisted her mouth. "Um, this is as good as it's going to get with me today. I doubt that there'll be any emergency tailors on hand to loosen the stitches."

Sasha seemed deep in thought. "Don't write that off too quickly. We may find one on hand. I have a sewing kit."

Jaslene shook her head. "Not happening. Believe me. Not happening at all. We have too much going on. I only have to wear this dress for a few hours. So . . . don't worry about it. I'll manage." She opened her file folder, which held the preprinted signs for each dressing area, and she posted them on the door.

"I can't tell that your dress feels uncomfortable." Sasha studied her closely. "You wear it well."

"Well, I'm not the bride. You're the star of the show. As long as I blend in with the bridal party, I'm good."

"You're walking down the aisle with Marcus, right?"

The humor in Sasha's voice was not lost on her. "Yes . . . that's correct. That's what I'm doing."

"All right. Well . . . you know that's kind of cool, right?"

"Cool" was her code word for *This is the most amazing thing to ever happen.* "Yeah, kind of sort of."

"Yes." Sasha's eyes widened. "It's super amazing, and I'm glad you two are finally dating."

"We're taking things slow to see how it goes for us. No rushing or nothing."

Sasha couldn't suppress the smile from her face.

"What?" Jaslene said.

"Eeee!!" Sasha jumped up and down, and her dress swished with her movements. "I can't believe that you can't tell that it's happening. It's happening. It's happening. It's happening!"

"What's happening?"

"The great meld." Sasha clapped her hands and jumped up and down more. "I'm excited for you. The great meld happens when a couple operates as one. They become in sync with each other, and they're in flow. I can see it happening between the two of you, and I love witnessing every moment of it. In my opinion, the meld between the two of you is just as important as my wedding."

Oh brother. "You're too much."

"It is." She smiled. "I remember sitting in the pews at your wedding, waiting for you to make your procession down the aisle. But you never appeared at the altar. I remember the shock in your voice when you called me that evening and told me that Hope died. When I saw you at the funeral, the joy left your eyes. That was hard to witness. You, of all people, deserve all the joy in the world."

Jaslene bit her bottom lip. It was the only way that she could hold back the urge to burst into tears. She needed to change the subject. "I forgot to ask you yesterday. Do you know what time *Southern Bride* will be here?"

"They should be here now."

Her tummy leapt. "Oh."

As if reading her mind, Sasha said, "Girl, don't be nervous. They already love your work. They said they want to interview you sometime after the ceremony. Be on the lookout."

"Cool. Cool. I'll do that."

"Remember, own your gifts. Don't second-guess yourself."

"I'll try. I'm gonna go do the wedding planner and bridesmaid thing. I love you." After giving Sasha a quick hug, she blinked to keep herself from crying. Why did Sasha always say things that made her teary-eyed? Maybe that was what a friend was supposed to do: read your heart.

Jaslene needed to get everyone lined up for the procession. She spotted the wedding party at the end of the foyer, and she walked over to meet up with them. On the way, she saw Greg stepping into the Du Bois room.

A bridesmaid handed her a bouquet. "This is for you. The florist just dropped them off. I held yours for you."

"Thank you." Jaslene stood on her tiptoes and looked out at the crowd. She checked the time on her watch. "Looks like we should be starting in a few minutes."

Just then, she heard the swishing of Sasha's gown. Jaslene opened the door for her, careful to ensure that she couldn't be seen by her groom. "Are you ready?"

"I am!" She was beaming.

"I spotted Greg after you and I spoke," Jaslene said. "He looks just as happy as you do."

Sasha nodded. "Marcus stopped by earlier today, and he looked pretty happy too."

She wasn't letting up. "Anyway, good luck."

Jaslene got back in line. When she did, music played, and they made their way down the aisle. Memories of her wedding came to mind.

Stop it. This isn't your wedding. That's over. This is for Sasha.

Still, a well of emotions bubbled from within. They were as much a part of her as the air she breathed. If only she could grasp the pendant that Marcus had given her, but the guests were watching them walk down the aisle.

She positioned herself to the left of Pastor Clark while Marcus stood on the right. Then the song changed. Imani and the cellist played Pachelbel's "Canon." The guests stood and turned their attention to Sasha as she walked down the aisle.

Jaslene glanced at Marcus. There was a light in his eyes that she hadn't seen since . . . their own wedding day. And then he mouthed a word: *Beautiful.*

Beautiful. He had said the same word the night before they were to be married. She could almost float.

After Sasha took her place next to Greg, Pastor Clark started talking. Sasha and Greg looked as if they were in rapt attention, but Jaslene couldn't seem to focus on his words. It all seemed like a dream, a dream that she had buried in her heart since her own wedding day. She hadn't realized that until now.

Thinking along these lines made her feel some type of way. Was she feeling this way because she stood close to Marcus at Sasha's wedding? Or was this truly the desire of her heart?

This could be her heart's desire. She simply needed to let herself fall into it.

Her mouth curved upward.

"I do." Greg's voice pulled her from her thoughts. The couple exchanged vows. It was time for Jaslene and Marcus to do their part. Imani stepped up to a microphone which was positioned near the floral arrangements.

"For this next part of the ceremony, I'll play Violin Concerto No. 2 by the late composer Lucrecia Kasilag. She was known for incorporating Filipino indigenous instruments into her productions."

Imani returned to her spot next to the cellist and began playing. As she played, Marcus held the traditional Filipino arras, thirteen gold coins, in a sachet. Greg handed them to Sasha. "This symbolizes prosperity for the couple and Greg's promise to provide for Sasha and their future children."

Marcus and Jaslene set the mourners' bench before the couple and covered it with a white cloth. Sasha and Greg had requested the use of this bench for their ceremony to symbolize the blending of Sasha's Filipino and African American heritage and how that heritage would influence their union.

The couple knelt at the bench. Seeing the two of them kneeling at the bench moved Jaslene. She looked over at Marcus who must've felt the same way. Jaslene and Marcus had planned to have these elements in their own wedding, but it felt great to be part of Sasha and Greg's special moment.

Marcus and Jaslene placed the traditional Filipino veil over Jaslene's head and Greg's shoulder. "This veil shows that the couple are dressed for the world as one," Jaslene said.

Finally, Jaslene took the yugal, the silk cord, and gave one end to Marcus. They twisted the cord into a figure eight. "This symbolizes the couple's everlasting fidelity and shows that they'll walk in the world as equals," Marcus said.

When Imani finished playing, Pastor Clark said: "By the power vested in me, I now pronounce you husband and wife. Greg, you may kiss your bride."

Greg and Sasha kissed, and the guests cheered. Marcus and Jaslene removed the cord and veil from the couple and set it on a side table, along with the arras. Jaslene got the straw broom from the side and set it before the couple. They jumped the broom, and the crowd applauded once again.

"Ladies and gentlemen, it's my joy and honor to present to you Mr. and Mrs. Smith," Pastor Clark said. Jaslene set the broom aside and stood next to Marcus. Mendelssohn's "Wedding March" played and the newly wedded couple walked down the aisle. The rest of the wedding party linked arms with one another.

People were busy taking photos and congratulating the new bride and groom. Jaslene reveled in the moment.

"Shall we, my dear?" Marcus said.

"Let's." Jaslene linked arms with him, and they walked down the aisle. The guests smiled at them. Jaslene imagined that they were beaming at her as if it were her wedding day.

They stepped outside and walked over to the right when they saw that Sasha and Greg were busy taking pictures. As they did, Marcus stepped closer to her. She could sense the warmth of his presence, and it sent her into a tizzy. She took a deep breath to steady herself.

"Are you Jaslene Simmons?" a woman with a brunette bob said.

"Yes. That's me."

"Hi there." The woman extended her hand. "I'm Kirsten Lee from *Southern Bride*. It's so nice to meet you."

Oh wow. "Nice to meet you as well. Sasha mentioned that you wanted to meet with me."

"Yes. Is this a good time? I just want to ask you a few quick questions."

Jaslene glanced over at the wedding party. They were all preoccupied chatting with the guests. "This is a perfect time."

Kirsten looked at her and Marcus. "I really enjoyed the wedding ceremony. You two were great for each other."

Marcus held Jaslene close. "I agree."

"I walked around to the reception area already and caught sight of your centerpieces. They were so unique. What's your inspiration?" Kirsten asked, opening her notepad.

"I take my inspiration from each client. At least that's what I did before."

"Before?" Kirsten said.

"Yes. I took a sabbatical from wedding design for a while. I'm restarting it again. I'll be getting my formal certification in the craft this summer." Jaslene and Marcus met eyes. He smiled at her.

"You're not certified?" Kirsten scribbled something in her notepad.

Uh-oh. Was that a bad thing?

"Your work is so professional," Kirsten continued. "I couldn't tell the difference, and I've seen lots and lots of weddings and receptions while working for the magazine."

Whew. "That means a lot."

"Tell me more. You mentioned that you take your design cues from your clients. Can you elaborate?"

"Oh yes. Every wedding is unique," Jaslene said. "I let the couples take the lead by telling me what they want. I specialize in incorporating African American and Filipino elements into my designs, but I'm well-versed in many cultural wedding symbols and rituals. I think it's important that these elements don't get lost in the actual ceremony and reception. They're a statement of the couple's history and identity, something that they'll pass on to their children."

"Love this so much." Kirsten scribbled quickly in her notepad. "Is it okay if I take a few pictures of you?"

"Sure thing."

"I'll be waiting for you out here," Marcus said.

"Cool." Jaslene kissed him on the cheek and walked with Kirsten to the reception area in the atrium. Kirsten took more photos of Jaslene by the centerpieces.

"This is all so perfect," Kirsten said. "I'm going to linger and take more photos. But you can expect this wedding feature, and your business, to be published in the June issue of *Southern Bride*."

"Excellent," Jaslene said. She gave Kirsten her business card. After talking details, Jaslene joined Marcus outside. "Thanks for waiting for me."

"Of course. Thank you for teaming up with me and being in the wedding party." Marcus wrapped his arm around her waist.

"I didn't really have a choice, given the circumstances."

"Ouch. That hurt," Marcus said, teasing.

"I didn't mean it like that. I was just saying. We were on the brink of a real emergency and all. I had to do something."

"And you did it very well."

Marcus knew just what to say. She loved that about him. "I'm glad that we were paired up."

"You are?"

"Of course I am. I mean, you and I have practiced for this. We're old pros at this wedding thing."

He chuckled. "I'm glad that you see it that way."

"After everything that happened to us, I can't see it any other way, not anymore at least."

Marcus smiled and kissed her on the cheek, and she responded by kissing him on the lips.

"I thought you didn't like PDA," he said.

"Well . . . one kiss didn't hurt." She winked at him.

"I need the bride, groom, and the wedding party to be present for pictures," the wedding photographer said to the crowd. "Please come here. The lighting is great right now."

Jaslene placed her hand in Marcus's, and they joined the rest of the group. Being next to him was perfect.

AFTER THE GROUP pictures, the wedding party headed to the atrium for the reception. Most of the guests were already there, either sitting at their assigned tables or walking around and chatting with other guests. Marcus was pleased to see so many people walking into the museum because, as Harold had said at the staff meeting, they counted as guests. Marcus still didn't know what to do about the situation with the ring and the exhibit. He would tackle that later.

The vibe for today's wedding reception was very different from that of the fundraising gala. While the fundraiser exuded a feeling of twenties reverie and fun, the wedding reception was pure elegance. Jaslene had designed both events very well.

Each table featured a spray of white roses as the main centerpiece. White rose petals also covered the black tablecloths. Each seat had a three-by-five-inch rhinestone picture frame which featured the name of the guest, along with a fun trivia fact about the couple.

Marcus spotted his name next to Carla's placard and sat at the place setting. Jaslene would sit where Carla would've been, but he didn't spot her.

To Marcus's left was Grandpa Clark's placard, along with one for Grandma Clark too. Marcus picked up the card and read his grandfather's name, written in calligraphy. Was he going to stay for the reception? Or was he too upset about yesterday's conversation about the ring? Marcus wasn't sure.

The sound of heels clacking against the museum's hardwood floor interrupted his focus. Jaslene walked toward the head table, waving at Marcus. "Sorry that we didn't get to walk in together. Kirsten had some additional questions for me."

"Not a problem." Marcus gestured to the table décor. "This looks wonderful. Where'd you get all of the white roses?"

"I had them brought in from Savannah." She inhaled deeply. "I love their fragrance."

"Me too," Marcus said, smiling.

Tuxedoed waiters carrying silver platters of appetizers walked around, serving the guests. One carried a bottle of champagne and poured it into each guest's fluted glass.

"I'm starving," Jaslene said, sitting next to him. A

waiter stopped at their head table and Jaslene filled her plate with dumplings and grilled mushrooms.

"You worked hard all weekend. You deserve to enjoy the reception," Marcus said, adding dumplings to his plate too, along with a spoonful of sweet potatoes.

The museum soon filled with more guests and the chatter increased exponentially. The DJ's turntable was a few feet from theirs, and the DJ put on his headphones and played smooth jazz. When Sasha and Greg entered the space, the DJ tapped his microphone. "Ladies and gentlemen, I'm pleased to introduce, Mr. and Mrs. Greg and Sasha Smith!"

The newly wedded couple entered the room, and the wedding guests applauded. Greg spun Sasha around on the dance floor and gave her a huge kiss. The crowd *ooh*ed and *aah*ed. The couple made their way to their seats at the center of the head table.

"Before we begin this wedding celebration," the DJ said, "I want everyone to know that we're having a double celebration. Today is Sasha's birthday!"

The DJ played Stevie Wonder's version of "Happy Birthday to You" and the guests sang along. A waiter brought the cake to Sasha's seat, and she blew out all of the candles. The crowd cheered.

After the birthday singing, Sasha waved to Marcus and Jaslene and pointed to the empty seats next to Marcus. "Did Pastor Clark and his wife return? I saw them drive away after we finished taking pictures. I thought they'd stay for the reception."

Marcus checked the time on his phone. Forty minutes had passed. If they left for a short break, then they would've returned by now. "I'll call and see where they are."

Sasha's eyes brightened. "That'd be great."

Wedding guests walked up to the head table to greet the new bride and groom. Marcus pulled up the contacts on his cell phone and dialed the number.

"You look worried," Jaslene said. "Is something the matter?"

"I have a suspicion, but I won't know for certain until I talk to my grandfather. Hold on a sec." His cell phone was ringing. "Be right back."

"No problem."

Marcus stepped out of the reception area and headed to his office. The phone rang and rang. Hopefully, Grandpa Clark would answer.

"That you, Marcus?"

The sound of Grandpa Clark's gruff voice brought a smile to his face. "Yep. I'm calling because we were looking for you. I saw you leave right after the ceremony. Will you return for the reception?"

There was silence on the other end.

"Tell him, Reginald!" Grandma Clark's voice could be heard in the background.

"We won't be at the reception today. I should've told Sasha before we left . . . but it would've been hard to explain."

"Is this because Harold wanted you to return the ring to Finch?"

"Yes. I officiated Sasha's ceremony because I promised that I'd do so, but I can't stay there any longer than I have to. Not with Finch wanting the ring back and Harold agreeing with the man."

"I understand." Marcus sighed. "We'll miss you."

There was silence for a few moments. "What do you think of your boss's views?"

"I don't like it. I told him so."

"You can do something about it."

"What's that?"

"Convince him to change his mind," Grandpa Clark said. "And tell Harold that he'll be losing a donor if he doesn't tell Finch that I won't return the ring."

Marcus's neck muscles tightened. "I tried to change his mind, but I'll also let him know that you will no longer donate to the museum."

"Thank you, grandson. I'm sorry that I can't be more of a support."

He took a deep breath. All this time, Marcus worked to try to show his grandfather the value in his work at the museum. Now that was jeopardized. "No need to apologize. You have principles, and I respect that."

After they hung up, Marcus tossed his phone on the desk. This wasn't going to be a fun wedding reception, at least not for Marcus. Grandpa Clark was right, and as pastor of New Life, he should have a definite say in how the exhibit went, but Harold wanted the grant.

The muffled sound of laughter and chatter from the reception filtered into his office. He got up from his desk, intent on enjoying the reception and not worrying about this issue, at least he wouldn't worry about it today.

Marcus made his way back to the reception and sat next to Jaslene. "What'd he say?" Sasha asked.

"My grandparents aren't staying for the reception, unfortunately. But he sends his well wishes."

"Did he say why?" A small frown formed on Sasha's mouth.

Oh yes, he most definitely said why. "Um, I think they're just tired." *Tired of Harold.*

Sasha squinted, as if trying to decipher his words. "Oh, okay. That's too bad."

"Time for the toasts," the DJ said from his microphone. He held up a glass of champagne. "We'll start with the best man."

Marcus pulled the small piece of paper from inside of his jacket pocket and began. "I want to wish the two of you the very best in life. I don't have any great advice to give on marriage, since I'm not married myself." He chuckled, and the crowd smiled at his self-deprecating humor. "However, I can give you some advice on being in love."

Marcus made a quick glance at Jaslene, and she lowered her eyes.

"As for being in love, you probably know about the honeymoon stage. But after that things will 'normalize.' Life becomes mundane and everyday. And those newly romantic feelings from the beginning fade. But the love won't fade. Feelings change. Hard times may arrive. But the love that you have won't change. No matter what life brings you, be sure to hold on to that love. Because it will carry you through the good and the bad times." He raised his glass. "To the new couple."

The rest of the crowd raised their glasses. "To the new couple."

Marcus and Jaslene clinked their champagne glasses, and then she sipped hers, not taking her gaze off him.

"That was a lovely toast," she said.

"Thanks. I spent a lot of time writing it up."

"I can tell." She set her glass down. "You seem distracted. You okay?"

He wasn't okay. He needed a change of pace. "Let's dance, love."

Marcus extended his hand to hers, and she gently grasped it. The DJ played Frank Sinatra's "Fly Me to the Moon," and Marcus and Jaslene swayed in time to the easy cadence. The strobe light from the DJ's turntable highlighted the flecks of gold in Jaslene's deep brown eyes.

"You look beautiful," Marcus said.

"I know." She giggled. "I saw you whisper the word 'beautiful' to me during the ceremony."

"Was I that obvious?"

"You were to me. But I don't think anyone else noticed because they were so focused on the ceremony."

"Ah, I see." He twirled her around. "So what you're telling me is that you, the wedding planner and designer, weren't paying attention to the wedding. You were paying attention to me."

"Don't think too highly of yourself. I could've been focused on something on the wall behind you," Jaslene said.

"Touché." Marcus pulled her closer, and their lips almost touched. "But even if you were focused on the wall, I was in front of it. You couldn't help but see yours truly."

She laughed. They swayed across the dance floor as Ella Fitzgerald and Louis Armstrong's "La Vie en Rose" played next.

The pendant which he had given to her sparkled under the strobe lights. His heart ached.

"You still haven't answered my question," she said as they did a promenade across the dance floor. "You okay?"

"No. The talk with my grandfather upset me."

"What happened? I thought you two were getting along just fine."

He needed to get this off his chest. "We still are. Can we talk in a quieter area?"

"Of course."

They left the dance floor and took the narrow, dim hallway to his office. The music faded to a soft din. Once Marcus arrived at his desk, Jaslene closed the door with a soft click.

"What's happening?" she asked. "You seem so serious."

"I have good news and not so good news. The New Life exhibit will take place." He sat and rested his forearms on the desk blotter.

"That's amazing news!" She clapped her hands.

"But there's a huge catch." Then he told Jaslene all that Harold said.

"What? That can't be. Let me get this straight. Robert Finch, a descendant of Odysseus Finch, is on the board of the Lee Ray Foundation. The jeweler told Robert that Pastor Clark has the ring. Robert wants the ring returned. Pastor Clark won't return the ring. And Harold thinks Pastor Clark should return the ring so as not to risk losing potential grant money from the foundation?"

"Correct."

"And Harold also doesn't want to display the ring in the exhibit because Robert says the museum will be painted as biased."

"Correct again."

"Wow. What did Grandpa Clark say when you spoke to him on the phone today?"

"Oh, he was still upset. If it weren't for Sasha's wedding ceremony, he wouldn't have returned to the museum. That's why he left so quickly today." Marcus shook his head. "It took so much for us to try to convince Grandpa Clark to lend us those items. Now it feels like I'm back at square one. It's frustrating to say the least. He wants me to tell Harold that he will not return the ring, but it's not going to work. I tried."

"Why don't we set up a time for Harold and Grandpa Clark to talk about this together? That way you don't have to be the go-between, and your grandfather can express his sentiments to Harold directly."

"Sounds like a great idea, but I'll have to convince my grandfather to speak to Harold. He can be stubborn."

Jaslene tapped her chin, apparently thinking. "How about we pay your grandparents a visit and try to convince them?"

"We can do that. I hope it works."

The music changed to a new melody, one that Marcus didn't recognize. The faint notes pulsed through the walls of his office. "Let's get back to the celebration."

Marcus reached toward her, and their fingers intertwined. Being with Jaslene was so easy these days. If he had a problem, she seemed to know the perfect solution, and vice versa.

They were like two complementary pieces of a puzzle. Amidst the troubles and confusion of life, they clicked. Marcus was starting to believe that some people were divinely made for another because, as the months passed, it became clear that their two hearts were becoming one.

Chapter Seventeen

*J*aslene and Marcus rode in silence to his grandparent's house. All she could think about was their time at the wedding and reception. She relished every moment with Marcus.

He made a right onto the narrow road that was a straight shot to his grandparent's house.

"This is the place where I found those sword lilies," he said. "Mary's garden should be coming up at any moment now. It's by the lake where Trey drowned."

"Who's Mary?"

"The woman who maintains the garden."

"Oh," Jaslene said. "How were you able to go there, given that it's near the lake?"

Marcus kept his focus on the road ahead. "I don't know. The garden was so attractive. I was able to see the lake from where I stood, and . . . it's tough to explain . . . but I just felt peace and a sense that Trey was okay."

His statement moved her. "That's beautiful." She glanced out of the passenger window, and the lake came into view. It was faint at first, but then it loomed larger in her sight. The lake gleamed as if it were made of blue glass. Then she spotted it, a garden of flowers of every single type. "I see it! How lovely."

"Would you like to check it out up close?"

"Sure."

Marcus pulled off to the side and parked.

After helping Jaslene out of his truck, they walked over to the garden. The soft fragrance of the place inebriated her senses, and she inhaled and exhaled deeply. "My goodness. This place smells divine."

"I know, right?" They held hands and walked among the different flora. Orchids, roses, tulips, sunflowers, and more surrounded them. "Trying to remember where those sword lilies were at. There they are!"

Jaslene glanced in the direction where Marcus pointed, and her heart skipped. The lilies were so alive. She released his hand and looked at them up close. "These flowers have the most beautiful fragrance."

"Don't they?" Marcus looked around. "Trying to see if Mary is here, but I don't see her. Too bad. It would've been nice if you could've met her."

"Not a problem. Being in her garden is a blessing in itself."

They spent a few more minutes in the garden, and then headed to the truck. Marcus turned on the ignition and they made their way to his grandfather's house. About twenty minutes later, they arrived. "I hope this works. I hope he listens to us."

"He will. You've made such strides in your relationship with your grandfather. I don't think that you'll fail."

They headed to the entrance, and Marcus knocked on the door. Moments later, Grandpa Clark answered. "Hey, Marcus. Jaslene. Wasn't expecting to see you here today."

"I wanted to stop by to talk with you. Do you have a moment?"

"Sure. I always have time for you." Grandpa Clark opened the door wider and gestured to the two of them. "Come on in."

They stepped inside, and the three passed by the plastic covered couches and sat on the folding chairs.

"How can I help you?" he asked.

"We wanted to help you. I told Jaslene about what happened with Harold. She thought we should stop by to ask if you wanted to talk with Harold about all of this. Tell him what you think about him agreeing with Finch concerning the ring."

"Can't do that." Grandpa Clark huffed and crossed his arms.

"I know. It's hard," Jaslene said. "But like he said, sharing about the ring's significance should come from you. You're pastor of New Life, and so you should be the first person consulted on anything related to the church."

"I'm glad that you think so, but Harold doesn't."

"And that's not right," Jaslene said. "You need to meet with him. What would it take to convince you to show up?"

Grandpa Clark crossed his arms, apparently deep in thought concerning her question. "I don't have a quick answer for that one. The simple truth of the matter is that, even if Harold welcomed my input on the exhibit, I wouldn't want to give it. Not like this."

Jaslene and Marcus exchanged a look. This was going to be harder than she thought.

"We need you to talk to Harold. Yes, we can have the exhibit without the ring, but it wouldn't be right," Marcus said. "We need you."

"You need me? You're being too presumptuous. Grandson, you've been working on this exhibit all along. You don't need me. You were doing just fine without me. Isn't that right?"

"I was working on the exhibit, but I was hoping that you'd be part of it." Marcus crossed his arms. "That's why we visited you. You and Grandma are more involved in the church than we could ever be. You are the steward of the sapphire ring, and you've made a free and conscious decision to not return it to the Finch family. I wouldn't feel right opening the exhibit without your blessing."

"You're wrong about that." Grandpa Clark glanced away. "Completely wrong. That exhibit would do well for me not to be involved in it at all."

"That's not true. Why say that?" Jaslene asked.

"I'm saying it because it's true." Grandpa Clark shook his head. "My not being there might be a good thing. After all, I was the one who failed my congregants that day." Grandpa Clark's voice grew quiet.

Pity arose in Jaslene. Pastor Clark might not ever be able to get over losing his congregants. Was there something she could do to convince him to still remain a part of it? Jaslene searched her mind for something, but nothing came to mind.

We were looking forward to welcoming the two of you into our family. Grandma Clark's words came to remembrance. The more time that Jaslene spent with Marcus and his grandparents, the more she wanted to be part of this family. "Pastor Clark, on our drive here, Marcus and I stopped at this beautiful little garden. It was by the lake where Trey died."

Marcus glanced at her, and the frown lines around his eyes softened.

"When Marcus had told me what happened there, I got worried. I thought it would be too much for Marcus, but he said he'd found his healing. His response made me think of the times when I felt as if I couldn't deal with hard things. But we find our healing, in some way. I think the people who died at New Life would've wanted you to find your healing too."

Marcus appeared to be focused on her, and self-consciousness took over. Did she say too much?

The sunlight which shone through the windows turned into shadows as clouds moved across the sky. "I'm not going to promise that I'll be there, but because you two are so persistent, I'll think on it a bit more. Not giving you a yes or no answer. Just gonna think on it. Understand?"

"Yes." Jaslene smiled. "We understand."

ON WEDNESDAY MORNING, Marcus awakened to the sound of his chirping cell phone. He grabbed it from his bedside table and read Grandpa Clark's name on the screen.

"Hello, Grandpa. Nice to hear from you . . . very early in the morning."

"I checked my schedule for the day, and I have some free time this morning. I can stop by the museum to see Harold around ten o'clock. Will that work?"

Marcus had no idea if Harold would be at the museum today, but it would have to work. Marcus would make it work. "Yes. It will. We'll see you then."

"Good. Looking forward to it."

After they hung up, Marcus quickly got ready and headed over to the museum. He needed to let Harold know of the appointment and, if needed, to convince him to stay and talk to his grandfather. That would be tricky, especially since the two had exchanged some uncomfortable words earlier.

The door to Harold's office was halfway open, and the faint sound of typing filtered through. The closer he stepped to the entrance, the more he braced himself for the conversation. No telling how Harold would react, but Marcus would talk to him about it.

"Morning. Good to see that you're here." Marcus sat in the empty chair across from him. "We need to talk."

"Sure. I'm finalizing the plans for the exhibit. It looks like we will have quite a few visitors. Which is a good thing, of course. How are things going on your end?"

"The exhibits are mostly ready," Marcus said, emphasizing the word *mostly*. "My grandfather called this morning. He should be stopping by here soon. He wanted to discuss the ring."

Harold was quiet, and then he set his pen on the desk. "We know where each other stands. There's not much more to discuss."

Sounded as if Harold wasn't budging, and that wasn't a good thing either. "I met with him yesterday. I don't feel right about us moving forward without his involvement. You should hear him out."

"Guess I'll have to since he's on his way."

Marcus nodded, not responding to his comment. Marcus already pushed by setting up this impromptu meeting. "Have you heard from the foundation?"

"I haven't. In fact, I'm waiting to get notification from them on the status of our grant application. I've been updating on our progress, so they're aware of what's going on."

They're more than aware. Marcus didn't respond. He glanced at the time on his cell phone. Ten minutes until his grandfather would arrive. They sat here, silently waiting for him to show up. Harold reached over and took the Royal typewriter from his second desk. "You might want to use this typewriter for something. I haven't had the time to use it. And so you're welcome to take it."

Marcus nodded. "Sounds good."

"Hello, everyone." Grandpa Clark stepped inside the office. "Glad to see you here. I'll grab some extra chairs from the empty office."

After doing so, he set them up and sat at the far end, and Grandpa Clark was seated in the center, directly across from Harold.

"Let's talk."

Grandpa Clark tapped his knee. "I wanted to meet with you today, Harold, not to convince you to change your mind, but to let you know what you're supporting by not changing your mind. Robert Finch called me at the church yesterday."

"He did?" Marcus said.

Grandpa Clark nodded. "He asked for the ring, and of course, I said no. He also knew that my grandson works at the museum. He said that if I didn't return the ring, then my grandson's job wouldn't be guaranteed."

Marcus's pulse pounded. This wasn't good.

Harold shook his head. "I'd never let go of Marcus over this issue."

"You sure about that?" Grandpa Clark said. "Because you've already insisted that I return the ring to Finch. I want you to know the full effects of your decisions."

Marcus nodded. His grandfather was right.

"And I'm not bowing to any intimidation tactics from anyone," Grandpa Clark continued. "The ring stays in our family. Solomon needed this ring to gain a freedom which he didn't have. After Solomon died, Janey wore that ring as a symbol of their love. I'd be a fool to return it now. And Harold, you're a fool for putting your stock in the Lee Ray Foundation. If they're funding you, they're controlling you. Like the Good Book says, 'Choose this day whom you will serve.'"

Harold looked away. "I've worked so hard to keep this place running."

"That doesn't mean that you have to compromise to keep the museum open," Marcus said. "Back in November, I said that we should think of other ways to be funded. Denmark Vesey's life served as an example for why the museum should do so. We don't need the Lee Ray Foundation."

"We can't do that now. It'll take at least two fiscal years for the museum to be funded from other sources," Harold said. "And the museum can also be closed in two fiscal years. Seems like I'm the only one who understands that. I have other business to attend to. Have a good day." Harold got up to leave.

"Hold on, Harold," Marcus said. "I'm sure we can still work this out."

"What's there to work out? Nothing."

"I can't believe this," Marcus said. "I can't believe that you're leaving. Regardless of how you feel about what my grandfather said, we need to listen to him."

Harold stopped and glanced at the two of them. Marcus was risking his job by standing up to Harold, but like Grandpa Clark said, Harold might fire Marcus anyway if it came down to it.

"What about sponsorships?" Marcus said. "Have any individual donors or companies agreed to sponsor the New Life exhibit?"

Harold twisted his mouth. "Not many. That was part of the original project plan, but I had set that part aside. I just didn't get around to finding people."

Marcus's eyes shifted to his grandfather. "Would you be willing to donate?"

"I was until Harold insisted that I return the ring to Finch."

"Would you be willing to help the museum out if Harold broke ties with the Lee Ray Foundation?" Marcus asked.

"The grant that I'm applying for would cover a lot of our operating expenses here. That's a hefty amount of money," Harold said.

Grandpa Clark appeared offended. "You talk as if you don't think that I have the money to cover it."

"I never said that." Harold shook his head.

"You didn't have to say it. I can see this written all over your face. It's quite clear to me."

If it wasn't one thing, then it seemed to be another between these two. Couldn't they manage to agree on anything? Marcus sighed.

"How much would you need to cover the expenses here, at least for the upcoming fiscal year?" Grandpa Clark asked.

Harold reached in his drawer and grabbed a file folder. "Here's a printout of our projected income and expenses for the upcoming year." He opened the folder and pointed to a number.

Marcus glanced over at it, and his eyes bugged out. That was a lot.

"The foundation covers all of this?"

"No. They don't. They cover about sixty percent of it though." Harold nodded to the figure. "If I don't get that from them this year, then we'll have to somehow make it up from other places. Or else close down."

"I can't cover that," Grandpa Clark said. "But I don't want my grandson to lose his job either. Marcus is doing good work here, regardless of my thoughts on you, Harold."

Hearing Grandpa Clark's support made Marcus feel emotional. "Thanks, Grandpa."

"I'm only saying the truth. You're doing good." Grandpa Clark sighed. "Our church has some money in reserves. We can afford to pay half of that sixty percent, but you'd likely need another generous donor to cover the other part. And of course, I'd have to meet with the board and the church finance committee to get approval to make that donation. So nothing is set, but I can definitely see what I can do . . . if you agree to not accept any more funding from the Lee Ray Foundation."

"You'd be willing to do that?" Marcus asked Grandpa Clark.

"Of course. Harold would just have to accept . . . and we'd have to get the board and committee approval, of course."

Who else could be another donor? Marcus tried to think of names, and then one alighted his mind. "Have you spoken to Heather Gates, yet?"

Harold nodded. "I did. She said that her father was going to make some sort of statement about the importance of our museum and highlighting it, but I haven't seen anything come though from their press office."

"I'll speak to her. Let her know our situation," Marcus said. "If Harold wants to go this new route."

There was a long silence. "We can go this route. I'll send an email to the Lee Ray Foundation requesting to pull our application for the grant. And if this new plan doesn't work then . . . well, I don't even know."

"It will work," Marcus said. "I'm confident that it will."

A COUPLE OF hours after the meeting with Harold and Grandpa Clark, Marcus dialed Heather Gates's number. He wanted to ask her about possibly funding the museum today. It was going to be a big ask, but hopefully she'd say yes.

He'd already rehearsed what to say. He probably over-rehearsed, in fact.

The phone rang and rang. "Please pick up," he said, whispering.

"Hello?"

Relief swept through him. "Is this Heather Gates?"

"Yes, it's me."

"Hi. I'm Marcus Clark from the Lowcountry African American Heritage Museum."

"Oh yes. I remember you. Nice to hear from you again."

"We so appreciated your presence at the fundraiser. I know that you're a big supporter of the work that we're doing here. Harold and I met recently, and we wanted to ask you a question."

Marcus took a breath. Then he went into his proposal about the museum and its needs. When he finished, Heather said: "That's a lot of money."

"I know. It's a big ask, but we want to take the museum

in a new direction. We're looking to get most of our support from donors who truly believe in our mission."

"How do you mean?"

Marcus then explained about the ring and its history and even the connections to their previous funders.

"Hmm. Hold on a sec. Let me check something."

She put him on hold for what seemed like an eternity. Marcus paced, wondering about what her decision would be. If she didn't want to go ahead with funding, for whatever reason, they'd be stuck. Yet Marcus refused to compromise the integrity of the exhibit, and he surely wasn't going to do so, no matter what.

"I can help with the funding, but I can only do so for this one year."

Marcus's heart leapt. This was really happening. "Really?"

"Yes. Most definitely. Like I said, this isn't a permanent fix. After this fiscal year, you'd have to find other sources. I can tell my father about it, and he might be able to see who'd be willing to contribute for the future. How does that sound?"

"That works for me." Marcus was smiling. "Thank you so much. This will really help us out. I'll connect you with Harold to work out the details."

"So glad that I'm able to help, and I look forward to the grand opening of the exhibit."

He hung up the phone, smiling. Marcus typed a quick email to Harold, letting him know of his conversation with Heather. He couldn't wait to share this news with

Jaslene too. Just as he was going to call her, a light tap on the door caught his attention. He did a double take when he saw Jaslene standing in the doorway.

"I was just about to call you," he said.

"Well, you're in luck. I stopped by because I forgot to get the storage box that I used for the wedding the other day." She sat at the chair across from him "What's up?"

Marcus told her about what happened with Heather Gates.

"Oh my! That's great." Jaslene clapped her hands. "This means that you won't have to rely on the Lee Ray Foundation?"

"That depends on New Life. Now all I need to do is work out the plans for the exhibit's grand opening. And of course, tell my grandfather. Hopefully the board and their finance committee will approve of making a donation to the museum."

"I'm sure they will. No need to worry."

Chapter Eighteen

Marcus drove to his grandparents' house right after work. He couldn't wait to tell his grandparents that Heather Gates had agreed to fund a portion of the museum's budget. Marcus hoped that by telling him this information today, he'd have more evidence to convince the board and finance committee to invest in the museum for the fiscal year.

"Hey there, Grandson!" His grandmother reached out and hugged him. "Come on in."

He stepped inside the house and walked past the familiar, plastic-covered couch in the living room. Marcus grabbed a metal folding chair from the kitchen and brought it to the living room to sit.

Shortly thereafter, his grandfather walked in. "Hey, Marcus. Wasn't expecting to see you so soon."

"I have great news. I couldn't wait to tell you. Heather Gates agreed to contribute to the museum's budget for the fiscal year."

"Great news." Grandpa Clark clasped his hands over

his potbelly and propped his feet up on the hand-carved footstool next to him.

"Yeah, I thought it'd help you to bring that information to the church when you met with them."

"It might. It might. I want to show you something, Marcus. I'll be right back." His grandfather left the sitting room and walked down the narrow hall leading to the rear of the house, the hardwood floors creaking underneath his footsteps.

"Do you know what he wants to show me?" Marcus asked.

Grandma Clark shrugged. "Beats me."

The swinging door to the kitchen swished back and forth, its sound filling the space. "Wonder where he's going."

"Your curiosity is getting the best of you. Let's go and see."

Grandma Clark left and he followed. Moments later, they were in the kitchen. Grandpa was riffling through a small closet that was usually locked. His grandfather kept that room off-limits when Marcus was a child, and young Marcus used to make up stories about what was hidden behind its closed door. He imagined it as a portal to another time in history. One step inside, and he could land in nineteenth-century South Carolina or in medieval Spain. He smiled. Perhaps those childhood musings led to his eventual profession.

"I just put it in here," his grandfather said. "Just yesterday."

A mishmash of carboard boxes were packed one on top of the other, and they looked like the Leaning Tower of

Pisa, only they were old boxes. Grandpa Clark lifted one box from the tower, careful not to disturb the others.

"What are you looking for, Reginald?"

Marcus sensed the exasperation in his grandmother's voice, and his mouth lifted in amusement.

"You'll find out soon enough." Grandpa searched through the contents of the box.

The intensity on his grandfather's face intrigued him. He was on a mission to find this mysterious object.

"Aha! That's where I put it." Grandpa Clark held up a velvet jewelry box.

"What's that?" Marcus asked.

"Janey's ring. I got it from the safe-deposit box the other day. And I wanted to put it somewhere for safekeeping until I saw you again."

"Reginald, why didn't you tell me that you got the ring from the safe-deposit box and put it in here?" His grandmother planted her hands on her hips. "You could've forgotten and it would've been lost."

"I know, I know. I'll do better." He smiled. "I wanted to give this ring back to Marcus."

Grandpa Clark handed the box to Marcus, and he took it. Upon opening the item, he let out a quiet gasp. It looked as beautiful as it did the day that he had used the ring to propose to Jaslene.

"Your grandmother gave it to me after all that happened between you and Jaslene. And I felt so sad when she did. Now I'm returning it to you."

Marcus gently pulled the ring from its holder and examined it. The sapphire still shimmered.

"If you ever want to propose to Jaslene again, then you have one less thing to concern yourself with. You'll already have the ring." Grandpa Clark stood next to his wife and wrapped his arm around her waist.

"I remember when I first proposed to Jaslene with this ring. When she said yes, I felt like the luckiest man on the planet."

"Second luckiest," his grandfather said, kissing Grandma Clark on the cheek. "You're the second luckiest."

"Aw, Reginald, you're too much." Grandma Clark giggled.

"It's been so good to see you and Jaslene together, especially at Sasha's wedding. Do you plan to propose to Jaslene?"

Marcus frowned. "We wanted to take things slow with our relationship. I don't want to get ahead of myself."

"The two of you look quite comfortable with each other," Grandma Clark said. "I think you need to give yourself grace and allow yourself to take that next step."

His grandmother was right. Jaslene didn't hold any resentment toward him over the past. Marcus needed to give himself a semblance of grace.

If he didn't, then he wouldn't gain the courage to propose to Jaslene ever again. Even though they were dating now, Jaslene could say no, but he needed to give himself another chance. After all, he got only one trip on this thing called life. Might as well do something good with it.

"I'll propose to her," he said.

"That's wonderful to hear. We will be rooting for the two of you." Grandma Clark reached for her husband's hand, and they smiled at Marcus.

"Maybe I'll be lucky enough to have what the two of you have, a love that lasts a lifetime."

"I think you will," his grandmother said, winking at him.

Marcus squeezed the velvet box in his hand. He was going to propose, again. Anticipation filled him, and for the first time in a long time, he sensed hope.

JASLENE RETURNED TO the museum bright and early on Thursday morning to help Marcus prepare for the upcoming exhibit. In many ways, this was a new beginning for her.

Sasha's wedding was complete. The museum was on its way to getting funding from other sources, and she was taking new steps with the business. She made a right into the parking lot of the museum and turned off the ignition. Jaslene headed inside the museum and down the now lit hallway to their office. Marcus was busy typing on his laptop. He did a double take when she stepped inside.

"Morning. I wasn't expecting you to be here today."

"I know. I wanted to help you with the exhibit. Two more days until it opens to the public." She sat across from his desk and glanced at him. "You need any help?"

"Not much. I was just putting the final touches on the program." He tapped on the keys of his laptop. "Can't believe this is actually happening."

"It's a miracle, isn't it?"

"Yes, a miracle. This could've only happened with the help of a few angels." He stopped typing. "Thank you for all you've done."

"You were the main one involved. I just helped."

"And you were a huge help."

"Okay, I'll take that compliment." She nodded, but Jaslene sensed that something else was going on with him. "Something the matter?"

"Nothing. I was just thinking, that's all."

"About what?" she asked.

"Doesn't matter now. I have to focus on this exhibit."

O-kay. This was awkward. Time to change the subject. "I have some good news. Remember Kelly Nielsen from the fundraiser?"

Marcus nodded.

"She gave my contact information to some of her friends. A few contacted me. They seem very interested in having me design and plan their weddings."

"That's great! And when the feature comes out in June with *Southern Bride*, you're gonna be a big deal in the Lowcountry."

Jaslene laughed. "Maybe."

"I know it for a fact."

Jaslene tapped her pen on her knee. "I'm kind of scared though. Not as scared as before. It's just weird doing this on my own. Hope and I were supposed to be in this together." She paused. "So there it goes. I guess this is the part where you tell me 'Don't worry' and all of that."

"I'm not gonna say that." Marcus reached over and grasped her hand. "I get how you're feeling. I really do. First of all, this is your calling."

"Perhaps," she said, her tone playful.

"And second of all, I'm proud of you."

"Proud of me? For what?"

"For how you faced your doubts about doing this work, but you went ahead and tried. Now it's paying off."

Hearing him say those words did something to her. He was right. She took a huge risk, especially given what happened in the past. She was blessed to have his perspective in her life.

"You're gonna do great with everything," he said. "How's Imani doing with applying to conservatories?"

"We're just in waiting mode now. She won't get any responses until spring. But she was invited to some performances around town. So she's just focusing on that."

His brown eyes lit up. "That makes me glad. I really do see beautiful things in her future and your future, Jazz. Just keep your heart open to whatever may happen."

Was she willing to do that? Yes, she was. "I will."

A ray of sunshine filtered through the now open blinds, and with it came a joy that she hadn't sensed in the longest time. She didn't know what her future held, but for the first time, she knew that she could handle it.

Chapter Nineteen

Somehow Marcus would have to figure out how and when to propose to Jaslene. He thought he would bring it up when she stopped by the museum the other day, but he got cold feet.

He could propose today, but he didn't want to have a proposal and the grand opening of the exhibit on the same docket. That would be stressful. Marcus needed to focus all his energies on ensuring the event went smoothly. Nonetheless, he kept the velvet box with the sapphire ring in his pocket for good luck.

Patrons lined up outside to enter. As they did, he sensed the anticipation in the air. The Governor of South Carolina had issued a glowing statement about the importance and significance of the Lowcountry African American Heritage Museum and so there was a lot of buzz happening. Today, the museum teemed with people who wanted to be part of today's event.

He headed to the atrium, and the chatter of people around him filled his ears. He waved to the folks, and that was when he spotted Grandpa Clark. His back was to Marcus, and he seemed transfixed on the timeline that he'd created for New Life Church.

Marcus smiled. Seeing his grandfather here on more than one occasion was nothing short of an act of God. "Hello there."

"Hey, Grandson. This exhibit is a work of art. The level of detail. The captions. Impressive. He pointed to the timeline. The lines and wrinkles on his forehead lifted. "I like how you put that together. You captured most every event since the founding of the church."

"I tried. Lots of research. And, of course, you." Marcus glanced over at the mourners' bench in the alcove. "Thank you for donating it."

"You're welcome, but the work was mainly you, the staff, and the volunteers. I'm honored to witness . . . and fully support it. Our board and finance committee met with one another, and I brought up what we had discussed during our meeting with Harold. We decided to help support the museum for the upcoming fiscal year."

"Really?"

"Yes. We're proud of you. Immensely proud."

He took one more look at the pictures of here. "And you know what? Don't worry about my approval. I know I made things a bit hard on you, but you've chosen a good career path for yourself. I'm honored to witness your work."

"You know, I wanted to show you something else with the exhibit. Follow me." Marcus walked to the other side of the timeline, to the modern day. A picture of the congregants who died in the mass shooting hung on the wall, with the phrase "In Loving Memory." Each victim's name was listed. "They are a part of New Life, and I wanted to show them here too."

"Thank you, Grandson." His voice trembled. "This . . . this is wonderful. Truly wonderful."

They stood in silence before the portrait. Everyone in the photo looked so proud and Black and beautiful. Moments later, they walked to the other end of the timeline. Janey's and Solomon's names were on the timeline.

"I was thinking that if you're up for it, you can work on our family tree too," Grandpa Clark said. "It would be nice to know a little more about Janey and Solomon and the children they had."

"Agreed, but that type of research may take years. I'd have to scour local records and everything. I hope you're up for the challenge."

"Of course I am. Wouldn't have it any other way." He smiled. "How are you and Jaslene doing?" he asked. "Did you . . . ?"

"I haven't. I'm waiting for the right time."

"The right time? Grandson, there's no such thing as the right time. You better ask her while you can. Tomorrow's not guaranteed."

He was right. "I'll try." Marcus checked the time on his cell phone. "Looks like we're about to get started."

"Good luck."

Marcus nodded.

After the visitors gathered in the central exhibit area, Harold stepped up to the podium to speak. "Good evening and welcome to the Lowcountry Museum of African American History. Thank you so much for showing your support of the museum today. As you probably know, our museum experienced a lot of challenges recently, but your presence here, along with the generous donations from our supporters ensure that we keep this history alive." Harold glanced in Grandpa Clark's direction.

Marcus tried to estimate how many were present, but they were too numerous to count. The room was packed. Jaslene stood off to the side, and he waved to her.

"I also want to recognize those who made a substantial impact on making this exhibit a reality. Marcus Clark is the archivist at the museum, and this was his passion project. Jaslene Simmons and Sasha Smith played key roles in ensuring that everything came together, along with our countless volunteers. Please give them a round of applause."

"I'd like to invite Marcus to the podium to say a few words about the exhibit." Harold nodded to them. "Please come forward."

Marcus wasn't expecting to make a speech. Everyone shifted their focus to them, so he made his way to the front of the crowd. "This event is the culmination of many years of work. So many people were instrumental in making this exhibit happen, some of whom are no longer with us. Hope Simmons was a volunteer here, and she was key in laying the groundwork for what you see today."

The crowd listened intently. He could acutely sense their attention on him. He took a deep breath. He needed a moment to take it all in.

"The story of Janey and Solomon, two enslaved people sparked my interest in this exhibit. They were in love, and they wanted to get married and live as free people. However, the social circumstances of the time prevented that from happening. Our journey with their story began with a record of a letter which Janey had written, along with a bench and a ring." Marcus motioned to the bench that was in the alcove, and then he continued the story.

As he spoke, Marcus's feelings toward Jaslene grew stronger. Talking about Janey and Solomon to this crowd made him know for certain that he didn't want to live another day without Jaslene.

"That's all I have," Marcus said, stepping away from the podium. "Thank you again."

"Is the ring also on display?" a voice from the crowd asked.

Marcus paused. How would he answer that question? "It isn't. My grandfather owns the ring, and he wanted to keep it in the family."

Grandpa Clark looked over at him, a smile on his face. Marcus stepped down from the podium. When Jaslene stood next to him, she whispered, "Great speech."

Shortly thereafter, Harold spoke to the crowd. "Thank you, Marcus. I have a short video of the folks who helped make this exhibit possible, and I'd like to play it now."

Everyone quieted down as the lights were dimmed. Then Marcus moved closer to Jaslene.

The reel played, and he was happy to see so many familiar faces there. Those employees who had contributed to this work in so many ways.

Then he saw an image of Hope, and she was smiling at the camera. The interviewer asked her what served as her inspiration for being part of the museum as a volunteer.

"My family: my daughter, my sister, and my future brother-in-law and his family. They all serve as my inspiration for working on this project. I feel as if doing this will truly bring us together and help my sister and my future brother-in-law begin the journey of joining their family trees."

And when she said those words, Marcus was stunned. He and Jaslene both looked at each other. Hope hadn't just done this for herself and Imani; she had done this for them.

The sunlight shone on the screen and Hope's face glowed. All was well.

When the video was over, Harold took questions from the crowd. Marcus was trying to pay attention, but he couldn't help but think about the words Hope had spoken.

Marcus headed to Harold. Jaslene was there too. "That was quite a video. Where did you get that?"

"I was going through the archives last week and I found it. I thought that it would be a good touch to add."

"Thank you," Jaslene said. "Just to see her face there again. I . . . thank you. It was great."

"You're quite welcome," Harold said. "I'm going to see the rest of the patrons."

"It seems like Hope was holding on to a vision of us being together, even more than we were."

They stood there, silent and taking in the weight of that. "I don't want to lose any more ground with you, either," Marcus said. He held Jaslene's hand. Everything seemed right, for the first time in years, he felt as if he was reuniting with the love he longed to have.

Harold's voice interrupted the moment, and they stepped back from each other.

"I invite everyone to take a look around and learn for yourself. Marcus and I will be giving small group tours of the museum in about half an hour. In the meantime, there are refreshments in the lobby, and of course, there's a wealth of knowledge to be gained."

Harold set the microphone down and walked over to Jaslene and Marcus. "All of this is turning out unexpectedly well. After everything that happened with Robert Finch, and especially after thinking about my natural response to Robert's request, I was thinking that it's time for me to retire."

"Retire?"

"Yes. This place needs a new person to steer the ship," Harold said. "I've been here for decades. You're the type of leader who can take this museum into its next evolution. I'd like to offer you the job of Museum Director."

"Museum Director? That's a big responsibility."

"You're capable. You helped to make this museum independent of the Lee Ray Foundation. Now we have supporters who truly believe in the work we're doing here. Your thoughts challenged me. And your thoughts proved true. This museum is more than capable of going at it on its own."

"I believe in you too," Jaslene said.

Her words tipped the scales. "If you believe in me, then I'll accept the position, Harold."

"Great!" Harold extended his hand to Marcus, and he shook it.

It was settled then. He was going to be the new Museum Director. The responsibility would be immense, but he knew that he'd do whatever it took to preserve and guide this place. It would be a beacon for those looking for answers.

"You deserve this, Marcus. It's your time," Jaslene said.

"It's our time."

He was ready for the future, and if luck kept smiling on him, then that future would be with Jaslene. Anticipation filled him. He would propose to her soon. "I was thinking, and . . . well . . . could you meet me at Battery Park tomorrow at noon? I have some administrative things I need to finish up, and then I want to talk to you about something."

"Can't you talk to me about it here?" Jaslene asked.

Marcus chuckled. "No. It's best if we sit down and have a heart-to-heart."

A heart-to-heart. "O-kay. I hope that it's nothing bad."

"Nothing bad at all." He gently grasped her hand. The look in his eyes confirmed his words.

"I'll be there."

As soon as Marcus arrived at Battery Park, he found a picnic spot where he and Jaslene could have a one-on-one talk. He set the picnic basket and blanket down on the grass and scanned the area. The sun shone brightly, and the clouds floated across a clear blue sky. He'd hoped that today—the day when he proposed to Jaslene—would have good weather. Luck was in his favor.

He practiced how he would propose to her, but he knew that whatever he practiced would be drastically different from the real thing, at least that's what happened the last time he proposed to her.

And there were no guarantees that she would say yes. But he knew that he'd have to ask her one more time. Maybe the two of them would end up getting married in the museum this time around. After having Sasha's wedding there, it didn't seem like a bad spot for nuptials. In fact, it was the perfect place for them, given that the museum was what brought them back together as a couple.

The joy in her eyes when she saw the finalized exhibit arose in his mind. He wanted to make her happy for the rest of his life. He wanted to spend the rest of his life loving her.

The possibility cemented within him and sent waves of wholeness to his heart. He loved Jaslene. The feeling rooted deeper inside of him even now.

"Marcus."

The sound of her familiar voice tugged on him. Even though he had seen her just last evening, he couldn't get over her beauty. She was divine in her peach pantsuit, and her hair was loosely held by a peach-colored ribbon as well.

He stood and headed toward her. The sunlight streamed on her just so, highlighting the flecks of auburn in her dark hair. Marcus led her to the picnic area where he'd set up the covered dishes, and then he gestured toward the plaid blanket. "Have a seat."

She did and then said, "What did you want to tell me?"

Here goes nothing. "I've been thinking a lot about us, and I'm sure you've done the same. I want us to try again. I don't know of a lot of things on which I would place my bets in life, but, my dear, I want to place my bets on us." He reached into his coat pocket and held out the velvet ring box. "Will you marry me?"

She gazed at the ring. "I'd love to marry you." Jaslene held out her hand, and her fingers were trembling slightly. But Marcus carefully slipped the ring on her finger.

"Perhaps Janey and Solomon will get their happy ending through us."

"I think they already have," Marcus said.

The sapphire ring sparkled.

Marcus leaned toward her and planted a kiss on her lips. If he could hold this moment in time, he would, but for now he savored it.

Chapter Twenty

Seven Months Later

*J*n the months following their engagement, Jaslene and Marcus grew closer to each other. After she accepted his proposal, their engagement period held more depth than when they were engaged before. Perhaps their experiences drew them closer together. No matter the reason, Jaslene treasured this stage.

In addition to preparing for their wedding, Jaslene was also helping Imani get ready to leave for Juilliard. For the next few weeks, Jaslene helped her shop for items for her apartment, and she ensured that Imani knew everything that there was to know about New York. The more she prepared, the more she settled into the fact that, yes, her niece was growing up and moving on.

The day came for Jaslene to take Imani to the airport. Marcus offered to accompany her, if only to provide emotional support.

"You ready to go, Imani? We don't want to be late for your flight," Jaslene said.

"I'm coming!"

Jaslene wheeled Imani's suitcase down the stairs and onto the street. Marcus should be there in a few minutes to drive them to the airport.

She was about to text Imani to tell her to get downstairs, but the door to their condo complex flung open. "I'm here!" Imani wheeled a paisley-printed suitcase with her. "Now where's Marcus?"

"Going to find that out right now." She scrolled to her text app and typed a message.

Beep. Beep.

Jaslene glanced up. It was Marcus. "Let's go!"

They hopped into Marcus's truck, and he put Imani's suitcases in the back. As soon as he slid into the driver's seat, he turned on the ignition. "Ready to start your new life, Imani?"

"As ready as I'll ever be." She clicked her seat belt into place.

Jaslene's heart flipped. This was for the best.

"How about you, Jazz?"

"As ready as I'll ever be too," she said.

The drive to Charleston International Airport was quiet . . . well, it was quiet except for the sound of nineties R&B music playing on the radio.

Jaslene's cell phone dinged, and she studied the screen. "Oh! I got another inquiry from someone who wants me to plan and decorate their wedding reception space." Jaslene pulled her tiny notepad from her purse and jotted down the information. "I'll return their message later."

"Things are looking up for you," Marcus said, his gaze focused on the road.

"And you too. Did Harold ever say when he wanted you to start as museum director?"

"In two weeks."

"Wow. That's fast."

"I know," Marcus said. "But I've been working on that strategic plan. I wanted to run it by you, see what you think, if that's okay with you."

She shrugged. "Sure. Not a problem."

"I have some room in my budget to hire a staff member who can focus on planned giving. So I'll need to put out a want ad for that. Hopefully, we can find someone good."

"I'm sure you will," Jaslene said.

Fifteen minutes later, Marcus pulled in front of the drop-off point for departing flights.

"Here we are," Jaslene said.

"Yes! I'm so excited!" Imani unclicked her seat belt and hopped out of Marcus's Ford F-250.

Jaslene waited for a few moments, and then she took a few deep breaths. This was the moment of truth. She got out of the pickup and helped Imani with curbside check-in.

"I'm going to miss you, Auntie." She reached over and hugged her.

"Me too. But you know you can always call me, text me, video chat, email, send a telegram, or send a note by carrier pigeon. I'm here for you, always."

"I know." Imani's eyes shone with tears.

"I'm visiting you too. I need to take a trip up there. I just won't be signing a lease for an apartment or anything."

Imani nodded. A tear trickled down her face, and Jaslene grew overwhelmed.

"You better stop crying now, or else I'll be crying too. This is a happy time. I can't wait to hear you play at Carnegie Hall one day. Practice hard. Study hard. And continue to be amazing you."

"I will." Imani nodded

She paused. "Good. Very good."

"And I can't wait for your wedding!" Imani smiled.

"Yes. That will be in a year. Lots of planning to do, and, of course, you'll be my maid of honor."

They gave each other one last hug. After Imani walked through the gate that was for passengers only, Jaslene instinctively reached for Marcus's hand. "I'm really letting her go."

"Yes, you are." He pulled her close. "You're doing a good thing. Imani might not have been able to make this step into Juilliard without you there to guide her."

"Oh, stop. You think too highly of me."

Marcus stepped back and looked her in the eyes. "It's true."

Jaslene smiled at him. "You're right. It's true."

"Do you want to grab a bite to eat? You can call back that potential client, and we can discuss our wedding plans."

"Sure."

Jaslene gently squeezed his hand, and they headed back to his pickup. This was good. Once they were back in the cab, Marcus leaned over and kissed her on the cheek. "You ready to go, Jazz?"

She relished his kisses. "Most definitely."

"Cool," he said. "Time for us to start planning our future, again."

"If Hope were here, I'm pretty sure she'd be smiling right now," Jaslene said. "I definitely am."

Epilogue

One Year Later

*T*he day of the wedding had arrived, and Jaslene was feeling all sorts of emotions about this moment. She remembered the joy and the anticipation she felt the first time that she was in this position, but instead of shirking away from those feelings, this time she embraced them. She let joy run through her like a marathoner, and she didn't want this journey to end. This was going to be the beginning of something good.

She looked at herself in the full-length mirror in the dressing area, and she smiled. As soon as she accepted Marcus's proposal, she knew that she would wear the same dress she had intended to wear if they had gotten married the first time.

The bouquet was similar too, but this time she added sword lilies to her bouquet in memory of Hope.

"You look gorgeous, Jaslene." Sasha stepped into the

dressing room, and she smiled. "Your dress is gorgeous. And you're even more gorgeous."

Jaslene laughed. "I love your enthusiasm, Sasha, but you already saw me in this dress the first time around."

"Yeah, but this is different. This wedding didn't come to you as easily. It was hard won, and you are the more beautiful for it. If Hope were here, she'd say the same thing."

The mention of Hope's name got her all teary-eyed. "Oh my gosh, now I'm going to mess up my makeup."

"My bad. Just know that I am proud of you for getting this far. You deserve it."

She deserved it. That wasn't something she would've been able to say to herself before, but she agreed. And she was not just doing this for herself, she was doing this for Hope.

"All right, girl. I'm going to have to line up with the rest of the wedding party, but just know that I'm so very proud of you."

They hugged one more time, and then Sasha left. Jaslene took one extra look at herself in the mirror and smiled.

She was ready.

Ready to spend the rest of her life with Marcus.

Ready to embrace joy in all forms.

Ready to follow her heart in all things, without inhibitions.

She stepped into the foyer of the museum and waited for the strains of Imani's violin to begin.

As soon as she heard the music, that feeling of joy returned. The door to the main area of the museum opened and the wedding party filed in. Jaslene, of course, was the last to enter.

Her eyes met with Marcus's.

When she reached him, Pastor Clark began to speak: "Dearly beloved, we're gathered here today in the sight of God to celebrate this joyous occasion where Jaslene and Marcus are becoming one. As we join together on this occasion, I want to remind you and the guests here today that our love is a reflection of heavenly love. Sometimes it's hard and it comes with its own share of difficulties, but beyond all of that, it is good. It is truly good. And I hope that no matter what comes your way that you two will be able to understand and reflect this love in your own lives."

Happiness zipped through her.

"Jaslene, do you take this man to be your wedded husband?"

As Pastor Clark said the rest of the words, nothing else mattered except being with Marcus.

"I do," she said, her voice trembling but filled with anticipation and excitement.

"And, Marcus, do you take this woman to be your wedded wife?"

"I do," Marcus said.

And Pastor Clark said, "You may kiss your bride."

Marcus leaned over and kissed her on the lips, and she returned the gesture. They found their happily ever after amid the regret, amid the pain, amid the hope. By dwelling and diving into the depths of history, they found each other.

Acknowledgments

*T*he idea for *A Sweet Lowcountry Proposal* first came to me in 2014 via two images: a wooden bench and a steepled church. With those two pictures in mind, I wrote.

A huge thank-you to my readers. It is a privilege and honor to write for you. Thank you for all the kind reviews, words of encouragement, and for taking the time to read my stories.

Thank you to everyone at Avon for all the hard work that you put into bringing this story to publication. I appreciate the support you provide to me as an author.

Executive Editor May Chen, thank you for always listening to me and for making my stories much better. I'm very, very grateful.

Nancy Tan, thank you so much for making my writing shine.

Deanna Bailey and everyone in the marketing and publicity department at Avon, thank you for your support!

Editorial Assistant Alessandra Roche, thank you for

your support as I worked through the steps in the publishing process.

To the amazing authors, Bethany K., Tif Marcelo, Mia Hopkins, Maida Malby, and Maan Gabriel. You ladies rock! Thank you so much for EVERYTHING!

To my friend Monica Hurley. Thank you for sitting with me at the late-night hour as I worked on my deadline. I appreciate you.

To my parents, Laysander and Maria Presentacion, thank you for encouraging me to dream big. I love you forever.

To my children, Samuel and Hannah, thank you for telling me: "Mom, you can write this book!" and for being my biggest cheerleaders. You bless my life every single day.

To my husband, Daren, thank you for your continual support. I don't know how you do all that you do, but you're amazing. I love you.

To my Lord and Savior Jesus Christ, *A Sweet Lowcountry Proposal* is another one of my small gifts to You. Lord, please take this story, which is the work of my hands, and do with it as You will. I love you.

About the Author

PRESLAYSA WILLIAMS is an actress and award-winning author who writes heartwarming romance and women's fiction with an Afro-Filipina twist. Proud of her heritage, she loves sharing her culture with her readers.

After receiving her undergraduate degree from Columbia, Preslaysa earned two master's degrees, the first in public administration from the College of Charleston and the second in writing popular fiction from Seton Hill University.

Preslaysa teaches writing and literature at her local university. Visit her online at www.preslaysa.com.

ALSO BY
Preslaysa Williams

A heartwarming Avon debut of love, forgiveness, and new beginnings set in the beautiful South Carolina Lowcountry.

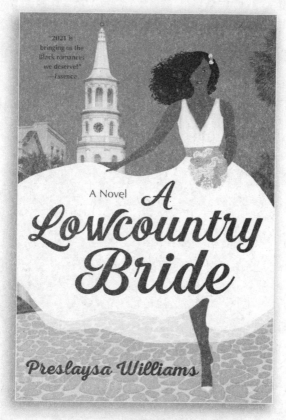

"I absolutely adore this book...love story begins slow—like a delicious lowcountry boil—but heats up to the perfect ending."

—KATHLEEN Y'BARBO,
bestselling author of *The Black Midnight*

AVONBOOKS HarperCollins*Publishers*

Discover great authors, exclusive offers, and more at HC.com.